GLOSSARY

Ach: Oh

Aenti: Aunt

Ausbund: Amish hymnal book

Bopplin: babies

Bruder: brother

Bwue or *Bu*: boys or boy

Daed: dad

Danki: Thank you

Dawdi: grandfather

Dochdern: daughters

Englisch: Non-Amish person(s)

Fraa: wife

Froh: happy

Gmay: The Amish church community as a whole

Grosskinner: grandchildren

Gute mariye: good morning

Gut nacht: good night

Hund: A dog, hound

Jah: yes

Kaffi: coffee

Kapp: prayer covering

Kichlin: cookies

Kind or *Kinner*: child or children

Nix: nothing

Maedel: young woman

Mamm or *Mudder*: mom or mother

Mammi: grandmother

Mei: me or my

Nee: no

Nix: nothing

Onkel: uncle

Ordnung: the written and unwritten rules of the Amish; behavior by which the Amish are expected to live; passes down from generation to generation.

Schee: pretty

Schwesters: sisters

Seltsam: strange

Wunderbaar: wonderful

Yer: your

An
Amish
Flower Farm

An uplifting romance from Hallmark Publishing

MINDY STEELE

An Amish Flower Farm
Copyright @ 2021 Mindy Steele

Print: 978-1-952210-50-1
eBook: 978-1-952210-37-2

www.hallmarkpublishing.com

To my family

Acknowledgments

Thank you, Julie and Stacey, for giving me a chance to write this story.

To Elizabeth, my editor, for making this an unforgettable experience.

To Sharon, Erica, and Jacqui, for inviting me to their farms and apiaries. Without your knowledge, this book could have never been written.

To Mirim, for giving me a glimpse inside your world.

Chapter One

BELINDA GRABER WIPED HER DAMP face with her short blue sleeve and stepped out onto the porch with her family. The blue van that had come to transport her parents skidded to a stop in front of them, stirring up a plume of white gravelly dust into the air.

On any normal Saturday evening, Belinda would've been in her flower garden, singing old hymns or daydreaming about a life far different than the one she had been given. But since they'd heard the answering machine message with *Aenti* Irene's pleas for help, nothing about this day was normal.

Belinda had wanted to go with her parents to Kentucky to tend to her grandfather,

Saul Graber. Dawdi was losing his battle with cancer...but her presence was needed here at home, in Havenlee, Indiana. Without their parents, each of the three siblings would have their hands full managing the family greenhouse business at the peak of the season.

Belinda would make hanging baskets and tend to the family's large gardens alone. Tabitha would continue selling their goods at the Amish market in town five days a week without Mamm to help her. And Mica would handle the farm and produce auctions, without Daed to guide him.

Belinda glanced over her shoulder as their mammi, Mollie Bender, limped outside to join them. Even her maternal grandmother would have to do more managing the house, despite the way her hip troubled her.

A short, pudgy man exited the van and began helping Daed load his and their mother's things. Belinda ducked into the shadow of her lofty brother, Mica, becoming invisible—a maneuver she had mastered in her growing years anytime unfamiliar faces drew near. He barely noticed her using him as a human shield anymore.

Her childhood unease—shyness, Mamm called it—stemmed from the port wine birthmark on her left cheek. She'd been stared at and heckled over it far too many times over the years. While she was no child anymore, interactions with strangers could make that unease surge again. The man offered a hello to each of them, sending a shudder through her.

Mamm offered up the last suitcase as they all joined her at the van. Belinda knew her mother would not be at ease until she was at Dawdi's side, willing him to defeat the odds. And Mamm's will was nothing to scoff at. At fifty, Hattie Graber had hardly a grey hair marring her auburn locks, but Belinda could see a prominent one doing its best to slip out from under her *kapp*. She reached over and tucked the wandering strand back into submission. Hattie took a breath, forced a smile, and gazed over her children.

"Is Dawdi really giving up on taking treatments?" Belinda whispered to Mamm. She was unsure how she'd feel about the answer, whatever it might be. She'd heard Mica and his friend Ivan whispering days ago that the treatments only prolonged the inevitable, that they made their grandfather sicker too. How could medicine make one feel worse than the disease? She didn't want him to feel worse, but neither did she want him to go on to glory.

Mamm took in an irritable breath. "Stubborn, that's what Saul Graber is. He thinks he can tell *Gott* when. Well, I have a thing to say about that." Belinda didn't doubt that for one minute. Her mother was certainly the most stubborn of the Graber and Bender lot.

"Your dawdi should not give up and re-fuse the help the doctors are trying to give," Mamm continued. "Where is his faith now?" She shook her head and knuckled away her tears.

Belinda closed her eyes and squeezed Mamm's shoulders. Her mother was the strongest person she knew, and here she was breaking down. They had all seen their share of loss, but it was one of those things a person never adjusted to. Death was cruel and robbing, and certain.

"Hattie. It's time." Mollie's voice broke the building tension.

Hattie nodded, straightening out any wrinkles of her dress that a few wayward emotions might have caused, regaining her composure. Belinda wished she could do more. But if Dawdi decided he was done with treatments, tired from trips to the clinic and the weakness that ravaged him...then, sadly, all she could do was pray.

Mamm and Daed explained to each sibling what they expected in their absence. Meanwhile, Mammi shuffled behind them to the open side van door. Her limp was growing more painful-looking every day. Stubborn ran as thick as winter sap in her bloodline; a new hip would have given her less grief than this old one, but she refused to consider it.

Belinda buried herself in the farewell hug her father offered. His pale blue eyes

4

were rimmed in red, but his arms were as strong and safe as they had been all her life, and he stood upright with a bearing that said he never doubted himself. Belinda had inherited Melvin Graber's eyes, but none of his self-assurance.

A damp late May breeze tickled the hairs on her lower arms, stirring a shiver. Rain-scented air mingled with the fragrance of a moist earth that would give her flower gardens the nourishment they needed to spring forth. Even thinking about her flowers and the joy they always brought her couldn't make this dreadful evening any better. She understood plenty about life and death at twenty-three, and the possibility she might never see her dawdi again, or hear his raspy voice sharing stories, broke her heart.

"We will call each afternoon and leave a message on the phone machine, if..." Daed began, his voice choked with emotion. Mica stepped forward and touched his shoulder. They no longer stood eye to eye, Mica having long ago surpassed Daed's height. In the absence of their parents, Mica would be head of the household, so Belinda knew Daed would worry little as he faced what the days ahead would require of him. Mica was responsible, levelheaded, and always did what needed done.

"Don't worry, Daed. Have faith and trust His will," Mica said solemnly. Daed looked up at Mica, visibly grateful that his teachings hadn't fallen on deaf ears.

"Take care of your Mammi and your *schwesters*," Melvin instructed, as if it needed to be said.

Tabitha threw two willowy arms around him tightly. They were very close, Daed and Tabitha, alike in many ways. Belinda didn't envy them that, for her parents loved them equally, but it was clear, the nearness between them; just as clear as it was that her brother and mother shared something tight-knit, too, which always made her feel like the fifth wheel. Belinda was the quiet one, and in a house with so many talkers, it often separated her from the pack.

Mammi Mollie patted her arm again, as if reading Belinda's mind. Her parents loved her, but it was her grandmother who evened out the unbalance. Mammi didn't pity her, like Daed, nor push her, like Mamm.

Her parents climbed into the middle seats of the van. "We cannot know how long we will be." Mamm poked her head out to see each of them clearly. Crickets chimed in, as if only now remembering they had a duty to perform. "Remember the things I have told you." Her mossy green eyes arrowed into Belinda's. "You have worked hard; don't waste all that effort. I know those gardens are going to be beautiful." She was speaking of the extra garden rows Daed had gifted his daughter to grow more flowers to sell, adding extra income for her family and herself. Belinda nodded, her face turning red.

She never should've told her family about her hope to have a flower farm someday. Mamm thought selling her flowers, freshly cut, was such a grand idea that they spent all winter planning for the right seeds to add market value to what had once been Belinda's hobby.

"Now Hattie, be on with ya. I'll see to them," Mammi Mollie said. "I might have all three married off before you return," she added, never one to let things get overly serious.

Tabitha chuckled at Mammi's playfulness. Mica suppressed a grin. Talk of marriage was never far from their mother's thoughts. It must be hard having three *kinner* full grown, and not a one even contemplating courting while all her friends were already bouncing *bopplin* on their knees. In this, the three siblings were equal. Having two stubborn children was just as much a burden as having one who feared speaking to others.

After a final farewell, Belinda and her siblings watched the van speed down the drive and onto the pavement. Across the street, Belinda caught a movement, and noticed Adam Hostetler, their neighbor, exiting his barn. He cast a long shadow across the field. At this hour on a Saturday night, Belinda would've expected him to be out courting Susanne Zook, as he usually did. She hoped all was well on his side of the road.

"She's gonna drag Dawdi into treatments against his will," Tabitha said to no one in particular, eyes fixed on the van racing down the asphalt.

"*Jah*," Mammi Mollie agreed. "Hattie always was a determined one."

"And we'll have at least four messages a day on our answering machine," Belinda added, pulling her gaze away from the barn across the way and the man who, oddly enough, was still standing there, gawking at them.

Mammi chuckled. "*Mei dochder* is thorough. She gets that from her daed."

Mica stepped in line with them as the van turned the bend from Mulberry Lane onto Whitley.

"What did she whisper to you?" Tabitha elbowed Mica gently. His smile came easily.

"She told me to find a worthy *maedel* before she gets back," Mica said, as the red of the van's brake lights disappeared. Belinda smiled. That wasn't a lot of time for Mica to find a suitable young woman. "Even with so much going on, she is still trying to get us married off."

"She asked me to *please* smile at Colby Plank next time he smiles at me." Tabitha shook her head. Belinda knew Colby Plank would not be receiving any smiles from her

8

sister. Despite his owning his own cabinet shop, little about him appealed to Tabitha.

"The good Lord sends what is needed when it's time, Mica. And"—Mammi Mollie turned to Tabitha—"don't be smiling at a Plank if you can help it, dear. I don't want *kinner* running around here looking starved. Those Planks can eat all day and never gain a pound. You will work your fingers to the bone for nothing." Tabitha laughed and promised she would never smile at Colby Plank, not ever.

It was a wonder their mother hadn't taken on full matchmaking meddling to ensure a marriage in the family. Well, she'd have to depend on Mica and Tabitha for that. If God wanted Belinda to have a family of her own, then he wouldn't have marked her as he had. Belinda sighed—and then set aside the care. Life was what it was, and who was she to challenge it?

"She told me to sell my flowers," Belinda muttered. Going to town, facing strangers, and striking deals was out of the question. When it appeared Adam was strolling their way, Belinda reached for her cheek. The ugly mark had driven her to live in the shadows, keeping her head down, careful to never draw attention to herself. It was the perfect defense to protect her heart...and maybe, if she was being totally honest, her pride, too.

She wasn't naïve. She knew that some thought her strange, given her quiet nature and timidity. But she couldn't change who she was or how she reacted. Talking to others meant letting them focus on her ugliness, and just the thought of that nauseated her.

Adam reached the pavement separating their family farms, locking eyes with her. At this distance she couldn't tell if he looked concerned or simply nosy, and she didn't care. She wanted no part of his curiosity, and skedaddled off toward her gardens.

Belinda wanted to be alone in the one place she always found solace. She didn't want to be stared at by her neighbor...and no one needed to see her cry for the grandfather she might never speak to again.

Adam Hostetler could tell something was wrong this evening when he returned home. As soon as his horse was settled into pasture, he'd glanced across the road and witnessed Hattie and Melvin Graber climbing into a van. It was awfully late in the day to need a driver for something simple like shopping in the next town over, so it must be something more urgent. Everyone knew Belinda's grandfather from Kentucky had been ill for some time. Since Adam's father had been in a terrible accident a month ago, he knew what it was like to worry over family. Adam whispered a quick prayer for the neighbor family before stepping out of the shadows.

If there was one thing his recent break-up had taught him, it was that he needed to be more present in the lives of others and less consumed with his own—currently disheveled—life. And that meant reaching out to those around him. The Grabers had been his neighbors for years. A normal man would walk over to offer comfort or concern. See that all was well. When he walked toward them, he didn't fail to notice how Belinda—just a couple of years younger than his own age of twenty-five—made a quick retreat, tucking herself under the shadow of her brother. Mica had always shielded her like a faithful dog standing guard over a kitten with no *mudder.*

When Adam reached the pavement, his gaze locked with Belinda's. For more years than Adam wanted to admit, she'd been the secret object of his affection. At one time, he'd hoped she would grow out of her shyness and finally welcome his attentions. He'd waited for years and watched for subtle signs from her, but she never gave them. Just as well, really. All that foolish hoping was behind him, now that he knew the female species better. He would steer clear, never to be made a fool of again.

Adam hadn't given Belinda a close look in years, and the distance between them was preventing him from getting a closer look now. But that habit of hers still lingered: She jerked her hand up and covered her cheek. Her eyes widened as he closed the distance. Before Adam made it to the gravel drive, she pivoted and scurried from the lawn, around the house, and out of sight.

Yes, change was inevitable; his current life was proof of that. Still, some things never changed. Belinda Graber would always be the girl who ran from him. Proof she was still as smart as she had been in school.

Mica ushered his remaining family indoors, not noticing Adam's quiet approach. Just as well. Adam shook his head and turned back to his own house and the late supper he knew awaited him. He hoped all on that side of the road was all right. If not, tomorrow was Church Sunday. If news was to be learned, he would know then. Nothing went unnoticed in Havenlee.

Chapter Two

AFTER A LONG WINTER OF biweekly church gatherings in cramped houses, Adam knew he wasn't the only one who appreciated the airy barn of the local minister today despite the dreary weather.

Once the final prayer was over, he stood, stretching out his stiff limbs. He collected his straw hat, walked to the barn opening, and peered out. Cool May rain drizzled down, matching his discontented mood. It was only a month ago that logs had slid off the loading skids at the mill, landing on his father's leg. It had been a terrible accident, and that grim day had been the beginning of everything shifting in Adam's life.

As an only child, Adam accepted responsibility for all the family's financial burdens while his father was laid low, but working multiple jobs left a man little time to sleep, much less do anything else.

But it wasn't sleep that was harassing Adam right now. It wasn't even the rejection he'd received from the woman he'd spent the last year courting, though it still stung that she had left him because he worked too much—as if that was even a plausible excuse. But no, none of those were what troubled him now.

Adam had a bee problem.

Under all the mounting responsibilities he'd inherited, how would he manage the summer honey harvest?

He glanced back and noticed his former girlfriend, Susanne, prattling with friends in a distant corner instead of helping the women ready the fellowship meal. She stood out with her blonde hair and fetching smile, mocking him. In the large open barn, tables lined the back while benches sat nearly empty beside him, nearer the open front. He waited for the weather to break, a chance to put some distance between him and the woman who made a habit of skirting chores like she did commitments. Susanne always hid when there was work to be done or promises to be kept. Instead of helping the women serve today, she stood giggling and gossiping in a corner. It made his blood boil.

One minute he was anticipating asking her to marry him and the next, he was alone.

Couples who endured the hard days with an equal love and gratitude as for the good ones were equivalently matched. Adam believed that wholeheartedly. He had been a fool to rest his hopes in a *maedel* who had other ideas. Watching his parents work so well together over the years had sent all kinds of fanciful notions into his head about marriage, but reality had taught him few could have what his parents had been blessed with. Susanne wanted a husband who made her the center of his world, but the world was too big for one to set any fallible human at the center of it, by his way of thinking. He should have seen the truth earlier, but he'd been blinded until it was too late. Betrayal, just like rejection, had a way of bruising a man deep. He knew he was better off, but fresh wounds were sore spots, and some sores tended to linger longer than others.

Few knew about the breakup yet, since it had been just days ago when Adam caught her holding hands with another man, but surely all of Havenlee would know soon enough. The gossip would spread that Adam had been passed over for Jerimiah Petersheim. It seemed Jerimiah had more time for porch-sitting and doting on her, and that appealed to her. Susanne had made it clear she had no intention of sharing a life with someone who raised bees for a living.

Hoping to avoid further sympathetic looks from Kathy Zook, Susanne's mother, Adam retrieved his hat and strolled out of the barn to seek solace under an old oak. The misty rain was tapering down, but even if it had been pouring buckets, he would have preferred being out here.

Tobias, Jacob, and Caleb, his closest friends, ambled out of the barn and joined him under the budding oak, which did nothing to umbrella them from the gloomy day. Since childhood, wherever he went, they had never been far behind.

"Looks to be about over." Tobias held out a palm up to prove it. Slowly, others began leaving the crowded barn, beckoned by the promise of summer carried on the winds.

"How's Atlee doing?" Caleb inquired.

"He handled the two surgeries and the two weeks in the hospital with the finesse of a bear awoken in winter." Adam grinned. "But now he's happy as a cat in the milk pail with all the pampering Mamm is giving him."

Adam surveyed everyone milling about. Faces he had known all his life. Somewhere in that sea of hats and white *kapps* had to be someone willing to lend an extra pair of hands. He was going to need more than the two he had if he was to keep things moving forward. Everyone had offered well-wishes and expressed their concerns for his father's well-being since the accident. Many of the local women had been by their home to lend a hand, making Mamm's life easier. It was one of the reasons Adam loved being part of his Amish community: how people went out of their way to help each other. Havenlee was a community where everyone took care of one another. There were five cakes, nine pies, and more cookies than three people could eat in a lifetime sitting on Mamm's counter presently. But not one of those sweets was going to help him manage his life right now.

He was at a dead end.

The bees were his future, and soon he needed to be pulling frames and harvesting their riches. But how was one man supposed to do all the things he needed to? He groaned inwardly.

He had asked everyone he could think of, but no one could help him out. He suspected some were more afraid of the bees than others, and he couldn't rightly hold that against them.

He ran his hands through his darkening blonde hair, glad Mamm had shortened it yesterday, and surveyed the faces more closely. He just needed one person, just one, and then he could manage.

He liked plans, following them; he was no longer a boy who believed things would work themselves out.

It was all...complicated.

After the meal, children scampered away in various directions and split into groups: some to play kickball, some boys who were overly fascinated with mud puddles, and little girls who just stared at the two groups, giggling. Men gathered into clusters to talk about the upcoming planting season and the weather. Standing between youth and age, Adam didn't want to play kickball or talk about planting. He wanted to find someone who could help him with his hives. The tension between his shoulder blades tightened.

"That one's still shy," Tobias said, jolting Adam out of his thinking. Tobias was working at the mill this summer for extra money, but he'd always preferred cattle over wood. They were nearly eye level, of the same build—only Tobias ate better, Adam mused.

"I asked her for an extra slice of pie, said *danki*, and still nothing." Tobias sounded a bit put out.

"Noel Christner asked Mica if he could drive her home, but she won't go," Caleb Esh added, though who he was talking about, Adam couldn't have said. Adam finally turned to face his friends. *Be present.* Something he knew he needed to work on more.

Adam followed their gaze to the Graber sisters clearing the dessert table. Tabitha Graber was as well-known for her beauty and her bold, forthright personality as she was for selling quilts at the local Quilters

Haven shop and running the family's produce stand at the local Amish market. She liked things in order, even the way the desserts sat on the table in sequence of color, or the way she arranged vegetables at the family's produce stand at the market. She never had a hair out of place and always walked with her chin tilted up. She projected confidence and demanded order.

He narrowed his gaze to her younger sister. Belinda was the complete opposite—as gentle and quiet as her sister was dynamic and outspoken. Belinda's fine looks weren't as striking as her sister's, but her beauty had a lovely peacefulness to it. Looking at her settled him, filled his heart with quiet warmth. His eyes caught on her hair, which didn't hint at red like the rest of the Grabers. She was blonde, but not the sunny color of Susanne's. Belinda's was somewhere between wheat and gold.

He pulled his gaze away firmly, deliberately. Women only complicated life, and he needed no more complications, especially from that one.

In school Belinda had been teased because of a birthmark on her left cheek, but Adam never noticed it much. He was more entranced by those large, expressive eyes of hers, and the way she would turn squiggling lines on her paper into plants, flowers, and scenery. He could count on both hands the number of times he'd almost approached her when they were students, but every time he came close, she would drop her gaze and he'd imagined he could literally see the anxiety run up her spine. No, Adam wasn't one for making others feel uncomfortable, and it was clear he made her *very* uncomfortable. Another reason he hadn't followed her last night, to query if her grandfather had taken a turn for the worse.

"You're talking about Belinda, aren't you?" Adam replied coolly.

"*Jah.*" Tobias smirked. He was an incorrigible flirt. "A man could catch a glimpse of those eyes if she'd stop staring at her feet all the time."

Adam refused to comment.

"I told her that strawberry pie was my favorite, offering her a compliment, and she walked off into the house like she hadn't heard a word I'd said," Jacob added. Jacob had a tendency to speak in one volume, a decibel just above actual silence. Adam suspected most *didn't* hear a word he said, but he was used to his friend's undertones.

"You know she's shy," Adam put in unnecessarily. Everyone knew her timid, quiet nature. Belinda never sought out attention like other single girls in the community. Still, it found her easy enough. Maybe *Gott* knew what he was doing, blessing the beautiful sisters with an older brother the size of a shed. Mica would never allow just any man to court one of his sisters. Adam shook his head and grinned.

"*Jah*, that too," Tobias conceded. "But still...she isn't getting any younger. You'd think she would look up once in awhile. Smile or bat her eyelashes like the rest do," he added in an irked tone. "Isn't that a rule or something?"

Caleb chuckled. "Maybe she finds you repulsive." Caleb had a uniquely deep voice, the kind that always stood out amongst others. Adam laughed too. He loved his friends, with their banter and their comebacks. They never said a word when Susanne broke off their relationship. In fact, they seemed pleased. Caleb had often voiced the thought that Adam and Susanne weren't a good match. His friends also never fussed when days went by and they hadn't spoken, which he was now regretting, considering the topic of conversation was Belinda.

Adam fixed his gaze on the subject of conversation again. He hadn't let himself look at her when he'd been courting Susanne. He preferred Belinda didn't look up and bat eyelashes at any of his friends, knowing them as he did.

She was far from the little girl who had first stirred his heart. Her pale green dress hinted at subtle curves that had not been present on her younger form. She whispered something in her grandmother's ear, guided her toward the house, and vanished. She was probably encouraging Mollie to rest. That limp couldn't be ignored, and at Mollie's age, the family matriarch had earned all the rest she needed.

"You just wish she stared at you." Adam pulled his attention away, toed the dirt around a dandelion.

"I remember when you wished that, too," Tobias countered, and gave his dark brows a wiggle. "You missed out on a lot fun back then since you were so stuck on pining over that one."

"I remember that too," Caleb added. "Never understood why you never tried harder."

"I didn't pine," Adam said gruffly. "We were *kinner* and she didn't care for my... *staring.*" No, she ran and hid every time Adam even *thought* to approach her during those years.

"Maybe you should give it another try," Tobias said, visibly amused.

"*Nee.* I'm not ever trying my hand at courting again," Adam said firmly. He had half a dozen responsibilities and not one would ever again include a woman. *Too much trouble.*

"Ever?" Joshua asked, his face distorted in shock.

"Ever." Betrayal, like rejection, left its marks.

To his surprise, they let the subject drop. Normally they teased, poked a thing with a stick enough that Adam's temper flared.

He appreciated their restraint in this case. These days it took little poking to get his temper going.

Nelly waved in their direction. "Guess that's my cue to go. See ya fellows," Caleb said, marching toward his sweetheart. Adam watched the perfect pair stroll off. Caleb was soon to take over his father's dairy business and Nelly worked at her *onkel's* store a few days each week and baked pies to sell for extra income for her family. They had a future ripe for the taking.

"I need to get going as well. Rhoda agreed to let me drive her home. If we leave now, we can take the long way," Tobias said, with a side-twisted grin.

"Staring at one girl and courting another?" Adam lifted a brow. "And how is that Yoder girl over in the next district?" he added, teasing.

Tobias tipped his hat, smiling to show off a row of slightly crooked teeth and a full-fledged charm that matched the twinkle in his dark eyes. "I'm in no hurry to settle down, and I like leaving my options open. See ya." Adam shook his head as his friends wandered off. He doubted Tobias would ever grow up.

"You look like a man who is thinking too hard. It wonders me if you have more than Atlee's health on your mind today." The bishop, Benjamin Schwartz, appeared out of nowhere. He was a short, stout man with more grey in his hair than a man his age had usually earned, and he'd always been keen on seeing to the needs of others.

Adam hoped the bishop hadn't heard him and his friends talking about girls.

"*Jah*," Adam said. "With Daed laid up with his leg, I took up work at the local pallet mill. I think missing a few extra hours of sleep is weighing on me."

"Your Daed has a long road ahead of him, for sure and for certain." That was the truth. Soon his father would begin physical therapy. Adam winced. He shouldn't be fretting over his own problems when his Daed was bending toward miserable.

"That's five days a week," the bishop tilted his head. "And do you still help Ivan Shetler in his construction business?"

"*Jah*, when he needs the help. He has a full crew and only calls for small jobs or if he's running behind on a project." Adam looked down at his hands, blistered from cutting metal for three days straight. The work wasn't easy or steady, but it paid well and didn't interfere with his honey business. He and Ivan had made a deal years ago.

The bishop cleared his throat. "You know the community has funds for matters such as these. You are stretching yourself out too thin, I feel." The community always collected offerings to help families in need, but Adam knew his Daed was a firm believer that accepting help should only happen in times of dire need, not to simply make life easier.

"*Nee.* I can manage. Others could use the money more." Like the Schmidts, who'd lost their barn, including livestock, in a recent lightning storm. The bishop agreed with a signature nod.

"So it is something else that troubles you today?" The bishop returned to stroking his beard, searching for the answers somewhere in the steady strokes. "You are worried about the honey business."

It wasn't a question. Everyone in Havenlee knew Adam had raised bees since he was sixteen. Many purchased his honey at the local Amish store or one of the *Englisch* stores in town, and there was hardly any surplus to stockpile over the winter months. Mamm had suggested he open a booth at the local Amish market. It was a good idea, but Adam had too many other responsibilities to work the stand so frequently.

He was itching to add more hives. It would be a good income. Enough, eventually, to sustain himself without the need for another income, now that supporting a family of his own was no longer in his future.

"*Jah*, I am. First harvest is June, then again in mid-August. With my other responsibilities, I could use an extra set of hands this year." Adam shifted his feet and searched the crowd as many began leaving.

"I've asked everyone, but with summer nearing, no one can help."

The bishop looked over his community as he ran his hands down his beard, forming a sharp point. Benjamin wasn't just the bishop, but a problem solver, too. His advice had helped the small community of Havenlee prosper and grow, with a busy Amish market where families sold their homemade goods. Tourists flocked to the largest Amish communities, but out here where roads ran narrow and pavement was scarce, their old roadside stands had barely seen a visitor. Havenlee had been fortunate the day he chose the lot.

Not all men were called to serve. The choosing was God's will. No Amish man was formally trained to lead a community, but when a position for a deacon, minister, or bishop needed to be filled, it was the man who unknowingly picked up the one Bible containing a slip of paper from a table of Bibles who was gifted a lifelong commitment of serving others. Benjamin Schwartz was made for his position.

"You've got time yet," Benjamin said. Adam did, but not a lot of it—a handful of weeks. "Mica Graber used to help his family back in Kentucky with their hives. He *is* mighty busy, but he's close by and has a strong back." The Bishop smiled and patted Adam's shoulder, before strolling away to the next group of men and whatever troubles they might have that needed mending.

Adam turned his attention toward the Bylers' barn. Mica was already helping his sisters into their buggy, and Mollie sat primly in the front holding a few empty dishes. Mica was a few years older than Adam and helped his family run their greenhouse business. In the colder months he served as the local blacksmith, and he *had* spent a few summers in Kentucky helping his dawdi with his beehives. Adam had even asked him a thing or two when he'd purchased his first two hives. How had he forgotten that? Mica had experience and was strong enough to handle the weight of the supers—the large wooden boxes used to collect the honey. What's more, Adam wouldn't have to teach him a thing.

It was the perfect idea. He felt his spirits lift, along with the tension that had been building up for days. Maybe he was being given an ounce of mercy, after all.

Chapter Three

O N MONDAY EVENING, ADAM PULLED into his drive, feeling as if he had just worked through a full week instead of simply starting one. He veered toward the barn and noticed Mica Graber sitting outside on the Graber family's wide wraparound porch, watching the sun fall behind Adam's barn. Adam often found himself watching the sun rise over his neighbors' home; their east and west positions were perfectly placed to enhance the view. Adam put Honey, his horse, in her stall, giving her a bucket of oats to keep her content for the time being. She needed a good brushing, not to mention a new shoe. But first, Adam needed to see a man about some bees.

Crossing the road, Adam raised a hand in greeting, and Mica waved him over. Adam wandered over the perfectly trimmed yard and the flowery path leading to the porch. Irises and flowers which he had no name for were in full bloom in an array of colors. Cool evening air delivered the sweetened scents abundantly. Adam, a novice in flora, but appreciative of all things sweet-smelling, inhaled. It was a sensory experience like no other.

"That horse of yours needs a new shoe." Mica was known for his blunt speaking. Adam preferred conversations not stuffed with idle chatter, too. Mica leaned back, legs stretched out and resting on the railing. He was a mountain of a man, all six-foot-too-many-inches of him.

"She threw it on the ride home." Adam removed his hat and noted an empty plate next to Mica that might have held strawberry pie. His stomach reminded him of another forgotten meal. The Grabers' front fields yielded rows and rows of strawberries to sell, and few people skipped the chance of trying out the Graber women's desserts at gatherings. All were excellent bakers.

"You need me to tend to it before morning?" Mica asked.

"*Nee*, I know my way around a hoof when necessary." Adam was not only a bee-keeper, but a Jack of all trades. There were few things he couldn't do when set to task. "I came over to ask a question."

Mica's thick auburn brows lifted. Adam

got right to the point, explaining his pre-
dicament, down to the fact that the honey
harvest would begin soon. Until he found
a moment to spare and check his hives, he
didn't know just how soon that would be.
"I'm not sure how to pull off doing all three
jobs. We need the income from the mill and
Ivan likes that I'm always available to help
him on a project, and I can't risk that. But
the hives can't go unattended. They are my
true livelihood," Adam concluded, masking
the tension in his voice.

"Sounds to me you're stretching yourself
mighty thin," Mica said. "A man can only do
so many things before the body wears, or
snaps." Mica sympathetic expression showed
that he was a man speaking from experience.

"I'm young and it's only temporary, until
Daed gets back to his feet." *Which might
not be for a full year.* The doctor had explained the lengthy road to a full recovery
for his father. A year was a long time. Adam
wouldn't complain, for as much as it would
stretch him out, it was still a blessing that
his father had survived with no worse hurt.
And anyway, Adam's crowded schedule was
nothing compared to what his father was
miserably enduring in the healing process.

"Well, you should know our parents are
gone to Kentucky to tend to Dawdi," Mica
started.

"*Jah*, I heard his health isn't getting any

better. I'm sorry." Adam remembered his own grandfather. Losing him when Adam had just turned nine had left an empty void.

"*Nee*, it's not getting better. Nor will it, since he isn't taking treatments any longer." Mica's jaw clenched.

Adam's heart went out to him and the rest of Belinda's family. It was clear her grandfather would be called home soon. Mica cleared his throat. His auburn hair glinted orange in the glow of the sunset. "I can't help much. Not as much as you need now, with me being responsible for the greenhouses, my shop, and what hay we've got, but I'll do what I can to lend a hand. Have you asked around, or am I the first?" Mica wouldn't say no, but it was clear he wouldn't be much help, having so little free time.

"I asked around," Adam said on a sigh. "Bishop Schwartz thought you could help, with your experience and all. And you really are the only other person in Havenlee who knows anything about extracting honey besides the *Englisch* teacher in town. I'd rather pay a friend and neighbor than an outsider." Mica agreed with an audible grunt.

After what felt like hours of awkward silence, Mica said, "Belinda could do it." He said it as if speaking to himself before snapping to attention, sounding more definitive. "*Jah*, Belinda could help, with all of it." He got to his feet, towering over Adam, who stood just below the porch. His fully stretched stance was as intimidating as it had been when they were in school. Even then, Mica had been years older and nearly a foot taller, reaching a lofty height in his boyish years.

"Belinda?" It came out like he'd just swallowed a handful of sand. Surely Adam had heard wrong. Belinda Graber would never consider working with bees, a task that many men hesitated to tackle. She had nearly tripped the last time he'd thanked her for refilling his *kaffi* cup at a gathering months ago. She was still the same frightened girl she'd been in school. The same one who ignored every look her way, every compliment paid her. She was fearful of everything—surely that included being fearful of bees.

"She knows as much as I," Mica said. "When I spent autumns in Kentucky, Belinda went and helped too." Mica thumbed his suspenders. How did a man nearing thirty look as if he was still growing? But despite his commanding presence, Adam didn't quite believe his words. Belinda couldn't know anything about working an apiary...and if she did, she surely wasn't about to help him. Her creature comforts were with flowers. Not thousands of bees.

"She helps with the greenhouse and the vegetable gardens, plus she has her flowers to tend to this year." Mica stepped to edge of the porch, pointing a thumb around the side. "Daed let her plant a few dozen extra rows of flowers this year to try making a go of something herself, but she can spare a little time to help another."

Adam peered out toward the three large greenhouses sitting adjacent to the Graber home. The lower greenhouse sat in the full sun closest to the road, a large watering tank at its side. The other two greenhouses were constructed in the shape of a very large T, closer to the barn. Even at this distance, he could see bold colors dotting the insides. The Grabers did well with their produce, and it never went unnoticed how fast they sold out of hanging baskets year after year.

They also owned a fair amount of land for growing vegetables and hay. Two large gardens were already sprouting green, and Adam noticed tomatoes already heavy in yellowy blooms, uncommon so early in the season. They were a family of green thumbs and blessed seasons, and Adam was fortunate his bees could forage for free next door. His gaze lingered over the flower gardens. *A few extra rows*, he mused, noting a separate plot from the two regular gardens stretching all the way to the fence line. Among bold blues and purply violets, the occasional pastel pink and withering daffodils, he saw her. In her white *kapp* and dull grey dress, she knelt between rows, nestled among the flowers.

"Are you seriously suggesting I ask your sister to help me?"

"I am. You've known her all her life, so why not?" Mica shrugged one large shoulder. "Belinda may be..."

"Shy, and has never said two words to me, even as *kinner*." Adam said too quickly. Was *Gott* playing tricks? Was the only person available truly a woman, when he'd just sworn off the fairer sex?

Mica pinned him with a look. "I was going to say, self-conscious, but she knows bees. I'm sure she would gladly help someone in need, and one who has so few options."

"Self-conscious?" Adam lifted a brow. What did Belinda have to be self-conscious about? Mica studied him for another hard minute as if the simple questioned perplexed him. The longer Mica stared at him, the tighter the pending threat squeezed Adam's chest.

"What?" Adam asked at last, when the silence had grown uncomfortable.

"*Nix*. She's in the garden." Mica pointed. "You can go and ask her. I'm not the one needing help." Mica smirked and turned away to scoop up his plate.

"I don't want to frighten her. She doesn't...like to be bothered." Adam felt his stomach form a loose knot. He wasn't the type of man who feared much, but he had a soft spot for the meek and he hated the idea of upsetting Belinda.

Mica chuckled. "Then don't frighten her. You *will* have to talk to work together.

I'm going for seconds. Strawberry pie is my favorite." Mica grinned as if he hadn't just added more weight to Adam's shoulders.

Adam pivoted, studying the figure kneeling in the garden. A thousand scenarios ran through his head, and not one would get him any closer to a solution for his problem than he was right now. He inhaled, slowly exhaled, and took one stupid step forward.

Mica slipped into the kitchen, empty plate in hand. "What?" Tabitha stood near the counter, arms crossed, brows raised in reproof.

"You sent him to talk to her, alone?" Tabitha's voice rose. "Don't try to deny it—we heard the whole thing."

"Then you heard the part about him needing help." Mica shrugged, fending off the impulse to laugh at her, and inched to the table, where one slice of pie lay, lonely. Tabitha was just as overprotective as he when it came to their youngest sibling. But Belinda wasn't a little girl anymore, running home crying day after day, convinced the other *kinner* hated and mocked her. She was a grown woman, and Mamm was right. It was time they all stepped out of their comforts. Belinda needed to test her abilities. She deserved more in life than the sheltered solitude she'd fallen into, and helping another would pull her out of that shell she stayed in. Help grow her confidence. Adam was a safe bet. He had a girlfriend and was an all-around decent fellow. He knew Mica wouldn't tolerate Belinda not being treated respectfully. Mica grinned. It was the perfect plan.

"She will be inconsolable. I should go." Tabitha made for the door, her controlling nature driving her.

"*Nee*," Mammi barked, halting Tabitha in her tracks. "You will stay put and mind yourself. Mica did the right thing. We can't coddle her for always." She placed both hands on Tabitha's shoulders. "*Mei* Belinda is not so little anymore. She knows her own mind and owns her own tongue. That Hostetler boy has known her for her whole life, and he won't harm her. He needs help, and it would be good for her to accept." *Blessed Mammi, always knowing how to deal with this house of women,* Mica silently mused.

"But you know how she can get," Tabitha continued, while Mica slipped the slice of pie ever so quietly onto his plate.

"You are a good *schwester*, but don't you think you should be focusing on your own future and not hers?" he asked. Mamm might be a couple hundred miles away, but her words and hopes sure weren't.

"And you," Mammi turned her attention

to him. Mica froze mid-swallow. "You are the eldest and not setting much of an example. Should've been married long before now," Mammi fussed.

So much for thinking he could escape without a reproach. But, he thought as he headed back to the porch, at least he was escaping with pie.

Adam brushed his sweaty palms down the legs of his dusty trousers as he neared the flower garden. "What are you up to now?" he grumbled heavenward. "Of all the people in Havenlee, why did it have to be this one?" No answer was forthcoming. He would do well to get this over with.

Adam homed in on Belinda, plunked down and tending her flowers, as she often did. Singing, as she often did too. Her voice was as soft and delicate as the woman it came from, caressing the air, enchanting the evening. He had forgotten just how sweet her voice sounded, how beautiful she looked nestled among the rows. Like her garden, she'd always been beautiful in flawless splendor, a distant vision of *Gott*'s good works. It was a serene picture, one that gave his chest a sudden jolt.

Adam focused on the reason he was here. He needed help with his apiary; that was all.

Cautiously, he walked to the edge of the garden, considering what he might say. How did one go about asking a woman like her for help? He stepped forward, careful of the flowers. No sense starting off on the wrong foot—literally. Mica insisted she knew a thing or two about bees, which probably wasn't enough for all he needed, but Adam had no other option. She had the time. Raising flowers couldn't be that demanding. If she agreed, it would be the perfect solution. So why were his palms still sweaty?

His very livelihood depended on his shy neighbor who barely whispered around others, but could sing a cricket to sleep, that was why.

Chapter Four

SUNSET THREATENED TO CALL DAY'S end, its crimson shadow etching over the earth and snaking past the greenhouses. Belinda had few moments to herself, and welcomed the free time to spend in her gardens. Here among her flowers, she could find some sanctuary from her assertive siblings. They were always reminding her not only that she had flowers to sell, but also that she was twenty-three with no prospects for marriage. Why was there so much emphasis on marriage, anyway? Couldn't a person just be content without it?

And why was Mica intent on shining a light on Noel Christner? Belinda wanted nothing to do with him. He was three years younger than she and far too bold for his own good. She huffed. What kind of man simply walked up unannounced and bluntly asked a brother to let him drive his sister home, without trying to carry on a conversation with said woman first? Granted, she didn't do conversations, so he wouldn't have succeeded if he'd tried for one of those, either...but that wasn't the point.

Belinda had learned long ago this was her lot in life. She'd lagged behind, letting shyness overrule what was considered natural for a girl her age. She never attended singings, youth gatherings or frolics, and after her school years the world simply shrank down to her family, aside from the occasional wedding or funeral. She didn't mind it—not at all. She preferred it. So why couldn't her family let it alone? No one seemed to care that Tabitha wasn't interested in youth rituals, either.

She rolled her shoulders, still stiff from making hanging baskets and scrubbing floors all day. She wouldn't think about Noel and his beady eyes here. She'd be thankful she was blessed with a beautiful garden.

Spotting where she had left off weeding on her last visit, Belinda knelt between rows and inhaled the mingling fragrances flooding the air. To her left, irises—bedecked in violet purple, creamy peach, and canary yellow—reached for any last drops of sunlight they could consume. To her right, zinnias poked out of soft blackened soil, rich and vibrant. She fingered the thick velvety leaves, anticipating the beauty they would transform into. Flowers were uncomplicated, yet their resilience was inspiring. Their only job in life was to be born, reach heavenward, and then be recycled. It was as simple as that. If they expected something more, in the in between, well, they would be sorely disappointed. She should follow their example, and be satisfied with the simple joys her life held.

But a girl could dream. And more often than not, Belinda did. Maybe she read too many novels, but she could easily let herself be drawn into a romantic chapter and imagine herself in the heroine's place. The lady of the house, tending her gardens just as a handsome suitor appeared to confess his heart. Someone with pretty eyes, perhaps, not beady and scary like Noel Christner's.

She plucked a small purple and yellow violet bloom, brushed the delicate petals across her cheek, and then tucked it between hair and *kapp*. She glanced around, felt the day's weight lift, and let herself sink into the world that belonged only to her. She loved the way the light raced over the earth each morning and then was swallowed up over the pastures across the road in the evening, as if reminding her another day was over and rest had been earned. What some called mundane, she called predictable and safe. If she wanted danger, she'd imagine it, and easily overcome it without getting so much as a scratch.

A few birds lingered nearby, darting for whatever insect dared to fly in their path. The last bees were getting their fill before calling it a night. This was such a small piece of a very large world, but she loved and appreciated the harmonious mixture of nature and humanity working hand in hand. This was her world, where she knew exactly what she was doing, and where she had a sense of control. Looks were unimportant out here, words weren't required, and no one had an opinion that they thought she needed to hear. Her heart lifted at the thought, and she began filling the evening with a melody. Maybe a handsome suitor would hear her voice, become enchanted, and seek her out. Maybe he could sweep her away and they would build a new life, a flower farm just as she had always dreamed of, and live happily ever after.

Yes, the imagination was a wonderful tool for the strange and impossible. She smiled as she hummed "I Give You Freedom," and then sang the verses.

"I set the bound'ries of the ocean vast,

Carved out the mountains from the distant past,

Molded a man from the miry clay,

Breathed in him life, but he went astray."

Belinda was just starting the chorus when the hairs on the back of her neck bristled.

A throat cleared, confirming she was no longer alone in her garden. She looked up, way up, as a dark figure stepped into the glare of the lowering sun. Mica was much larger than the shadow before her. For a second, she had the wild idea that she really had conjured up a suitor by singing.

Sliding a hand in place to shield her eyes, recognition slowly registered, and she found herself staring at the last person she expected in her garden. Adam Hostetler, her neighbor.

The slow tremble started in her belly and inched into her fingertips. Lowering her arm, she paused, feeling the urge to hide her birthmark. Since her schooldays, she had nearly shed the old habit, but just the sight of Adam Hostetler, this close without another soul around, stirred up the need again.

"The whippoorwill song," Adam said, speaking first. His voice was deeper than she remembered. He took a cautious step to her left, drawing closer. Her muscles tensed and she instinctually hunkered in on herself, like a rabbit hiding under a bush. But there was no bush, only anxiety curling her stomach, sharpening her nerve endings. Why was he here, in her garden, her perfect sanctuary?

"I hope I didn't startle you." *Startle* was too kind a word for what she was feeling. "Weather seems to be warming up." He sounded uncertain, lacking his normal confidence. Not that she paid him much mind, because she didn't...much. She'd simply noticed over the years that he chatted with others without a care, laughed out loud when something struck him as funny, and a handful of times over the years, had even offered her a thank you for a glass of something to drink. None of which Belinda dared to respond to. Not after the way he used to stare at her all the time when they were in school.

Ten years should be long enough to forgive the foolish antics of boys. Forgiveness was the center of their faith, and it was a tenet she worked hard to practice. But while she could forgive, she couldn't so easily forget. She might have grown out of those urges to run away, but the urge was never far from her thoughts, especially right now.

Adam kicked a clod of dirt and stared at the sky. He clearly wasn't leaving.

"*Jah*," She tried on a smile—Mamm insisted that all hellos needed a smile attached—but it felt like a grimace. Smiles that weren't genuine took a lot of effort.

"Mica said I could find you here." *Of course he did.* She released a slow sigh. Why were her siblings disrupting her quiet life so? Stirring a pot with nothing in it made no sense at all. Her stomach twisted a bit tighter, part nerves and part anger with her brother. She focused on weeding a row around a patch of young zinnias. If she was going to take seriously this new venture Daed had dropped into her lap, she needed all the flowers she could grow. Once she figured out a way to sell them without going to town, that was. *One problem at a time,* she told herself. *Get rid of your neighbor, first.*

"These look nice." His blue eyes glanced about. He looked almost as uncomfortable as she felt.

"Your bees think so." Belinda continued weeding, though she had barely a weed to pull, and began searching them out desperately.

"What are they?"

"Delphinium," she muttered, wondering why he cared. Adam was taller than she remembered. Seeing him across the road, tending to his hives and the family's few horses and head of cattle, she hadn't noticed how he'd grown. Though he'd never been short, either. Tall and handsome, that was Adam Hostetler, though he was nothing like his friend Tobias, a well-known flirt. Adam went to gatherings when he was sixteen until after his baptism, but never showed signs of holding an interest in anyone, including her dear friend Nelly, who used to go starry-eyed any time Adam drew near. Then last spring Belinda had watched him drive Susanne Zook home from church. Her friend Salina had told her Susanne had even been so forward as to ask him for that ride home. Belinda could never have spoken to a man so brazenly. In fact, speaking to one at all right now was making her itchy. And this one just stood there, disturbing her quiet. If one of them didn't say something soon, would he keep standing there?

What did one say to someone who never spoke to you? She could ask about his father. "How is Atlee?" Her gaze slid toward him again, cautiously. His long legs traveled some distance to a pair of narrow hips before his torso fanned out again into two broad shoulders. She swallowed back the sudden awareness of him. What had made her look, she couldn't say. All this talk of courting and time having limits, peppered with an active imagination, perhaps. Certainly, not something she would've usually done.

"Better, now that he is home. His leg was broken in four places." He removed his hat and ran his hands over his sandy hair. "They had to put pins and screws in it." His sharp brows gathered, but his eyes remained fixed on her. He looked to be searching for something—her birthmark maybe. She returned her focus to the imaginary weeds.

"The doctor says he will have a long road ahead," he added. She felt for Atlee Hostetler and for Ada, who would be taking care of him. It was no small duty to care for others, and Atlee would need months of care. "Mamm says *danki* for the dishes your family sent over. It was kind of you."

Belinda nodded. Tabitha had delivered the dishes before going to work over two weeks ago. If "Thank you" was his purpose for coming over today, he could've knocked on the door and delivered it straight to Mammi. She lifted one shoulder higher, hiding the mark, not gifting him the chance to see it clearly, say something cold. Adam might not have teased her about it like most, but the way he stared had hurt nearly as much. Avoiding him had worked for years, so why was he here, staring at her again? And where was Mica? She could always depend on Mica to know when he was needed.

Adam moved through the garden and she watched his steps weave through her flowers, until he was facing her straight on, leaving her more uneasy than ever.

"I heard your parents are staying the summer in Kentucky to help with your dawdi." His voice really was deeper than she remembered, rusty, and maybe tired. Not as deep as Caleb Esh's, but weighty enough to unsettle the air, force things to attention.

She nodded, declining to reply. It was none of Adam's business how long her parents would be gone. Just thinking of her parents again made her think of her grandfather. Mamm had left another message on the answering machine last night saying Dawdi was in good spirits and eating better, but the doctor's prognosis was still the same. Without treatments, his time was narrowed down to a painfully small number. *Four months.* That was all he was expected to have. Of course Daed had no intention of leaving his side for a single day of them. It would be a hard summer without her parents around to see things done well, but nothing was more important than what her parents were doing.

"I heard that he stopped taking his treatments," he said with genuine empathy. "I'm sorry."

Biting her lip, she managed another courteous nod. She wasn't about to cry in front of Adam Hostetler. Belinda focused on the flowers. Another stretch of quiet lingered, only broken by an owl clearing his throat before nightfall. Adam remained, hovering like a schoolmaster. Normally people found her too quiet, too skittish, for them to be comfortable in her company for long. They said their hellos and went on their way. Even Noel Christner was learning to stop wasting time on her. She'd even given him a full on "No thank you" the last time he'd asked to take her home. Tabitha had been awfully happy that Belinda had been brave. Could she be brave now and perhaps tell Adam to go? She mentally shook her head. She was shy, but not purposely rude.

Taking a deep breath, Belinda spoke, though she didn't dare give him eye contact. "Is there something you need?"

"I just wanted to stop by, say hello." His tone was uncertain. Lying was a sin, and yet, Belinda was certain she'd heard just one.

"Why?" she asked, befuddled.

"Would you like me to go?"

Yes, I would. She could be in the house in ten seconds flat. His head tilted toward her and she dared another glance. He didn't look like he was here to spy on her ugliness or tease about her singing in the garden. In fact, Adam looked worried.

"You never came to say hello before." *Where did that come from?*

Adam's eyes widened into something looking a whole lot like surprise. His unease did wonders to nurture her confidence.

"I don't like making you uncomfortable," he said. Did he not? "And the distance is the same, both ways." He quirked a brow, bringing with it a one-sided grin. Something in that smile caught her off guard. Adam Hostetler was handsome, no denying that, but it wasn't like Belinda had ever thought about going across the road, knocking on the door, and saying, *Hi, we went to school together. I see you every day and you see me, but I wanted to be the one who said hello first.* No, she never once thought about doing that.

"Well," she said, and hated the slight tremble in her voice. "I've got work to do, and I have an early morning."

Chapter Five

ADAM KNEW HE WAS GOING about everything all wrong, and Belinda looked about two cows from a conniption. But at least she wasn't running away, which was what he'd been expecting. To think that all these years he'd worried about her sensitivity, when all he had to do was march over here and strike up a conversation. To be sure, it was an uncomfortable one, but she had in fact spoken to him.

"I could use your help," he said.

"Help?" Her perfectly lined brows gathered, but she still refused to look at him. If he had a pet peeve, it was someone refusing to make eye contact when talking to others. It seemed so dismissive, as if she wanted to emphasize that she cared more about some green leaves with not a bloom showing than talking to him. He had half a mind to walk away, leave her to her precious flowers. If he wasn't so desperate, he would have, too.

He shifted his stance, faced her. It was now or never. "I took work at the mill to manage Daed's medical expenses, and I already work part-time helping Ivan on the side. That leaves me with not enough time for my hives. I've asked friends and even Mica if they could help with the honey harvest, but none have the time to spare."

"But Atlee got hurt at that mill." Her voice trembled slightly.

Adam was stunned. Was Belinda concerned, for him—for his safety at the mill? That was a silly thought, and he quickly squashed it.

"Tobias has helped you before," Belinda said in a voice barely audible, still not giving him the courtesy of her full attention.

"He's helping at the mill for the summer and tending to his daed's cattle, and he only helped pull frames for a few days one fall." In fact, Tobias had fooled around more than he'd helped. How did she know about that, anyway?

"Susanne?" Belinda suggested. Adam bristled. She must not have heard of the breakup, keeping to herself as she did.

"She's allergic," he said, before clenching his jaw tight. Or at least, that was what she'd always told him when he'd tried to get her to help. Susanne was certainly not

interested in bees, him, or anything resem-
bling work. *Just Jerimiah Petersheim.*

"Is she." It didn't sound like a question.
"You're a beekeeper and courting someone
who is allergic to bees."

He couldn't help but be taken by
surprise again. Belinda Graber was more
practiced in sarcasm than he'd expected. He
hadn't expected that...or that he might like
it. Here, in her garden, surrounded by famil-
iarities, she was different. And even though
her words were unexpected, Adam agreed
with her skepticism. Susanne's claim that
she was allergic had been just another lie.

"Belinda," her name came on a weary
sigh. "I can't afford to pay much, but I was
hoping you could help. I will be gone a lot,
but I'll help every hour I'm home. I have an
inspector coming soon and then there's Zimmerman's general store to deal with. They
have less than a dozen jars left to sell and
I can't let them buy from someone else and
lose my place. Mica says you helped your
dawdi with his hives and know a lot about
them. I don't have time to teach anyone everything there is to know."

"Mica said that?" Her voice sounded
a bit husky, indicating anger. Cocking his
head, for a better look of her, he still could
only see the top of her *kapp*. Was that all
she heard from his mouthful?

She rose, turned and knelt again, this
time to pluck dead blooms with her back

toward him. "Why is an inspector coming? Have you got mites or something?"

Well. She *did* know a little about bees.

He maneuvered to a short section of puffy pink blooms and stood before her again. Talking to someone who avoided looking at you was a chore. Especially when he didn't understand the reason for it. It seemed like more than just shyness.

Mica had said Belinda was...self-conscious, but Adam still couldn't figure out why. She didn't stutter like little Katie Jo Shetler or have a tic like Ivy Lapp did, rubbing her fingers together in odd circles. She no longer bore as dark a mark on her face as she had as a girl, not that it had ever bothered him; it was lighter and less noticeable now. She was witty, and if he was being honest, she was even prettier than he remembered. What did she have to be self-conscious about? She was a gentle spirit wrapped in beauty, with eyes that had the power to entrap a man's good sense. He averted his own gaze. *Focus on your troubles, Adam, don't go adding to them.*

"The state sends out an inspector every so often to all beekeepers, checking the health of the hives. It doesn't cost anything and it's voluntary, but they let you know if other keepers in the area are having problems with mites, beetles, and such. Its routine, but someone has to be there, and

Mamm wouldn't know how to answer any questions, should there be any."

She didn't seem the least bit enthused to help. In fact, Adam wasn't sure she was even listening. She was still pretty, even at this angle. Susanne had been pretty too, but something about Belinda drew him closer. Her innocent vulnerability, her delicate movements, the way she braved a look at him when he knew she hated doing so. It was all tempting, but he was man enough not to take the bait.

Her eyes snapped up to meet his equally. "So Mica and you figure I have plenty of time on my hands?"

The earth went quiet. Not a frog croaked, not a bug dared to zoom by. He was pretty sure time simply halted, giving him time to regain some sense of composure. Those big blue eyes, a dazzling violet matching a small flower tucked into her hair, made Adam's mouth go dry. He was trying to stay focused, but all he could do was stare helplessly at the way she really had grown into those eyes, and the small delicate point of her chin, the way her lashes encased those...*Snap out of it.*

"*Jah*, I mean I hoped, I'm hoping," he stuttered foolishly, pulling his gaze away from those eyes and the tiny flower in her hair. She sang to flowers, and wore them, which should've made him think her a foolish *maedel*, but it seemed adorable instead.

She had freckles, too. He hadn't known that. Three made a cute line down the right side of her button nose. Adam knelt to see her more clearly. Maybe he looked too intimidating standing over her as he was. Maybe there was more of her to see in the dimming light of the day.

"There is no one else. I really could use the help," he said with complete honesty, uncomfortably aware that he was just east of begging. Asking for help was harder than it looked. Add guilt, and it was pure torture. He was putting pressure on her and he didn't like himself for it, but he was desperate. "I will compensate you fairly for any help you can offer."

"I'm your last choice," she muttered. Adam knew better than to answer that. She bit her bottom lip—a little fuller than her top one—as she considered his request.

Adam waited, wishing he knew what was going through her mind, wondering how he could tip it in his favor. He was the worst neighbor, using her good heart to get what he wanted. Mamm would have his hide if she knew he used his circumstances to apply pressure for his own personal gain. But he needed this help too much to walk away.

Belinda yanked a few blades of grass that dared to grow too close to the garden's edge, and contemplated. Not only had her brother sent Adam out here, but now her good moral sense told her she might just have to accept helping him. It was the Amish way: helping out those in need.

The sun was nearly gone, the moon casting a warm scarlet hue over the landscape as he waited for her answer. She'd always enjoyed harvesting honey for Dawdi, but could she work with another, someone who wasn't family? On top of that, could she take money for it? With Atlee's injured state, the Hostetlers needed every dime they could rub together.

"You can't pay me." She started to get to her feet, and Adam followed. "It wouldn't feel right. I know Atlee's surgeries and future needs will be costly."

"You can't do the work for nothing. *That* wouldn't be fair." Adam offered her a hand up, but she ignored it, brushing dirt from her drab chore dress. When she looked up to him, Adam was again staring. Life had taught her to wilt under such looks. Unexpectedly, Adam took a step back, a gesture to address her natural-born reticence.

"I won't do it for nothing."

His eyes flickered with surprise. "What do you want, then?"

Belinda swallowed the flock of sparrows trying to make its way out of her belly and took a deep breath. What she wanted was not to be looked at like she was right now—especially by him. Adam's eyes had always intrigued her. From a distance, she'd thought them to be green, but as sure as she stood there looking at them now, they were blue, a pale dusty color like a sky nearing the brink of change. She needed to think, and that wasn't easy with those magnetic eyes hanging on so tightly.

She was inexperienced in matters of attraction, avoiding worldly temptations easily enough, but Belinda was bewildered by what those eyes were doing to her. Maybe she was coming down with something. A summer cold, perhaps? Or maybe she had been spending too much time reading and daydreaming.

One thing she did know for certain, though: He wouldn't be here, asking her for help, if he wasn't desperate for it.

Adam had a lot of responsibilities. Working two jobs while trying to run his own business, and having not a soul he could depend on. Belinda could always count on her family if she needed them in anything, but Adam was an only child. All of these responsibilities fell on his shoulders alone.

She knew so little about work troubles, except one. How to find a market for her flowers without actually speaking to strangers. A thought hit her like lightning. *Yes!* She could do this. He needed her, and she needed a way out of doing the one thing she feared most.

"I'll help you harvest your honey, and you'll help sell my flowers." She spoke loudly and lifted her chin to show him she was serious. It was a moment of bravery. If only her siblings were here to witness it.

"Flowers," Adam said, less enthusiastic. "I don't know a thing about flowers."

"You can pack a bucket, can you not?" She gripped her apron and twisted it in her hands. "Tabitha agreed to sell a few cut flowers at the market with our greenhouse plants and early vegetables, but Mamm insists I find buyers, like the florist in town. I'm not comfortable doing that, but I can tend to the honey harvest."

"You want me to talk to buyers and sell your flowers? Is that a thing?" His voice betrayed his doubts. She brushed her cheek out of habit. Maybe he thought her silly, raising flowers for sale, but it was no less important than being a beekeeper.

"The florist might be interested. I mean, I'm local." She tried to sound confident. "Mammi Mollie mentioned a baker," she started down the list of possibilities. "There's also a soapmaker in town. They use flowers for that too," she added.

"Soapmaker I get, but why would you sell flowers to a bakery?" His brows gathered in bemusement.

"They're edible," she began, walking toward the house. "And *I* can't sell anything to them, but you can."

Adam had no idea how to respond to that. Who would eat a flower? Was it a vegetarian thing? Curiosity piqued, he trailed behind her, surprised how fast her stride was and how she managed to not get tangled up in her skirts moving like that. "Besides packing a bucket, what do you need?" Her pace slowed ahead of him.

"Simply speak to the florist. The baker, too. I can have Tabitha speak to the soap-maker. If you can get them to accept, you can deliver my flowers before you go to the mill. You go by all those places, anyway, to get to work, and I can meet with your in-spector and begin seeing to harvesting the honey."

It sounded perfect, coming from her soft rosy lips. How hard could it be to ask a couple of folks to buy flowers? And if they were willing, she was right to say it would be easy enough to drop off a bouquet, or bucket, here and there to appease her. He'd be getting much more than he was offering, and he could still tend to his family needs.

"Deal," Adam quickly said, without thinking too hard on it. She was all he had.

Belinda pivoted, smiled, and held out a hand. Adam barely had time to stop, and nearly smacked into her. With their bodies mere inches apart, he sucked in a breath, heavy in floral notes and rich earth. Her audible gasp rattled him even more than nearly toppling her over. And she had four freckles on the right side of her face, not three. Her eyes held something soft and vulnerable, with hints of childish excitement over getting her way. It reached into the deepest recess of his soul and lit a spark. Adam all but found himself enchanted, just as he had been at ten, staring at her across a classroom; at sixteen when he went to gathering after gathering hoping to see her there. He should look away. Last thing he needed was to be beguiled by blue eyes and soft features. Being alone meant protection from rejection. Never again would he gamble with his heart, let someone pull the wool over his eyes. Never again would he taste the bitterness of betrayal. With rawness still fresh in his thoughts, the spark fizzled easily.

"Deal. We are now a team." She gave one hard nod and took a very obvious step back. Despite the slight tremble in her outstretched hand, she was smiling proudly over her accomplishment, striking a deal with him. It was a good look on her. He thought himself a sturdy sort, a man who could focus on the job at hand without getting distracted, but Belinda Graber was standing before him, agreeing to become his partner for the next few weeks. How did one put a spark out for good?

"A business partnership," he said, more for himself than to her. Who would have thought Belinda Graber would be the one to help him? Tobias would be laughing his hat off when this came out. Adam reached out and accepted her hand as it slipped perfectly into his. *One less worry*, he mentally whispered. He either was the luckiest guy in all of Havenlee...or he'd just made his life a lot more complicated.

Chapter Six

THE KITCHEN SMELLED STRONGLY OF cloves, vinegar, and summer heat. Belinda set down her basket of freshly picked peas and a handful of crisp lettuce and went to the sink to wash her hands. Tuesdays were just Monday's repeats. First she gathered eggs, and then she worked in the greenhouse for a spell, transplanting seedlings and putting together more hanging baskets, before heading to the vegetable garden to plant more seeds. Now the sun was perched high, bending toward the neighbors. The time was between lunch and supper, she knew by its position. All her work had made her thirsty.

She took a glass, filled it under the faucet, and gulped in a most unladylike manner, glad Mamm wasn't there to see her. The only witness was Mammi, who was pickling the last of the cellar-stored beets. Such work always lifted her grandmother's spirits. Mollie Bender loved the kitchen, her sanctuary. Belinda figured everyone had one: a place where one went and found peace, satisfaction. Tabitha's was the upstairs sewing room. Daed often walked the last fields where a murky pond hid. And Mammi loved canning in the kitchen, almost as much as she liked her Sunday visits with friends. Belinda took another drink. Did Adam have a sanctuary?

"You've got something to share." Mammi continued stirring, not looking up. Belinda set the glass aside for later and went to fetch a large bowl to soak the peas in. Belinda had nothing to share. Not a thing.

"*Nix,*" she replied, standing on tiptoe to retrieve a large metal bowl from the top of the hutch. "Would you like me to clean more jars? Looks like we had more beets left over than last year." She pointed a thumb toward the table where freshly washed jars awaited filling.

"*Nee,* I washed plenty," Mammi said flatly. "*Yer* dodging the question."

"You asked a question?" Belinda smirked playfully, lifting one light brow.

Mollie Bender shook her head and did what she always did when she felt unheeded. "Lord, give me strength to deal with these *grosskinner* in my last days. They are a task for sure and certain, and you know how hard Hattie and James wore at me." Belinda giggled. Mammi talking aloud to *Gott* always amused her. Mammi turned around, fisted one hand on her healthier hip and said, "Here is *yer* question. What was that handsome fella next door doing in the garden with you last night?"

The pickling spices were clearing her sinuses, but in response to that question, she was glad to have the excuse to hide her face in her pocket handkerchief. "Asking for help," Belinda mumbled, giving her nose a pat.

"With?" Mammi stood waiting. Her patience shortening.

"Harvesting honey," Belinda replied.

"And?" Mammi's tone grew taut.

"And that's it. He asked me to help." Belinda shrugged, turning off the faucet once the peas were completely submerged.

Mammi looked heavenward. "Lord, help this one get to the point before I soak her in beet juice and send her to town for staple goods." Mammi lowered her gaze. "And *yer* reply was?"

"I agreed," Belinda caved, having no more teasing left in her. In fact, she was still reeling over agreeing to help Adam. As Belinda washed the peas and helped her grandmother ladle the bloody beets and vinegary spiced liquid in jars, she shared the details of her new arrangement with Adam. She left out the part where she had looked foolish with a flower tucked in her hair. Alone time with Mammi gave Belinda a chance to talk out her thoughts, without a sibling around to prune them.

"I worry what some might think of us helping each other," Belinda confessed, and bit her lip. She really wanted to help with the bees, help someone who certainly needed it, but it was Adam, the boy next door. And since when did he get so muscled and tall, and distracting?

"You agreed to help another, as is our way." Mollie waved a wooden spoon in the air. "You pay no mind to what others think, just what the Lord does."

Belinda nodded, agreeing with the logic. "I was nervous talking with him, but it wasn't so bad," she admitted, gathering pots stained crimson and heading toward the sink.

In the windowsill sat a dying arrangement of daffodils, two limp dull-red tulips with wide-faced pedals, and one faded purple hyacinth. She needed to collect fresher ones. She'd barely slept a wink all night thinking about the hives and the look of desperation on Adam's face. There had been moments when their eyes collided and she didn't even feel the need to run or shy away. She actually felt pity for his hard circumstances, and a desire to make things better for him. But as much as he needed the money from all his jobs, it was certain that his hives weren't just a hobby. A man didn't worry like that over a hobby. His bees were just as much a part of him as her flowers were to her. It was nice to not be the only person who felt that way.

"He's a good fellow," Mammi added. "And he isn't a stranger. Maybe that is why it was easy." Belinda wished that were true. Despite him living just across the road, he *was* nearly a stranger. Boys like that didn't talk to girls like her, and just because they were adults now, that didn't change.

"You always liked helping Saul with his hives. This is good." But was it? Before Belinda could respond, Tabitha came bursting inside, her arms heavy with the empty trays the family used to display their vegetables.

"I sold all the hanging baskets, potatoes and lettuce, and most of your flowers too." Belinda noted a small collection of remainders lying in the bottom of a basket. She would put them in a glass on the table, give them time to flourish, then toss them in the compost in a few days. She loved the smell of fresh flowers throughout the house. Tabitha brushed back her loose hairs from her milky skin. Belinda wished she'd inherited her sister's skin instead of being sun-touched and freckled.

"Tulips are a customer favorite, but I think if you have any hyacinths left, they will do well. When all those sunflowers bloom, I imagine they will be even a bigger seller. Oh, and Mirim Petersheim said when your lavender blooms, she would love some to dry."

"I can do that," Belinda said, slightly stunned. So she was in business, at the market at least.

"I smell fresh bread." Tabitha kissed Mammi's cheek affectionately. Belinda couldn't smell anything but the strong pickling spices.

"Mica had three sandwiches at noon today. I could bake three loaves a day and he would find somewhere to put them, I tell ya," Mammi said, starting supper now that she'd finished the canning. Always busy, they all were, from sunup to sundown. Belinda almost felt guilty she'd agreed to help Adam when she was sorely needed at home. Almost.

"Mica said he'll be cutting hay tomorrow." Belinda eyed the sky out the kitchen window, a chicory blue color without a hint of threatening clouds. A few more days of this kind of weather and she would be carrying water for the gardens. "How will he get that done without Daed?"

"I'm sure Ivan will help, as usual. I do enjoy watching them work themselves weary." Tabitha chuckled. "But perhaps we should help with Daed gone."

"Those men can handle it. You two have plenty to do," Mammi said, peering into the oven. Satisfied with the progress of supper, Mammi limped toward the fridge, tossing a wink over her shoulder toward Belinda. Was Mammi making sure that Belinda didn't have added duties so she could help with the hives?

"Daed left a message this morning." Belinda turned to her sister. "He said Dawdi is feeling better today. Mamm got him to eat two meals yesterday."

"That is *wunderbaar* news." Her sister's green eyes glimmered with joy, and Mammi nodded in agreement. "I still pray for his healing, but I know how hard those treatments were on him."

"So, what's the latest news from the market?" Mammi prodded, always eager for the latest gossip.

"Well," Tabitha began, "I heard Deacon Moses gave Lynn Christner a visit. It seems she insists Lake Drive should be off limits to all Amish teenagers."

"But the Deacon, the Shetlers, the Glicks, and the Beilers all live on Lake Drive," Belinda put in.

"*Jah*, but her fuss was that she fears too many young couples take advantage of hiding among the trees surrounding the lake to kiss until the sun comes up." Tabitha clutched her heart in dramatic fashion.

"Stuff and nonsense," Mammi barked, slinging a towel in the air. "Couples have been kissing there for years. She thinks to stop it? They'll just find another spot."

"Mammi," Belinda said, taken back. "We shouldn't speak of such things." Kissing was private, and Belinda felt her face heat just thinking about it.

"Then I'll change the subject. I heard today that my sister is going into the honey business." Tabitha kicked off her thick-soled shoes and stomped toward the laundry room to tuck them away in their usual place. Mammi shot Belinda a knowing look.

How did Tabitha find out at the market about her helping Adam? Gossip traveled awfully fast.

She hadn't spoken about her agreement with Adam last night with either sibling, mostly because it was none of their business. She was twenty-three, for crying out loud. Besides, she hadn't wanted them to get the wrong idea. She'd snuck back inside, hurried upstairs into her room, and when Tabitha went to check on her, had faked sleep just as she had when she was young. She hadn't wanted to discuss it. Adam was doing her a big favor, and Tabitha didn't need to know what it was.

"I'm just helping him out. You know Atlee will be out of work for months, and Adam did ask Mica first." Wasn't Tabitha the one who begged her to try harder to speak with others? Belinda finished scrubbing the last pot and set it aside to dry. Mammi had potatoes peeled and boiling on the stove. She was always one step ahead, preparing for the next day before this one had even completed a half turn.

"Is he paying you fair? Don't let your shyness be taken advantage of, little sister."

"Sort of." Belinda went to stir a mixture of vegetables in a pot, added salt and pepper, and then turned the gas burner on low. The scent of pork and thick gravy slowly wafted in the air.

Tabitha began setting the table. "What does 'sort of' mean?" Her eyes darted between Mammi and Belinda.

Belinda blew out a breath. "We are to help those in need, ain't so?"

"We are," Mammi seconded. Belinda could always count on her grandmother for support.

Tabitha frowned. "You two know what I'm saying. Helping Ada with the house or weeding their garden is neighborly. But this is bees, Belinda. They sting."

"Not me. They fly around here all day and haven't stung me yet. And we are helping each other." Her voice lost some of its certainty.

"Meaning?" Tabitha began tapping her bare foot against the floor as hard and quick as Mamm with shoes on. "You know I can do this all night." And she could. It was that Bender blood—stubborn to the end.

"Might as well tell her. Nothing goes hidden," Mammi reminded.

"He's going to try to sell my flowers in exchange for my helping him harvest his honey and tending his hives." Belinda crossed both arms across her chest. Tabitha's scowl pinched so tight, it looked as though she was fending off a swarm of gnats. "And I do have to meet an inspector for him, so there's that," Belinda added.

"I can't say I'm *froh* you found a way around dealing with others, but I am impressed at your business sense." Had Tabitha just complimented her scheme? Belinda's shoulders relaxed a little. But there was no way she would tell Tabitha that when Adam had nearly knocked her over and their eyes locked, something in her insides had suffered a mighty shock.

"*Danki*. We probably won't start for a couple weeks. He works a lot, but he mentioned showing me all the hives soon." Just the thought of a second encounter made her nervous and excited at once. "I know he has some by his house, but he wants to show me the ones in the other fields too."

"I bet he does," Tabitha said in her typical teasing way.

Belinda blushed. "It isn't like that. Adam is courting Susanne. They will probably marry next year. What we have is just a partnership. He helps me and I help him."

"Adam is a smart fellow. He'll figure it

out." Tabitha went to the refrigerator and pulled out a pitcher of lemonade, a hint of something playing on her lips.

"Indeed he will," Mammi added, still eyeing the gravy that was reaching a nice thick texture. She adjusted the gas underneath.

"What does that mean?" Belinda studied both of them for clues.

"It means that while he's so busy taking care of his family and working around the clock, he might find out his girlfriend isn't such a catch after all. In fact, he might've figured that out already. I haven't seen them together for a spell. They used to eat lunch at the market together." Had they broken up? *No*, Belinda quickly decided. If they had, Adam would've said so.

"I'm proud of you for helping," Tabitha added. "Mica says pulling honey is hard work. I heard Mamm and Daed talking before they left about how expensive Atlee's surgeries were, and his rehabilitation will be costly as well."

"Our Belinda has always had a soft heart for those in need. Thankfully, she wasn't born picky, like some." Mammi pinned Tabitha with a look and her sister responded by playfully sticking out her tongue.

Belinda carried food to the table as Mica began stomping his boots clean on the porch. "I just wish Adam didn't go to work at the same place where Atlee got hurt."

"We all do what needs to be done."

Tabitha said. She worked hard to sell the family's products, when it was no secret that she preferred to spend her time quilting and baking. If given the chance, Belinda suspected Tabitha would quilt and bake all day. "And being picky is better than settling for something you don't really like." Tabitha aimed the comment to their grandmother. "I won't settle."

"Dawdle and get nothing but a drowned heart," Mammi quipped. She began flipping the cooled jars of beets upright, now that they had sat long enough for the caps to seal.

Neither sister had a worthy response.

Chapter Seven

A RAP AT THE FRONT DOOR jolted Belinda nearly out of her skin. Dishwater splattered all over the floor and a gasp squeaked out.

Mica chuckled. "I'll get the door, jumpy sister." Belinda ignored him, annoyed that she was so easily rattled. She grabbed two nearby hand towels and began mopping the mess on her freshly scrubbed floors.

"Wonder who that could be?" Tabitha asked as she began clearing the table.

"Adam's asking to see you," Mica announced, entering the kitchen. Belinda glanced up and Adam was there, standing next to Mica in the doorway. They both wore similar smirks. Here she was, a sight for sure and certain, down on all fours, mopping up a mess. He just had to choose now of all times to come see her.

Adam was just a few inches shorter than Mica, who had reached six-foot-four long ago. The rolled-up sleeves of his powder-blue shirt exposed strong forearms that she imagined had no trouble working three jobs with ease. He wasn't skinny like Noel Christner, nor plump like Tobias Miller. And he was staring again.

"How's your folks?" Mammi asked, limping toward the sink with another handful of empty dishes. "We sure miss them at *gmay*."

"They're good," Adam replied. "Daed hates being stuck in one spot too long, but he likes Mamm fussing over him." Adam grinned, his eyes not leaving Belinda. Under his gaze she felt a trickle of perspiration descend down her back. She scrambled to her feet and dropped the dishtowels in the sink.

"I was hoping to show you the hives," Adam said. "But no need to rush—I'm in no hurry." He sounded more sincere than she could deal with right now. He had a girlfriend and shouldn't be making her feel so off-kilter this way. In the full light streaming through curtainless windows, she could see him more clearly. Adam was looking at her like she'd put the first smile on his face all day. The air suddenly grew still and suffocating. Was he waiting on a reply? *Did he ask a question?* She seized her bottom lip between her teeth, vacillating between words and retreat.

"*Nee*, we can handle the rest of this. Belinda is awfully excited to see all the hives." Tabitha said in a surprisingly delighted tone. "So she can help you better." She gave Belinda a slight hip bump, urging her forward.

Adam nodded, a grin still on his lips. Belinda ducked her head and quickly slipped on her flip flops at the door, hoping her flushed cheeks weren't noticeable. Adam held the door and she quickly slipped out ahead of him.

"*Danki* again for helping," Adam said, as they crossed the yard toward the road. A strong scent of sawdust caught Belinda's nose, making her realize they were walking too close. She inched away slowly, establishing what felt like a proper proximity between two unwed people.

"I heard Tabitha sold out today," he said. Her sidelong glance revealed him smiling. He had a wonderful smile. When they were *kinner*, his smiles had made her want to cry, run home and tell her Mamm that boys were making fun of her. She'd outgrown that phase...kind of.

Maybe he'd think her prideful, but she said what she was thinking, anyway. "Tabitha said the customers really liked my tulips."

"Your two lips?" Adam asked. Belinda's

face flushed with heat. Then he gave a low chuckle, deep and warm, the sound mingling with the evening air. It had been a silly joke, and nothing more. "I wouldn't know a tulip from a lily," he added quickly. She didn't dare tell him that tulips were actually from the lily family—though he should probably learn that if he was going to sell her flowers. "I stopped by the florist, but they had a sign on the door that they were closed until Friday. Do you ever go help your sister at the market?"

"*Nee.*" She had no desire to go to the market, where crowds were.

"You should sometime. There are so many booths and so much to see, especially on Saturdays. There's even a man who brings puppies sometimes." Belinda gave him another sidelong glance. Did he think her a child?

"I'm surprised you have time to go yourself, as busy as you are." That earned her a different kind of smile. Who would have thought Adam was capable of looking embarrassed?

"Tobias and I eat lunch there sometimes." He didn't mention Susanne, and Belinda wondered if her sister's words might be true. "They have a nice place between two food vendors where you can just sit in the shade of the oaks near the old clock tower." Why was he telling her this? She didn't need to hear about the things she missed out on. All they needed to discuss was what he expected from her in forms of harvesting honey.

"Tabitha has mentioned such," she replied, not knowing what else to say.

Adam continued describing the booths, the food trucks, and the Amish owners who sold their goods there. She was a much better listener than talker, and his voice had a way of drawing her in, as did his stories. How had she lived all these years and not known so many of her community members sold goods at the market? Tabitha always talked about how busy it was with people milling about, but Adam made it sound exciting, as if crowds and strange faces were simply a different landscape, worthy of viewing. To him, maybe they were. In the six years since her family had opened their own produce stand at the market, Belinda hadn't been tempted once to go see for herself.

"There's an older woman who sells books. Like hundreds of them. If you like that sort of thing." He shrugged. She did. Since childhood Belinda had found bravery between the covers of her favorite books. There was safety within those pages, even when the stories got scary. They fed her imagination, allowed for a sense of normalcy.

They crossed the Hostetler yard. A flagstone path led to a dainty front porch. The house was a small two-story with a blend of wood and stone. Belinda always found it quaint and not too big for the person cleaning it. Maybe she could have a house like that someday—cottage style, with acres and acres of flowers surrounding it. It was a beautiful vision, that dream in her head.

Around the side of the house were the first beehives. "I have ten here," Adam explained. "We won't get close, since you're not wearing protective clothing or real shoes."

"They won't bother me. They buzz around me every day while I work." Adam tilted his head. He had to know bees foraged her flowers daily. It was her family's gardens, her very flowers, which fed his bees so well.

"I get stung even wearing the suit." He sounded a bit wounded.

"Mammi used to say it's because I smell like my flowers." Why did she say such a silly thing out loud?

"I read that you are supposed to make certain you *don't* smell like anything, especially flowers." Was he questioning her methods? If she wasn't so uncomfortable, she would tell him he didn't know everything. Bees swarmed her head on a daily basis and the only time she'd been stung was by accident, after forcing a poor bee to its sudden death underfoot.

"And you do smell like flowers," he added casually, as they moved toward the pasture. Belinda wasn't sure how to respond. He most certainly wasn't being fresh, but a man shouldn't openly comment on the way a *maedel* smelled—especially when he was courting someone else. It could give someone the wrong impression.

Adam opened a gate leading to pasture. "So you know all about drones and queens and workers?" Belinda stepped through and he closed the gate.

"*Jah*. Dawdi was a good teacher, plus I read a lot."

"I thought so," he muttered. What was that supposed to mean? He probably thought her fanciful.

She struggled to keep up with his long strides in the rutted pasture, but she didn't ask Adam to slow down. The faster he showed her the locations of all his hives, the faster she could get back to her side of the road.

The next fourteen hives nestled near a grove of birch and maple. "Mind your footing. Don't want you twisting an ankle," he said over one shoulder. Falling now would be even more embarrassing than Adam walking into her house and finding her sitting in a pool of dishwater. She focused more diligently on the terrain.

The wind played coolly with the grasses. It was a beautiful evening with a brilliant sunset and a perfect breeze as she walked four steps behind her neighbor toward his grandmother's land.

Belinda knew May Fisher well. The stout, spunky older woman had taught her and Tabitha how to crochet years ago, though Belinda had long since forgotten how. May had once told Belinda that if she didn't attend her quilting frolic, she'd drag her out of her house by the root of her tail. Belinda had attended two for good measure that year. No one wanted to be dragged out of their house, and even though she didn't have one, tails certainly didn't have roots.

"You're so quiet," Adam said, slowing down so she could catch up.

"Sorry." Belinda kept her head down, searching for ankle-twisting dips in the terrain. She hoped it wasn't warm enough for snakes yet.

"It wasn't a complaint." Adam was an only child. Did he prefer the quiet, too? He glanced over to her again and let out a sigh. "I worry you might change your mind. I have asked a lot more than I will be giving. But you won't have to do it all alone—we'll work together some days. Are you still sure about this arrangement?" It was sweet that he thought he was taking advantage, when it was she who would gain the most from this partnership.

His clenched jaw was slightly shadowed. Belinda tried not to imagine what he would look like in a beard, but she had a good imagination. If he and Susanne decided to marry, he'd look just as handsome with a beard as he did without one.

"I won't change my mind unless you do,"

she assured him. There was no way she was going to talk to *Englisch* bakers and florists herself. The *Englisch* stared enough at the Amish, pointing out their strange clothes as if wearing jeans with holes and makeup that changed your whole face wasn't strange. The last time Belinda went to town with her family, she had observed at least six souls in torn jeans. At first she'd felt sorry for them, that they didn't have the money to buy better ones or someone capable of giving them a good mending. That was until Tabitha explained it was considered a fashion. Well, that was ridiculous.

"How many hives do you have altogether?" she asked, as the hum of the evening rose around them. She kept a good two arms' lengths between them. He didn't try to close the distance.

"I have forty-six." Belinda swallowed her surprise. That was a lot of hives to tend to.

"Really?" Her voice pitched into something horribly similar to a chicken in distress.

"You can back out. I won't hold it against you," he said, coming to a stop. "It was stupid of me to ask so much of you. With your parents away, I'm sure you barely have the time for your own chores." Adam yanked his straw hat from his head and smacked it on his britches leg.

Belinda faced him straight on, and for the first time since he'd asked her for help, she looked directly at him without pulling away. Adam was normally a confident man, but right now he looked exposed. She knew a little something about how that felt. Right now, she couldn't think of herself and what she was gaining with this partnership. Belinda could only think about how she could possibly make a small part of his life easier.

"*Nee*, I think it's amazing. Forty-six hives," she said. "I cannot believe you've never needed help before now."

Adam narrowed his gaze. "Some don't find it a worthy trade."

"Like selling flowers, but here we are," she replied, without giving it much thought. It was hard to ignore what felt like bees swarming in her belly when one corner of his mouth hitched ever so slightly.

"*Jah*, like selling flowers." He resumed walking. "Actually there are only forty-four. I had two colonies swarm off last week. They don't like being ignored."

"I'm sorry. You've been busy, *jah*. I am sure you simply missed changes in the colonies, unhappy queens, or unsatisfied workers." She shrugged.

"*Jah*," he said, shooting her another surprised look. "You understand what would cause a brood to swarm?"

"You act surprised."

"I am," he said flatly. So was she—but not by her knowledge. Belinda had never said so many words to another person outside of family and friends in her whole life. "It's good to know Mica was right about you." What else had her brother told him about her?

"I'll do everything I can to make this season a success. I know how important the income is to your family." They'd gone to school together, joined the church together, so why was he looking at her like she was a newcomer, someone he'd never seen before? Like she was someone he wanted to keep looking at?

"And I'll do my part as well," he pledged. Another stretch of silence followed them as they closed the distance to his grandmother's.

"I want more," he declared. "Hives, I mean. I want more hives." She smiled as he shared the personal thought with her.

"In Kentucky," she told him, "there's a man who rents his bees to others. To pumpkin farms and the like. You could put hives on other farms, nearby of course, and people would pay you to do it. It is growing trend, using bees to help pollinate crops." He stopped again to study her. Why did he keep doing that?

"I know. I have been thinking on it." Their eyes remained locked, steady on each other. "I've never told anyone that." *Not even Susanne?* Belinda didn't know what to say, or if saying anything was proper. Instead, she smiled up at him, appreciating his trust in her, and he smiled back.

They prattled on about some of the local areas that could be possibilities, including her family's farm, which seemed to surprise him. It felt good to spend time with someone who didn't focus on the things that made her different. In fact, Belinda suspected Adam was a bit different too. Getting to know him like this was nice.

"To anyone else, this talk would sound absurd," he said. She agreed with a slight laugh. They both had chosen more unusual trades. Was that why talking to him came so easy?

"So, how many?" She started walking again, more cautious of her footing than looking down as a way of retreat. "How many hives would you like to have one day?"

Chapter Eight

H E SHOULDN'T HAVE MENTIONED SHE
smelled like flowers. A man only
spoke of such things when he was
trying to flirt—and Adam most certainly
wasn't flirting. Fine, so she liked to read,
smelled like a garden, and knew plenty
about hive keeping. He should be happy
about the latter, but it was the former that
was messing with his head. Worse, she was
surprisingly easy to talk to, pulling more out
of him than he cared to share.

"A hundred," Adam answered. He
watched Belinda's reaction. Susanne would
be frowning right now, sharing her doubts
about his trade, but Belinda's expression
didn't waver. Wasn't it a good thing that
the person helping him knew what she was
doing? Or was he just being sweetened, be-

cause she needed him, too? He studied her intently for clues. Susanne had played his heart, derailed his future plans, and betrayed his trust. Thanks to her, Adam now knew to walk cautiously. Behind seemingly innocent blue eyes lay the power to disarm any man, and he had no intention of letting that happen to him again. He would maintain his equal stake in their partnership, not allowing for failure on his part. That was how he would ensure his own success.

"I always wanted a full acre garden," she told him. "I want to have my own flower farm." Did flower farms even exist? But of course they must. "You can sell plants and bulbs and even dried flowers and herbs. There are so many routes you can take to make it profitable. Did you know there is only one tree nursery nearby, and that's in the next county?"

Her eyes actually sparkled as she shared her dreams with him. "Well, maybe we will both have what we want, eventually," Adam said, tamping down the rush of warm blood running through his veins.

"Maybe we can," she said softly, but he heard it all the same,

After weeks of long days blending into one another, Adam was dog-tired. He knew himself well enough to know he wasn't the ideal person to be around as of late. The fact that Belinda was still going along with this arrangement, that she was willing to help him, surprised him. If she didn't fret about the next showing of hives, then he would have his help and maybe sleep more peacefully tonight.

The flowery scent of the woman walking nearby was eroding his good sense. A tired mind had a way of messing with a man's priorities. He picked up his pace again. He would simply show Belinda the location of the remaining hives, walk her home, and then get to bed. He should take advantage of every wink of sleep he could get. Beside him, Belinda looked out across the fields, a glow of sunset on her face. Adam did his best to keep looking forward.

"I don't want you lifting anything too heavy by yourself, so we can pull the frames into an extra super that I keep on hand in the evenings when I get home. Do you know how to use the extractor?"

"*Jah*, but I can lift them. I'm stronger than I look." He doubted that, but kept the thought to himself. "Some of Dawdi's weighed as much as eighty pounds, and I handled them on my own." Adam tightened his jaw. How could her family ask such a thing of her? How could he?

"You could get hurt."

"I assure you, Adam Hostetler, I can handle it. I know how to do things the right way." She let out a breath, clearly annoyed. "I have the greenhouse wagon I can use to tote them. All it takes is some planning. Not everything requires bigger muscles. We made a deal." She strode ahead of him toward his grandmother's house.

Why she was being so insistent about this? Was her fear of dealing with strangers and selling her own flowers messing with her common sense? Well, he'd have to add a few rules in this partnership. One, no heavy lifting. She could agree or deal with *Englisch* bakers and florist herself. Two...well, once Adam wrapped his head around Belinda Graber freely talking to him, he would figure out number two.

He caught up with her and they walked together, Adam posing probing questions, continuously testing her bee cunning— which continued to impress him. She was as smart as a whip. He had no idea she could talk so much, either. As long as the conversation centered around bees or flowers, that was. He made a mental note to remember that.

Descending the rise, he saw that a lamp flickered in the front window of his grandmother's house, indicating she was still up. Mammi seldom waited until nightfall to go to bed, but of course on this night of all nights, when he had Belinda with him, she would still be awake.

"Just let me tell her we're out here. Don't want her coming out with Dawdi's old shotgun thinking we're a pair of fool kids up to no good." Adam laughed, recalling the near heart attack she'd given him the first time she came barreling out the front door holding the gun longer than she was tall. By now Adam was accustomed to her opening the door with it, but it would surely give Belinda a fright.

Realizing Belinda was no longer strolling alongside him, Adam spun around and immediately spotted the look of terror on her face. He instinctually marched back to her and reached for her hand.

"It's not loaded, Belinda. I'm sorry I scared you." He shook his head. Stress and fatigue were making him dumb. What was he thinking, talking about something that would upset any woman, especially this one?

He squeezed her hand, adding an extra measure of assurance, and urged her toward May's front door. "She just keeps an *unloaded* gun by the door. She likes to have it handy after some kids in town smashed in her mailbox, like, five years ago." He patted her shoulder with his free hand.

She shuddered and finally looked up at him. "Why would she dare use one?" He offered a smile, trying to push back the urgent need to make her feel safe that had come without even a hint of warning.

"She only uses it as a prop, truly. Don't worry, there aren't any bullets in the house. I checked." He squeezed her hand again. "It's okay. I promise. I wouldn't lead you into harm's way," Adam urged tenderly, and slowly coerced her all the way to the front door before Belinda's nerves ebbed. She peered down where their hands were joined and immediately pulled herself from his grasp. Adam knocked on the door, then rubbed his hand down his britches leg as if he could wipe away her touch and his own boldness in taking her hand.

No man had ever touched her, aside from Mica and Daed. Belinda had no time to dissect the gesture or how she felt about it before movement stirred inside and the door opened. May Fisher bounded onto the porch, unarmed. Belinda exhaled slowly.

"Well hello, sweetie, and oh, you brought a friend." May did a sidestep around Adam and wrapped Belinda in a hug, causing her to gasp in surprise. She wasn't used to such affection. Embracing was an uncommon greeting, unless among kin. May smelled strongly of lavender and soap, and happy thoughts. Despite her surprise, Belinda's smile came easily, though her stomach was still a riot of emotions.

"Belinda Graber, it has been three months since you came to see me outside of *gmay*. You shouldn't ignore your elders, dear,"

May winked, shaking a finger at her. Something soft flickered in Adam's green eyes. Or maybe they were blue. Belinda looked away before she could tell for sure. Was it possible she wasn't imagining the changing colors? Did eyes change colors?

"Sorry, May, but with Mamm and Daed gone and the growing season peaking, Mica can use all the hands we've got, and I only have two," Belinda said with a shrug, sending May laughing. She wasn't used to people laughing *with* her, only *at* her appearance and shyness. The change felt nice, in an awkward kind of way.

"Well, we all can't be spiders." May patted her cheek affectionately. "Always was a helper. Another week and I might have been tempted to come drag you out here for tea and *kichlin.* I have only one *grosskind* and he never has the time for me." May shot a stern look toward Adam. One could see the love between them, displayed rather than disguised by the playful banter. Belinda mentally noted to set aside some time this week for tea and *kichlin.* It must be awful lonesome living alone this far from anyone. May's little parcel was the last house on Mulberry Lane, a mile to the nearest neighbors—her family and Adam's.

"I can't say I'm surprised that my Adam here brought you over for a visit. I always thought..." Adam cleared his throat before May could go on. Belinda wished she knew what May had been about to say, but brushed off the curiosity.

"Belinda is helping me this honey season since I'll be working at the mill." The grandmother and grandson exchanged a look.

"Oh she is, is she?" May smiled cunningly. "Well, that's nice. I did wonder how you would manage working, tending to the livestock, helping Ivan on jobs, and your honey business. I have been needing that old chicken run repaired for months, but didn't dare mention it." Now that May *had* mentioned it, Belinda watched Adam immediately give the small chicken run a quick study, clearly making plans for its repair. How would he do so many jobs and when would he sleep? Realizing she was gaping at him, she quickly lowered her head.

"I came to show her the hives here at the orchard and didn't want to startle you if you heard us walking about. I can look at the coop over the weekend, perhaps. I also wanted you to know that Belinda will be over here often, so it would be nice if you could leave Dawdi's shotgun behind the door and not frighten off my only help." Adam gave May a wink.

"Mighty kind of you, and I can try. But I won't promise." She waved a stubby finger. "Those pesky kids may return, wanting to smash this mailbox too." May turned to Belinda. "I've had three smashed to pieces, and mailboxes aren't cheap." Her voice snapped with anger. Belinda shuddered to think someone would destroy an old lady's mailbox. Another reason to avoid outsiders, she reminded herself.

"Adam's helping me sell my flowers," she mumbled. She didn't know why she said that. It was no one's business, but suddenly she felt the need to say something.

"Well, Adam has always had a good head on his shoulders. It's kind of handsome, too." May reached up and patted his cheek. Belinda knew better than to agree to her words but couldn't help but grin when Adam's jaw tightened and his head shook. Family could be embarrassing at times.

"I'm sure he will do his best to see your flowers fetch a good price." May tossed a wink back to Adam. "I think you two will make a good match." Adam shot her a frown.

"Business partners," Adam corrected. Belinda nodded in agreement, even as she winced a little at his firm, unhesitating correction.

"I see. Well, I think you will make good business partners then. You both need each other. It's *good*." She patted Adam's shoulder. May liked patting to show affection and approval—and dragging someone out of their house by roots and tails to show affection and *dis*approval.

"We should get going." Adam stepped off the little porch.

"*Jah*, make sure to walk her home. We

95

wouldn't want our Belinda here to trip and fall. It's getting dark." She quickly slammed the door before Adam could say more.

"Sorry about that," Adam said, as they began walking toward the orchard. "Mammi has a habit of speaking her thoughts out loud. It's hard to be the only kid in a family, and unwed, without *kinner* for her and my parents to dote over."

"It's okay. You cleared up any curiosity she was having," Belinda muttered, watching her footing. "Family can be pushy in such matters." She may have been blessed with siblings, but that just meant there were more people to put pressure on her when she didn't move through life fast enough to suit them.

"So you have a pushy family too," he jested. Belinda didn't feel comfortable having such a personal conversation with him, so she kept her reply neutral.

"We are expected to court at a certain age, marry, and have *kinner*. At least you are courting, so that should make your family happy."

"*Jah*," Adam said on a sigh. Well, Tabitha must have heard wrong for sure, or Adam would have clarified his and Susanne's break-up right then.

When they reached the orchard behind May's house, a new world came into view. The "small orchard" Adam had referred to consisted of more than twenty trees, all in a full and glorious bloom. It was a hidden treasure as perfectly painted as a postcard. "I've never been here before." Belinda stopped and inhaled deeply. There was nothing like the fresh scent of apple blossoms to make spring linger. Two long rows of hives nestled just south of the orchard.

"But it's only a mile from your house, and you do visit here sometimes." Adam stopped and stared at her. He must think her a *seltsam*, an oddity. He would be right. Her ignorance about this area was her own doing, of course. She was always purposely hiding herself, staying unavailable, which meant she'd had fewer opportunities than most to explore the area. It resulted in her not knowing her surroundings well enough. She didn't attend singings on Sunday evenings or gatherings in warm weather months, or frolics, unless threatened. Why would she, after barely surviving the heart-break of cruel words and harsh looks until she finished her schooling in the eighth grade?

"I don't make it a habit to go wandering around people's properties," she said flatly, and continued toward the hives. And with what she'd recently learned, it was a good thing, too. If May had pulled a gun on her, Belinda surely would have died of shock.

"You haven't been to the market and you haven't seen the orchard a mile from your house." Was he asking a question?

Belinda just shrugged, unwilling to answer either way. It was none of his concern why she preferred staying at home. Fortunately, he didn't push for a reply.

"I checked on these just a couple days ago and I think I can start in the next week or so. I'll let you know, but feel free to see for yourself anytime. These are a good distance from my honey house, so I can fetch them early when we start."

A honeybee landed on Belinda's shoulder, and she carefully fingered it back into flight. "I can meet with your inspector and start some this week, if you'd like." She nervously twisted a *kapp* string. "If you try to do too much, you might wear yourself out and I am here to help, ain't so?"

"*Jah*, but I could say the same about you," he said. staring at her intently again. For a moment they stood there among the hives and low buzz of evening. A chill climbed up her spine until it tickled the hairs on the back of her neck. She broke the gaze first, telling herself that she had nothing to prove by holding it. Adam Hostetler had no idea how she spent her time or how those long looks bothered her.

"What are those blocks for?" She pointed to the hives sitting firmly on cinder blocks. All his hives were elevated like that.

"Skunks," he muttered. Noting her confusion, he continued. "Skunks are a top predator of honeybees. By putting the hives up on blocks, skunks have to stretch to reach into the escape hole to snatch a free meal. It also exposes their soft spot." Belinda listened intently. She knew skunks raided honey hives, but not that they had soft spots.

"Their stomachs are where they're most vulnerable. Forcing them to stretch out for a free meal gives the bees a chance to defend themselves. A few stings send the skunks running."

"That is a good idea. I didn't know that."

Adam watched Belinda out of the corner of his eye as they walked back toward the house. Not only was she offering to help, but she seemed eager to start. "I still need to show you the honey house." He needed time to think. Working with her was going to be trying, that was for sure. He was a man of his word and he had already made a deal with her, but if he could, Adam would erase it all right now. Belinda was going to be far too much of a distraction.

He walked her home as Mammi had insisted, hands in his pockets, his mind playing his last conversation with Susanne over and over. He wasn't good enough. He had too many responsibilities. He was a beekeeper. All the reasons why romance was not meant to be an option for him. Anything to distract him from walking alongside Belinda and her quiet innocence and big charitable heart, and those eyes that could almost make a man forget his troubles.

Chapter Nine

FRIDAY MORNING SUNLIGHT PEEKED through barn gaps, descended on leafy branches, and washed over dew-kissed grass in shimmers. Belinda carefully pondered which blossoms to gather for Adam to present to the florist today. In her pocket, she'd already prepared a list of specific plants he could bring. She had a feeling he would need all the information she could provide—she knew better than to expect him to have looked up the names on his own. His lack of enthusiasm for her chosen trade was evident.

With scissors in hand, she snipped a perfectly mid-blooming snapdragon and closed in on a row of tulips begging to be shown off. There were so few left now. She selected a pink one along with a late blooming hyacinth, adding them to a small bucket where a few pussy willow sprigs awaited in fresh water. She stared at the array of colors and shapes. Something was missing.

In the greenhouse's far corner where her parents let her toy with wintering new sprouts, Belinda stared at the flowering hibiscus. A large pink dinner plate bloom would make a perfect addition to her collection, she concluded.

Content with her choices, she stepped out of the greenhouse and caught sight of the figure strolling through the morning fog toward her garden. His long strides were purposeful and quick, his erect posture solid. She wasn't sure how she felt about seeing him. Their encounters left her befuddled, yet craving the next one. Taking a nervous breath, marshalling the thoughts swirling through her head, she stepped out.

"*Gute mariye.*"

Adam halted at the soft sound and began walking toward it until all of her came into view. Just as he suspected, morning light did her the same favors as the glow of dusk. Even in drab grey, she was freshly crisp, a morning jolt to the senses.

"Do I really have to walk into a florist carrying that little green bucket?" His grin quirked to one side as he pointed to the bucket in her hand. He didn't allow himself to compliment her morning smile. This was a partnership, nothing more.

"A deal is a deal, but no. It is just for the travel. You can carry them in your hand and ditch the bucket if you feel better doing so." She giggled. It was clear even she thought a grown man walking into a florist's shop with a bouquet would catch some attention.

Little did she know that before he joined the church, Adam was well known for accepting a good dare. Tobias had always liked stretching the limits of their upbringing as far as he could without crashing over a cliff. *Well, there was one cliff,* he mused. Adam took the dare and dove right into the lake, earning him "king of the hill" status for a good year or better. He also took full responsibility for hiding all the bishop's tack early on Sunday morning on the occasion when it had occurred to the twelve-year-old boys that no bishop meant no three-hour church service. And yet, as sure as they'd been that the idea would work, the bishop was standing in the center of the Planks' living room when they arrived that morning.

Adam peered up from the flower bucket, pondering. Had quiet Belinda Graber ever done anything reckless in her whole life?

"The things we do for help around here,"

he teased, and took the pail from her hands. "Now what kinds of flowers do I tell her you have?"

Belinda dug into her pocket and presented the list. Her smile turned into a grin, but a small dimple still winked to be noticed. Something was different about her today. He couldn't quite put a finger on it. She still had that habit of dipping her chin and lifting her shoulder as if hiding an expression—that much hadn't changed. He wondered if she did it to hide the cute little mark on her face.

"Are you always this prepared?"

"I am." Her chin tilted upward. She had more pluck than he'd counted on.

"So am I," he said, before tipping his hat and disappearing across the road into the mist of waking day.

Adam secured Honey to a telephone post in the empty parking lot. He reached in and pulled Belinda's flower collection from the small green pail. Honey snickered. "Yeah, I know. I should have thought this out better." He looked like a fool, not for talking to his horse, but for carrying a bouquet of flowers in his hand walking down the street. At seven in the morning most of the inhabitants of Havenlee—primarily *Englisch*—were only just waking up, but that didn't make the situation any less awkward. He hoped the early fog would linger before he was noticed by a familiar face.

He walked swiftly past the old bookstore, the bakery, and a small brick front that boasted a sign for the best lawyer in town, before he fixed his gaze on the grey siding attachment with floor to ceiling windows.

At the sound of hooves clopping on pavement, Adam turned. *Tobias heading to work.* Tobias hadn't been early for a solitary thing since he was born, and yet he had picked today to head to the mill forty minutes before clocking in. It just figured. Adam groaned inwardly, tightening his hold on the ridiculous bouquet in his hands.

Tobias tilted his straw hat upward for a better view and threw up a wave, a wide grin spread over his face. Adam scowled and half-waved in a surrendering gesture. Yep, he was going to hear about this for months to come.

The sign on Swift Florist and Gifts said they didn't open until eight, but the light inside accompanied by movement urged Adam to knock. Through the glass door, a middle-aged *Englisch* woman strolled toward him. She wore a cheery smile beneath a head full of brown curls that needed taming desperately.

She opened the door and stared at him in puzzlement, before her brown eyes landed on the flowers. "Well, it's not every day a man walks *in* here carrying flowers." She chuckled easily and reached out a hand. "I'm Marcy. Marcy Swift. Are those hyacinths?" She stepped out from the doorway, coming closer. "Oh, and you have calla lilies and pussy willows. Where did you find such delicious hibiscus in bloom this time of year?" Her eyes lit up. Adam felt his throat tightening. He had no idea what a hibiscus was, but she seemed impressed he had one. He loosened his grip, hoping he hadn't caused any damage to the flowers.

Just as he started to speak, something inside crashed. Marcy's face immediately creased into a scowl. "Please come in," she urged, stepping back inside the shop. "If you could just give me a moment—I need to check on something." Adam followed her inside and was suddenly overwhelmed with the floral scents that flooded the shop. Marcy disappeared around a corner, and after a few moments reappeared with the same welcoming smile as before.

"So, where were we?" She brushed her hands together, as if something sticky had covered them.

Adam needed to get this embarrassment over with before he was late for work. He wanted to do his best for Belinda, but he still felt that selling flowers was too silly for words.

"My friend owns a flower business." Adam cleared his throat, wincing as the words left his lips. He never had a problem selling honey. Everyone liked honey. But more importantly, he knew what he was talking about when it came to honey. Could this woman tell how out of place he felt here?

"How wonderful. It just so happens I'm on the lookout for a new supplier. Does your friend have a name?" Marcy was sensing his unease, but that did little to lift it.

"Belinda Graber," he replied.

"Graber? Like in the market stand Graber's Greenhouse?" Adam nodded and grinned. Marcy was impressed by the flowers, admitted needing a supplier, and now recognized the family name. They were all good signs. "I buy all my fresh produce from Ms. Graber. I didn't know she grew flowers too. She is always sewing pieces of material together when her stand isn't busy."

"That would be Tabitha, her sister." Adam relaxed.

"May I?" Marcy reached out and took the flowers from him. She inhaled and walked casually to the counter. "What other flowers does Belinda have?"

Adam perked up and quickly fumbled in his pocket for the list Belinda had given him this morning.

"I have done business with the Amish in the past when I found myself in a pinch, but would it be all right if I visited, so I could see her selections?" Marcy accepted the list and began studying it.

"Meaning?"

"Her gardens." Marcy chuckled again. Her wildly colored blouse was distracting, especially when paired with her mismatched pants. Adam imagined this was what a hippie looked like, all colorful and disheveled. Her deep throaty laugh sounded more manly than feminine. He dug for a reply, but she wasn't done speaking. "Yours as well, I suppose, even if she does the actual gardening. I assume you are her husband." Adam didn't blink.

"She's my neighbor," he corrected. "I'm simply helping her out."

"Hmmm." Adam couldn't decipher the meaning behind that, but the smile on her face made him start to get all uncomfortable again.

"And what is your name?"

"Adam Hostetler, ma'am." He finally had the common sense to remove his hat.

"Well, Adam." Marcy shifted behind the counter, her eyes skimming the list in her hands another time. "I take it Belinda knows her stuff, by the looks of this list. Dusty Miller, dahlias, salvia, and eucalyptus. Not common garden variety things like pansies and petunias."

"She's very knowledgeable. She has been growing flowers for a good many years." *And she wants to own a flower farm,* he withheld. It wasn't his secret to share.

"Could you possibly come back later today? I'm about to open and still need to get Jackson—my son and the source of the racket in the back—settled. I will work up some numbers that you can show her."

"I get off work at five. I can stop by then." Adam could barely manage to keep his excitement contained. This was easier than he'd thought.

"Perfect. I have been disappointed lately with my regular two suppliers. I'm so glad you stopped in today." She closed the space between them, offered a hand. "I have a feeling your Belinda is an answer to my prayers." Adam smiled at her words and shook her proffered hand.

He walked out of the florist shop feeling happier than he had walking in. He'd barely had to say or do a thing. Belinda's flowers practically sold themselves. He couldn't wait to tell her the news.

"Not every day you see a man walking into a flower shop carrying flowers," Tobias announced, as Adam walked into the pallet room where five other men worked.

"Funny," Adam scoffed, waving them off before they even started.

"Two weeks ago you swore off *maedels* and courting. Your recovery time is impressive. Got a secret you want to share with us?" Tobias spread out his arms, indicating the men around them, all red-faced, ready to burst into laughter.

"No secret. Let's get to work. That is why we are here, is it not?" Seeing Adam was tight-lipped on the matter, the men began their day. Within minutes, hammers were driving nails in a chorus of production.

"You aren't the romantic type, so give it up. Why were you walking down the street this morning carrying flowers? You got a new interest you're keeping hid or something?" Tobias started again.

Adam lowered another armload of pre-cut boards and wiped his forehead. "I was seeing if the florist wanted to buy them. There's no new love interest. I have no time or want for such. You, on the other hand, seem to have plenty time to waste."

Tobias's gaped at him, hammer suspended in air, clearly trying to read between the words. "Did it work, though? Did they buy your flowers?"

Adam chuckled. Tobias was his best friend, but he wasn't the only one who liked teasing. For the rest of the morning, the two talked about Adam's partnership with Belinda Graber. Adam left out the part about Belinda smelling like a fresh spring garden, nor did he mention that her eyes had a way of dancing like chicory blooms in an autumn breeze.

"Well, I'm glad you got help with your honey. So, does she have much to say to you?" Tobias probed. Adam couldn't fault him for his curiosity. Most any single man in the district would jump at a chance to have a full conversation with Belinda Graber.

"When you pick the right topic, *jah.*" Adam trod lightly. Tobias had already tried convincing Adam to get back out there, start dating again, instead of letting one rejection turn him into a lonely being. He didn't want his friend fixating on the idea of Adam becoming interested in Belinda. His grandmother was already bad enough.

"And what topic is that?" Tobias wiggled his brows.

"I'm not telling you," Adam chuckled. "Don't you have your hands full enough?"

"I do, and it would seem now you do too." Tobias was going to make a big deal out of this, as sure as anything.

"It's not like that. She's helping me and I'm helping her. That's it," Adam made it clear. No way would he risk his heart again.

"I'm not convinced. You still like her, don't you?" Tobias asked.

"I don't dislike her, but *nee*, we are just

partners." And that was all they would be. Innocent smiles and piercing blue eyes would have no effect on him ever again. Ever.

Chapter Ten

BELINDA CHEWED A FINGERNAIL IN nervousness as Mammi, positioned behind her, chattered on about bacon grease and greens. Today, Belinda didn't care about food. All she could do was wonder if Adam found at least one person willing to buy her flowers.

"You should get changed and get going if you're going to meet that bee inspector today," Mammi said, as if Belinda could forget she had to speak to a stranger. It was a small price to pay, considering the people Adam would speak to on her behalf, but still her stomach rolled with a tremendous quiver.

"Mammi, do you think anyone will want to buy my flowers?"

"I do. Who doesn't love flowers?" Mammi

was never one to exaggerate. "I think Adam will see to finding the right person. Now stop biting *yer* nails."

Belinda dropped her hand and shrugged. "He doesn't think a flower business is a real thing. Maybe it isn't." She added salt and pepper to a roast Mammi planned to cook for supper this evening. Taking up a small paring knife, she began peeling garlic and onions to add to the roast.

"Our bishop thought it a good one, as did the ministers. Did that *bu* say otherwise to you?" Mammi growled.

"*Nee*, not in so many words, but the look on his face said it for him," Belinda replied. She remembered that look well enough, something between a scowl and shock.

"So *yer* a mind reader, are ya?" Belinda tossed her a frown. "You best concentrate on your side of it and let him do his. The Lord will see you both find what you're looking for in the end." She turned back to the stove, adding flour to the oily skillet. Mammi insisted on gravy as a side dish to every meal.

"Looking for?" Belinda paused in her dicing of garden vegetables.

"Oh, nothing, dear." Mammi took up a worn-out whisk and began working the flour in. "I'm just an old woman rattling off a head full of thoughts. Get along with ya. I can finish up here before tackling Mica's laundry. That one still rolls around in the mud just as much as he did as a *bu*. You would think he would outgrow that. How will we ever get him married off?" Mammi sputtered those last words heavenward.

"I think you would have better luck with a tree," Belinda jested. "He doesn't even care that every single *maedel* in the community has tried gaining his interest. Salina used to beg me to invite her for supper, hoping to catch his eye."

"That one talks far too much for Mica. The right one is out there, though. I just haven't found the right *maedel* willing to put up with his big appetite yet. Tabitha will be a chore when it comes to finding her match as well," Mammi murmured, deep in thought. "Some divine intervention may be needed on that one." It seemed Mammi was taking seriously her promise to *Mamm* before she left for Kentucky. Belinda had no worries. Mammi wouldn't dare play matchmaker with her.

"He would have to be perfect for Tabitha to notice him, and no one is. If you think to marry them off before Mudder returns, you are certainly going to need intervention," Belinda chuckled, and Mammi agreed with a laugh.

"Oh, I'm not a woman who rushes in when it comes to matters of the heart. A marriage for just one of you will do fine for now." Belinda could see her grandmother organizing a surprise visit from one of the community's fair maidens soon. Mica didn't stand a chance. Belinda could warn her brother, but decided against it. It would be entertaining to watch him sweat after he'd put her in such a position with Adam.

"Mammi?" Belinda pushed the chopped onions aside with her knife before they brought out tears. "How did you know Dawdi was 'the one'?"

"I didn't. I was courting another." The smile that covered her face, deepening lines and wrinkles into folds and creases, caught Belinda off guard.

"Mammi!" Belinda let out a surprised chuckle.

"It happens." Mammi waved her off. "*Gott* knew best for me, and for that I am thankful," she said, matter of fact. "Anyhow, your dawdi was helping his *onkel* who had fallen into troubles. I was also asked to help the family, being as there were few who could spare the time. They had nine *kinner* and *nee mamm*," she said in a sadder tone.

"That's awful."

"It was indeed, but weeks and weeks of tending to the family, serving meals to your dawdi and his family, we got to know each other. He made me feel..."

"*Schee*?" Belinda quickly put in.

Mammi's forehead wrinkled into a disappointed V. "Appreciated." Belinda imagined her grandmother as a beautiful woman in her prime, her pale grey eyes highlighting her lighter hair. "Looks aren't everything, dear. We are to be drawn to what is on the inside, not the out," Mammi reminded her. Belinda knew she was right, but looks sparked first impressions, and first impressions often set the stage for friendships or interest. Could she not see the logic in that?

"I know," Belinda muttered.

"Does Adam appreciate you?" Mammi asked next.

Belinda hiccupped, the question catching her off guard. "He has a girlfriend," she replied.

"I'm not sure that's true. Seems to me that Zook girl spends more time over at the Petersheim house these days."

Belinda's mouth fell open.

"Why would she prefer spending her time with Jerimiah Petersheim?" Her words came out so quick she had no time to wrangle them back.

Mammi shook her head in annoyance. "Lord, help these *kinner* know how to do the simplest task." She turned to face Belinda again. "Please answer the question I asked you and stop getting distracted. Does he appreciate you?"

"I don't know, but I can tell he wishes he had someone else helping him." Like Mica, who wasn't afraid of May and her shotgun, or any number of others.

"Why would you think that?"

Belinda sighed heavily at the simple question. "Well, sometimes he says things like, 'I can do that so you don't have to be here too much,' and sometimes he looks at me like he is trying to find something, or maybe to figure out if I'm normal. It's quite disturbing." And quite nerve-tingling, she wanted to add.

Mammi's face shifted into a sly grin. "He probably wonders how he got so lucky to have such a sweet, *schee maedel* working alongside him."

"I don't think so. Susanne is *schee* and well-liked." Belinda was not pretty nor well-liked. Susanne's company was always in demand, but few wanted to spark up a conversation with Belinda.

"Don't ever compare yourself to others. There is only one you, and you were made special by *Gott*. I have a feeling your handsome neighbor is discovering that."

"You shouldn't say things like that, Mammi." Belinda felt her cheeks flush, but quickly gained control. "Besides, *Gott*'s plan for me has nothing to do with Adam Hostetler." Belinda tapped her cheek, the ugliness there, to punctuate her point.

"And how can you know His plan for you?" Mammi snapped.

"Well, He put this mark on my face, didn't He? It puts me on a path for a different life than one with a husband and *kinner*. And Adam deserves better, like Susanne. They are perfect together."

"Fiddlesticks and nonsense." Mammi

slammed down the whisk, sending gravy all over the counter and stovetop. "Appearances are nothing in matters of the heart. And he won't find better than you, I say, someone who will work hard to help him."

"He is helping too; that was part of the deal." Mammi was getting this all wrong. If Adam hadn't gotten himself into such need, they wouldn't even be having this conversation. To her neighbor, the only thing that set her apart was that she'd said yes when everyone else he'd asked for help had said no.

"*Jah*, but two people who see to each other's needs before their own, that means something. You best get those silly thoughts out of *yer* head. Adam would be a fool to not see you for the gift that you are."

Belinda appreciated her grandmother's positive thoughts and devotion, but reality was that no man wanted a wife like her. With the roast fully seasoned and loaded with vegetables, Belinda set it into the oven to cook slowly, and kissed her mammi's cheek before heading upstairs to change into her bee outfit.

Bees did most of their foraging in the warmest parts of the day, which would make checking the hives easier at those times, considering they'd have other things on their minds and wouldn't give her presence a second thought. Adam said the inspector planned to come today around two, and that this coming week might be a good time to start pulling frames and extracting the honey. Excitement was wearing down all her natural-born patience. She had yet to see inside the honey house, where he extracted honey from the cells and readied it in jars to sell. Surely he would make time to show her soon so she could get started.

She slipped into her jeans and one of Mica's white shirts. Bees were easier to deal with up close and personal if you wore white, Dawdi had taught her. She removed her *kapp* and pinned on a kerchief so her veil would fit properly. She slipped on her sister's rubber boots, and eagerly headed out the door and across the road.

Belinda took a shuttering breath before knocking on the Hostetlers' front door. She couldn't recall Atlee Hostetler ever owning a shotgun, nor could she believe Adam's mother, Ada, capable of using one even as a ruse, but one never knew, now did they?

Laughter inside spilled out. She bit her lip, hoping she wasn't interrupting Ada and Atlee having a pleasant day after so many bad ones.

The door opened and Ada greeted her warmly. "Belinda. How nice to see you." Ada was a short woman and slightly curvy, but she had a wide, open smile and a kind heart. She was a *gut* friend and neighbor. Mamm often traded recipes with her.

"Who is it, Ada?" Atlee called from inside, his deep voice filling each room before spilling out onto the porch. Belinda had always been fond of Atlee, a gentle giant who had often silently reminded her to smile when he grinned her way in public and lifted a playful brow. It had been a game when she was young, but on occasion, when they caught one another's gaze, he still reminded her to smile with one of his own infectious grins.

"Belinda is here to meet the inspector." Ada opened the door wider to invite her in.

"It's not necessary to have me in. I won't trouble you with an unannounced visit, I just didn't want to go walking across your property and not tell you. The inspector should be here soon."

"How considerate." Ada's blue eyes gleamed. "Adam has been working such long hours, I'm glad he has a special friend like you to help." *Friends.* Were they friends? Belinda hadn't considered friendship.

"Well, tell her to come in. I could use a chat." Belinda couldn't refuse, not with Atlee asking. He'd once helped her out of a tree when she was ten. She'd been brave enough to climb up, but too scared to climb down before Atlee came to her rescue—and he even promised to keep it a secret. Her parents still hadn't a clue she'd climbed up there in the first place. Her family had hosted church that day, and she had become so overwhelmed with the eyes on her, whispers she thought carried her name, that she'd bolted. Mamm would have surely protested her hiding in her room through the whole fellowship meal. At the time, going up the tree seemed like a safe idea. Atlee had found her, brushed away her tears after helping her out of the tree, and told her to smile. "Life is sweeter when you're smiling," he had said. She had forgotten that part, but was glad she remembered it now. She stepped inside, and smiled.

"I'm sorry, I dressed to check the hives and meet the bee inspector. I know I look..." She fidgeted nervously with the veil in her hands.

"Like a woman not wanting to get stung by a thousand bees." Ada waved off her worry.

Belinda had never been inside the Hostetlers' house before. Anytime it came their turn to host church, the large barn usually offered ample space. The home was overly tidy, even by Plain standards. Not a speck of dust anywhere. Belinda had heard that Ada's overwhelming need for cleanliness stemmed from her terrible allergies. Dirt didn't dare take up residence here.

The lemony scent of Thieves oil mingled with the scent of baking bread. The small sitting room to the right held two couches and two puffy green chairs. Atlee lay across one couch with his leg in a contraption that must have made it impossible to move. One suspender hung loosely over his right shoulder and his britches had been cut just above his knee. Belinda expected him to look out of sorts, but his gleaming smile proved quite the opposite. Adam had his father's smile and deep-timbered voice.

"Hello, neighbor. Tell me, how is your grandfather? I heard he had to go for more cancer treatments."

Belinda cleared her throat, preparing to speak up. Mica often said she had a voice like a rock, meaning he could hear more of what a rock had to say. "Tabitha spoke with our parents last night. He is doing as good as expected, but he isn't taking treatments any longer. Mamm and Daed are staying until..." Belinda pushed back unbidden tears. It would do no good to cry in front of Adam's parents, even if thinking of all her dawdi was going through broke her heart.

"Your dawdi is a good man. He will be rejoicing with your mammi soon, my dear. Think of that when it troubles you." Atlee was kind to coddle her oversensitivity. Sometimes it was hard to simply accept things as they were. "Even flowers die. Everything has a season," Mamm always said, but Belinda found no comfort in that when it came to losing her dawdi.

"Adam says you're helping with the honey harvest this year. I see you take your job seriously." Atlee gave her clothing a careful study. He had strong, sharp brows like Adam, but unlike Adam, his eyes didn't seem to be searching for anything.

"Now Atlee, we can't be having our Belinda here getting stung. Adam would be terribly upset." Ada touched her arm and smiled. *Our Belinda.* That was the second time his family had referred to her as *our* Belinda. It was sweet, but terribly unnecessary.

"If a bee dared sting her, that is," Ada added with a laugh. Belinda flinched, wondering if she was being mocked.

Sensing her confusion, Atlee chuckled. "Adam says you sing to the bees, charming them. I think our *sohn* is smitten by your talents."

Belinda's face went crimson, more in response to the suggestion that Adam was smitten than because of the comment about her singing.

"He does?" Her skin grew damp, just thinking Adam found anything about her appealing.

"I'm glad you could help. With Atlee in such shape, I wouldn't have the time needed to do much myself, and I can't imagine lifting those screens of honey," Ada said a bit regretfully. Belinda didn't correct her mistake in calling hive frames screens.

"You leave the heavy lifting to Adam," Atlee said sternly, waving a long finger at Belinda. "No sense hurting yourself, especially after being so kind to offer."

"I've done my share of it before," Belinda quickly reminded them. "He can't possibly do everything." Adam's parents eyed her with appreciation.

"Who would have thought you and Adam had so much in common?" Ada smiled. "I worry terribly about him, working so many hours, taking no time for himself." Ada's eyes started to glisten. "We have been blessed with a selfless *sohn*, but I fear it costs him much." Was she speaking of him having time for himself, or something else? Was Mammi right about the end of Adam's romance with Susanne?

"Now Ada, he knows his limits. And he has Belinda here now to help. All is as it should be."

Belinda nodded in agreement. It was clear Adam's mother worried for him, and Belinda couldn't blame her. Adam was stretching himself out rather thin. "I will do my best to see some of the load is lifted." Belinda lifted her chin in determination. Adam's parents needed reassurance. She could offer that much.

"You always were a respectful *maedel*." Atlee smiled. "And a whole lot quieter than those others, too."

"I should go. The inspector will be here soon." The last thing Belinda needed was for Adam's parents to get the wrong idea about her reason for helping. And she didn't want to get the wrong idea from them, either—no matter how she liked the idea of Adam finding her interesting. It wasn't true. He needed her; *wanting* had nothing to do with it. She was smart enough to know the difference.

Belinda left the Hostetlers' doorstep and put all fanciful thoughts out of mind as a white truck pulled into the drive. She had all afternoon to think about Adam, if she dared think of him at all. Right now she had a bigger problem. She had to talk to a stranger for Adam's sake. She took a deep breath, whispered a prayer for control, and stepped forward.

An hour later Belinda had bitten her nails to nubbins, but Steve, the state inspector, had been very kind. His tan trousers needed a hem and his buttoned-up shirt looked two sizes too small, indicating a man who hadn't missed many meals. Three pens rested in his breast pocket, but his fingers held a fourth as he made little check marks over a healthy stack of papers clutched in his hand.

"Adam has a decent setup here. Have you seen inside the honey house?" Steve scribbled a few more notes on his clipboard stack of papers and looked up.

"*Nee.* I mean no."

"Well, it's a beaut. The fellow is a real engineer. He is even considering adding a generator to run most of it. Will shorten the harvest time," he said with a wink.

If Adam upgraded whatever setup he currently had by using a generator, he wouldn't need help at all. Strangely, that made her wish generators went against *Ordnung*, but they didn't. Many local Amish businesses used generators as a form of alternative energy.

"I have everything I need. I'm pretty behind today and have three more stops just in Havenlee." He pocketed the pen and looked at her more intensely.

"You just put those," he motioned toward the two plastic packages in her hands, "where we noticed a problem, and let Adam know what we discussed." Belinda stared down at the beetle traps he had gifted, hoping that as she checked more hives there would be no more surprises.

"Thanks for meeting with me while Adam was at work. I never knew he was married, but I'm glad I finally got to meet the other half of his business." Steve reached out and Belinda hesitated before shaking his hand. He smiled widely and let go just as quickly as possible. Maybe he sensed her unease.

"I'm just helping out. Adam isn't married." She couldn't let him leave thinking she was Adam's *fraa*. That wouldn't be right. "We're neighbors," she added.

Steve lifted a brow. "Oh, I see," he said.

It sounded as if he didn't altogether believe her, but he didn't say anything else before he got back into his truck. As the truck speed down the little drive and veered onto the road, Belinda touched her cheek.

"He didn't even seem to notice my mark," she said to herself. Tabitha's words flowed into her heart. "You don't see what we do."

Chapter Eleven

E WAS WORN DOWN, LIFE challenging his resilience, but Adam was looking forward to delivering good news to Belinda—while also getting an update from her about her appointment. He hoped meeting with the inspector hadn't been too hard on her. He felt guilty that she'd had to do it, considering her history with strangers, but it couldn't be avoided. When he reached the front door and knocked, Adam barely had time to blink before it opened with a swift jerk.

Just under five feet tall, Mollie Bender stretched her neck up to meet Adam, eye to eye. Her gaze lowered and settled on the empty green pail in his hand. "I take it you had a good day." Her grey eyes twinkled with delight. Belinda had that same twinkle, minus the cunning.

"It was a day, that's for sure," Adam bantered. He liked Mollie, her hospitable smile and easygoing nature. Her tendency to talk openly to the Lord baffled a few, but she wasn't the kind who paid any mind to what stumped others.

"Don't think flowers are so foolish now, do you?" She folded her arms. Adam winced. It was clear Belinda had told her grandmother of his less than enthusiastic reaction toward the idea of a flower business.

"Not anymore," he conceded with a smile, having learned his lesson. "I found two buyers—actually, I found one, and one found me." He peered over her *kapp*. "Is she around? I have a list and some numbers to discuss with her." Mollie beamed even brighter. He wished Belinda would smile that easily.

"So the florist, and who else?" Mollie asked.

"A baker, if you can believe it. She saw me walking into the flower shop this morning and when I went back after work to talk to Marcy—that's the florist—she was waiting for me. Apparently bakers really do use flowers too." Adam had liked the baker immediately. Both she and Marcy, the florist, were more than excited to strike up a deal. Marcy had given him a list of flowers for which Belinda had a high demand, and had given him a second list that she and

Mia, the baker, hoped Belinda could provide. When Marcy quoted a price and the baker agreed on the same numbers, Adam knew he was in a whole different world. Flowers were very profitable. Who knew?

"I knew that foreigner would want them," Mollie slapped her hands together happily. "But who doesn't love flowers?" Adam knew better than to respond. "Belinda has you to thank for much today."

"None needed. We had an agreement. I'm just keeping my end of it."

"Oh, posh." Mollie swatted the air between them and he nearly stepped back. "Everyone likes to know they are appreciated. Do you feel appreciated, Adam Hostetler?" Her grey eyes narrowed, compelling him to respond.

"Um, yes? I do." He hadn't thought about it. Of course his family appreciated him, valued all the hard work he was doing.

"Do you also appreciate? This world can't stand one-sidedness." Taken aback, Adam didn't know what to say. Where was she going with this rambling? His brain was too tired for deep-seated questions, probing intentions. Sensing his bewilderment, Mollie continued. "Your bees need what she has, and she needs that smooth-talking tongue of *yers*. You can't have one do better than the other. They are joined, your bees and her blossoms, you and her. A man must feel appreciated and know how to return it to keep the balance." Adam hadn't a clue how to respond. Mollie looked up, frowning. "Lord, this one needs a lot of work yet. I've got one summer, but that might not be enough."

He blinked twice before gathering a bit of composure. Belinda's mammi was a complicated woman.

"It's the oldest romance told." Mollie waved her chubby finger toward him again. "Bees and flowers. The good Lord couldn't depend on just the wind to work around the clock." She leaned closer. "So He devised a plan for his beautiful plants to multiply." *Who talked like this? What did it even mean? Was he the wind or was Belinda?*

"I...um..." Mollie had rendered him speechless.

"You two make a fine match, as far as these old eyes can see," Mollie added, smiling as if holding a thousand secrets. Adam's neck grew excessively warm. He took a step back, let the sun hit him. Even its full-on blaze felt cooler than Mollie Bender and her squirrely thoughts.

"We are helping each other. That's all. I'm not..." Adam fumbled with his words.

"Not yet. But soon, perhaps. Been a lot of years since I could make a young man blush—I take that as a promising sign." Mollie laughed. He couldn't help but wonder if she might have lost some of her wits in her old age. "She's out there now, with the bees. I never thought anything would come before her flowers."

Adam shifted nervously. Inside, he had to admit, knowing Belinda enjoyed the same passion as he did had recently snuck into his dreams and interfered with his realities.

What would it be like to be married to a woman who walked beside him in faith and in interest? Working alongside one another, sharing the joys. Someone who didn't mind the quiet but could also talk about the things he loved with no judgments or soured expressions. He shoveled the thought back, buried it. No way would he let his guard down to even tinker with such an idea. He might not be able to control his wandering thoughts, but he could control his own heart.

"Well, *yer* wasting daylight." Mollie rattled him back to the present. "See ya on Sunday." She slammed the door.

"Uh, *danki*," Adam stuttered. He placed his hat back on his head and strode to the back pasture, but slowed when the reality hit him. Putting distance between himself and a meddling old woman was closing the distance between him and her granddaughter. Why had he let Mica talk him into this in the first place?

When Adam didn't find Belinda behind the house or in the horse pasture, Adam knew she had to be at the orchard. He needed to tell her about the florist and the baker so she could prepare for Monday morning's order. *It's business. Just business. I'm not the wind. Mollie Bender's not the wind. There is no wind.*

He heard the sweet humming hanging on an afternoon breeze long before he saw her. The wind captured her sound, carrying it a fair distance before swallowing it up. She always did have a pleasant voice. Now, standing in the wake of it, he recalled a time when a younger Adam had snuck over to her family's farm and hidden behind the barn to hear her singing. He'd grown out of that right quick when Melvin Graber made him muck stalls for three days as punishment, after he was caught on his second attempt. Fortunately Belinda's daed never squealed on him, but he was ten and she sounded like an angel. At least what a ten-year-old imagined angels to sound like. How had he forgotten that?

Adam recognized the old garden hymn, but didn't dare join in the singing, despite wondering how their voices might accompany one another. As he closed the distance, he suffered a mighty shock. There in the center of his world stood a stranger. In fact, if not for that sweet voice, Adam would have thought a thief had found his honey hives.

This new version of Belinda stood on a spray of apple and pear blossoms, covering the ground like a fresh snow. The setting was familiar—the woman was not. Gone was the plainly dressed woman he had known most of his life. In her place was someone wearing denim britches and a shirt that looked three sizes too large. *Charming bees and me* passed through his mind before he shook the thought clear from his head. He needed to tread lightly, stop letting others' words affect him so. Mollie Bender had gotten into his head good and deep. *Mollie was the wind*, he decided, settling that debate for now. But he would not let her stir up trouble for him, no matter how she huffed and puffed.

Regardless of these thoughts, Adam realized he wouldn't mind standing there all day, listening, watching Belinda toy with bees as if they had no bite to them at all. He'd once read about a woman in Kansas, "the bee charmer" according to the article he'd read, who could walk among swarms as free as a breeze. He imagined Belinda capable of the same.

He discarded the fancy, replacing it with common sense. She might welcome the bees around her, but no man was given such liberty. Everyone knew where she stood. A reclusive spinster, Tobias called her. Rejection stung worse than a few bees, and he wouldn't be thrilled to receive either.

He narrowed his gaze, noting Belinda wasn't using the smoker he'd set out for her. No matter her obvious ability, she had no business ignoring safety. The smoker calmed the bees, prevented them from growing angry. It was a necessary precaution. He couldn't be responsible for her getting hurt. Here she was dressed like a boy and ignoring her own safety. He couldn't decide which he would address first as he marched forward.

"You're supposed to use the smoker," Adam said, in a not-so-tender voice. There were rules when dealing with bees, and her carelessness couldn't be ignored.

"What are you doing here?" Belinda's head shot his way, her voice shaken and distant-sounding under the covering of her veil. In her bare hands, she held a frame covered in bees, thick with bulging cells, capped and waiting for harvest. He approached slowly and stopped twelve feet away.

"I live here," he responded. Denim britches, bare hands, a shirt three sizes too large. All three made him growl under his breath.

"You're usually not home so early."

"It's not early." Yep, she was in her own little world. "Mr. Shetler is letting me have a few days off here and there, so I will be here to help with these." He motioned to the hives.

She slid the frame back into the hive with long bare delicate fingers. Under the veil he couldn't see her blue eyes or that little dimple that had a way of appearing on a rare grin. He stepped closer, resigned to stings at this point. Surprisingly, none came.

"I have extra gloves. Left them right by

the smoker. You should be wearing them," he reminded.

"It's easier this way." A few dozen bees crawled up her right arm. Her brother's shirt would offer little protection if they decided to defend their homes. Fatigue and disappointment needed little fertilizer to grow into a temper.

"It's not a suggestion." She looked at him, gave his expression a long study, and then pulled another frame from the super. Adam stepped closer.

"Being stubborn will get you stung." Was she purposefully ignoring him? She didn't look up, focused on the frames and their careful placement so as not to harm a single bee.

"Barking orders will get you ignored," she said, with the same sweet voice she used when she spoke to bees. There was that pluck again.

"Why are you dressed like that?" His gaze made a slow sweep over her. But even as he stated the question, he figured out the answer. A dress would certainly invite a few dozen stings. Why hadn't he thought of that sooner?

Belinda glanced at her clothing. If she was grinning, he couldn't tell. "Oh, these are my pants Mamm purchased for me." She said it as if it meant nothing at all. "Can't work out here all day in a dress, can I? Are you always this grouchy at the end of the day?" Adam nearly choked on her defiance. Since when did the shy girl next door talk back? She stepped away from the hives, lifted her veil in slow movements.

"Hattie paid for you to wear denim? Belinda, we took the same baptismal classes, joined the church when we were twenty." Belinda knew the rules, the responsibilities they'd committed themselves to when they'd been baptized. Just because she didn't mingle socially didn't mean she could pick and choose which to follow.

"You remember that?" Her voice rose. "I mean, what does our baptism have to do with anything?"

"The bishop doesn't allow this." Adam motioned toward her chosen apparel.

"He allows it for me," she said smugly. "And what I wear is none of your concern. You have too many hot and cold moods, Adam Hostetler. You could just say, *danki.*"

His mouth opened, but nothing came out.

"And I am permitted when helping my dawdi with the bees," she added. "Mica spoke to Bishop Mast in Kentucky and our bishop years ago."

Adam had seen plenty of *Englisch* females in denim in town, but the last thing he needed was this mental image of Belinda Graber in jeans to intrude on his long, stretched-out days. Despite his hard shell, she was getting under his skin.

"Okay then. But what if someone sees you? People might ask questions."

"No one ever does, and I wear a veil most of the time, so I doubt they'd even realize who I am. No one pays a care to who is under it," she retorted. "Mica says I look like a *bu* anyway."

There was that slight smile, the timid one when she wasn't trying to be funny, but was. It weakened his temper. "I can't imagine you being mistaken for a boy," he mumbled, earning him a frown. But he stood by his statement. Who wouldn't notice that way she stood, her delicate stride, even the way she tilted her head so often? And the curves that womanhood had gifted her obviously gave her away. "And what are those?" Adam asked, pointing toward two yellow squares of cloth that looked more like something Mamm cleaned the bathroom with than tools for a honey harvester.

"These are beetle traps. The inspector said you needed them in one hive, but after looking, I think this one needed it too." She backtracked, lifted a lid from the ground, covered the hive she had been inspecting, and stepped away. All without her veil. Adam thought he might just explode at her careless behavior.

"Stop doing that," he said between clenched teeth. Belinda had seen to a potential problem that would protect his bees, but that still didn't mean she could ignore safety when it came to her own protection. She walked back toward him, head down, lip captured by her teeth. He considered reining in his temper, sensing he was stepping on her delicate nature. But it couldn't be helped. If she got stung, attacked by a thousand angry bees, he could never forgive himself.

"The inspector wants me to use those?" he asked, pointing to the wrappers in her hands.

"*Jah.* Dawdi uses those plastic ones you put oil in, but the inspector had a couple of these on hand. He said they work like magic." Clearly she wasn't upset with his harshness today.

"I read about these, but heard the bees might trying pulling them through the escape hole and get trapped. You should have asked me first," he said firmly.

She bent to gather the packaging from the Beetle Bee-Gone pads. "If you check your hives regularly, as one should, that won't happen." She turned to face him. "You asked me to help you, trusted me to do the job— and since you haven't been around to speak to, I did what I felt was best, for the bees." There was a hint of vinegar in her tone.

He reached for the plastic bags the yellow pads had come in, brushing her fingers lightly. The jolt of electricity affected them equally. She jerked away from the contact, dropping everything in her hands. Quickly tossing her veil aside, Belinda went to gather up the mess, but Adam had already knelt and began collecting them.

"*Ack*," she sputtered. When their eyes locked, Adam's chest pounded like a runaway team of work horses. In the absence of her veil, those blue eyes had captured him again, and he was completely aware she was also displaying cheeks tinted an appealing peach shade. He was a fan of peaches. He could no longer deny it. Belinda Graber still intrigued him. Quite a bit. And that wouldn't do at all. Wasn't he still angry with her?

"Blue," she muttered, then quickly got back to her feet. Did she read minds too? He surely hoped not.

"What?"

"Your eyes. I thought they were green, but they are blue—at least for the moment. I think they change depending on the light." She tilted her head. "It's fascinating they can do that." She lowered her gaze again. "Sorry." She was blushing, and now he was too.

Adam swallowed. Other than Mamm, no one had ever spoken about how the color of his eyes did tend to change under various lights. Susanne certainly hadn't. With that thought he turned away from Belinda. It would do no good to keep letting her affect him like she was. He was angry with her, wasn't he?

"They tend to lean one way or another, depending." He should be addressing her lack of safety, not discussing eye color.

"Depending?"

"On the light, the color shirt I wear, my mood—or so Mamm says," he said, stuffing the trash in his pocket. It was hard to focus around Belinda.

"Your mood," she whispered, but he heard it still.

"Belinda, you really shouldn't ignore safety. I can't have you getting hurt."

"What makes you think I will get hurt?" she said stubbornly. Those blue eyes had the ability to soften a man's mood and shoot fiery daggers in the same look. He could tell her she was irresponsible, careless, and treading a fine line between proper and defiant, but his lips wouldn't budge.

"I should go," she said, and began walking toward home. Without her *kapp*, Adam couldn't help but admire the long braid of hair under a small white kerchief. It hung down her back, between thin shoulder blades that Mica's shirt draped over like a waterfall. Not wheat-colored, but honey-hued, he decided. Her hair was as rich as honey, and the thought of touching it, toying with the strands, disrupted his thoughts. He had never had to chase after a woman before, but found himself helpless to catch up with this one.

Chapter Twelve

BELINDA HAD HALF A MIND to tell Adam to find someone else to help him. Instead, she kept her head down and picked up her pace. The faster she got to her side of the road, the better.

"Belinda, wait!" His voice reached out. She kept her pace. "You didn't tell me everything the inspector had to say."

She glanced over her shoulder. "He said you had the best hives in the state." That should make him happy, she thought.

He reached her side. "I can see to getting you a bee jacket. It would be wiser than just thin linen sleeves." She glanced down at her clothes. Mica's shirt worked fine. How dare he speak to her as if she were a child with no idea what she was doing? She picked up her pace. The bishop approved her attire, so Adam Hostetler's opinions didn't matter.

"It wonders me how Susanne puts up with you." How anyone put up with him.

"The florist, Marcy, says she would like a few dozen tulips and wanted to know if you had a certain kind of petunia—I think she called them million bells." Adam's voice slowed her steps. Here she wanted nothing more than to rid herself of this stubborn man, back out of their arrangement, and then he had to go and remind her he had done just as he was supposed to do.

"And any daisies that you've got," he continued. "She has orders piling up and a couple weddings next weekend." She slowed to a stop.

"She really wants to buy my flowers?" Belinda said, shocked. Had he really worked out an arrangement with the local florist? The news snuffed out her current anger with him.

"*Jah*, she does." He let out a sigh, clearly happy he had stalled her.

"That's...it's *wunderbaar*. I can walk them over to you at first light if you can drop them off before your shift."

"I'll come get them. She doesn't need them until Monday," Adam said. Belinda bit her bottom lip and stared at her boots as they walked back toward home.

"You should meet Jackson, her *sohn*. He is a hoot. Asked me about three dozen questions before I could leave," Adam said, chuckling. Less than a minute ago he had been questioning her safety sense, and now he was gossiping away like they were the closest of friends. Did all men have such ever-changing moods?

"I'm glad you like him." Her voice remained steady, but her insides were anything but.

"And the baker, Mia, she's Italian. Talks funny. I think you would like her. She said she wants pansies, enough to do four cakes. What does that even mean?"

Belinda glanced over and tried not to look overly shocked. "The baker? You made a deal with the baker too?" She would kiss him if she thought he wouldn't get the wrong idea, or if she thought kissing an appropriate thank you, which she didn't.

"I must have a knack for sales," Adam jested. Belinda couldn't argue that fact. Adam had secured her two buyers for her flowers. "So what does a baker do with flowers, exactly?"

"She sugars them and puts them on her cakes. It makes them look...*schee.*"

"It wonders me what kind of person eats flowers." He shook his head.

"It's safe to eat all kinds of them; weeds too." He made a face. It was hard staying angry with someone who made faces at you. The breeze carried on it all the magnificent scents from her family's gardens, mingled with sawdust wafting off her partner. It was a strange but invigorating mix.

Adam had held up his end of their partnership. Belinda needed to show him she was doing hers. "I can start pulling frames from your hives in the morning."

"I can't Saturday. I have plans. We will start Monday. It should go faster with two and you won't have to be here so long."

Belinda bit her bottom lip at an unexpected twinge of disappointment. Reminding herself that she was being foolish, she huffed out a breath, straightened her shoulders, and clutched her hands together.

Her reaction clearly surprised him. "What?" he demanded. "Why do you look offended? I just meant I know you like your space." He was back-pedaling, badly.

"Just because I prefer keeping to myself doesn't mean I don't understand when someone doesn't want to be around me." Her chin lifted a notch. "I know you wish it was Mica here instead." Her voice trembled.

"I didn't mean it that way, Belinda. I meant I'm sure you have plans on a Saturday. I heard Noel Christner has been pretty eager to see you. I thought maybe..."

"*Nee*, I don't have plans with Noel. Not tomorrow or any other day." Just the thought of it made her stomach curl. "You shouldn't listen to gossip."

"I guess I shouldn't." His tone deepened. "Noel is a nice fellow, you know."

"Noel is scary," she said. Noel was more than scary; he was too bold for his own good. *Like rude neighbors who smile one minute and scold the next.*

"How so?" Adam asked coolly. Belinda glanced up, noted her home lights in the distance, and picked up her pace again. She just wanted to get back to her side of the road.

"He hasn't talked to me before, and when we were kids, he used to stare at me all the time." She tipped her shoulder upward instinctually, hiding her cheek.

"Maybe it took a lot for him to ask you out. Maybe he was nervous." Adam gave her a sideways glance. "Some boys are more nervous talking to girls."

"You know that isn't true," she snipped.

"Why?"

His obliviousness irked her into being more blunt than she might have been otherwise. "*Buwe* didn't talk to me in school unless it was to say something cruel about my looks. I don't figure they've changed much just because they grew taller and started to shave." She fidgeted with the veil in her hands and watched her house come into clear view. When they entered the Hostetler yard, she hoped Adam would simply leave her to her own devices and go inside, but no, here he was, sticking to her side like jam on a biscuit.

"A couple were cruel, *jah*, but not all.

Trust me, most wanted to talk to you, to be your friend. They just didn't want to upset you when you seemed like you wanted to be left alone."

"I didn't want to be teased—that doesn't mean I didn't want friends. Yet by not talking to me all those years, they *did* upset me, and left me nearly friendless, to boot. *You* didn't talk to me in school." She meant the words as she said them to be an arrow straight to his arrogant male heart. When he stopped she kept walking, glad to be rid of him. How would she manage working with such a man?

An instant later, guilt ravaged her, piercing through her indignation. Still, she could not entirely regret her words, though she wished she'd given them a kinder tone. She was not a cruel person, but truth was truth and he hadn't had two words to say to her until he found himself in a pickle and needed her help. And he did not endear himself to her by scolding her like a child for not wearing the gear he seemed to think was necessary—gear she'd never required before.

She knew he was weary and overworked, but that was no excuse. Adam should have never sought her out tonight. Not until he at least had food and rest. His tongue had a mind of its own, it seemed. But her hopes that they would be parted now were dashed.

"Not for the reasons you think," he argued, as he quickly caught up to her again.

"You were so shy in school. I wish now I had talked to you then. I'm sorry if I upset you."

"I don't want to talk about this," she muttered, her voice trembling. His heart plummeted, and he knew he had awakened old hurts she had hoped to forget.

"I'm sorry. I know I have crossed too many lines this evening. I'm just tired. Then seeing you not taking precautions set me off. It's no excuse, I know, but I really just want you to be safe."

Belinda swiveled and took in a deep breath. "I'm not a child."

"*Nee*, you're not." He shifted. "Forgive me."

He was apologizing for his sharp tongue. Forgiveness was required. and surprisingly she didn't mind giving it. "My safety isn't your concern, but that was kind of you. I guess."

"I can be kind, and humble, and I'm strong too." He flexed his muscles playfully to make her smile. Why couldn't she just stay mad at him?

"And modest, I see." She rolled her eyes. When they reached the pavement that separated their homes, Belinda stopped. "So you and Susanne have plans Saturday? She could help with the hives, you know."

"No plans like that. I'll be repairing a chicken coop."

So he was going to help his grandmother. Despite his sometimes moody behavior, he cared for his family's needs. Maybe she would show up, help. She had promised Ada and Atlee she would do her best to make his jobs easier. How hard could repairing a few rotten boards be?

It had taken less time to get back than either had expected, and suddenly neither was eager to budge one way or another. "I can walk alone from here," she assured.

"It's no trouble," he replied.

"It wouldn't be proper," she said softly.

"It would be less proper if I didn't walk you safely to the door." He cupped her elbow and escorted her across the road before she could protest further.

"Because one can never know when a bear might attack," she said with a dry humor.

Adam gave her a quick look. "You never know," he replied playfully.

"Adam, I forgot. On Monday, Mica is forcing me to go to Shipshewana to the produce auction."

"Then we'll start Tuesday." He paused, and she wondered what he was thinking as their eyes held on one another. Did the contact send a thousand improper thoughts dancing in his head, the way it did hers? She saw his eyes drop to her lips...but no, that must be her imagination. A man who was courting Susanne Zook would never look at a Belinda Graber and think of a kiss.

"Well, *gut nacht*, Belinda, and *danki* for helping." He turned and walked across the road without waiting for her to say goodbye. She told herself she was glad to see him go, taking all the confusing feelings he roused in her away with him.

"I see you walked Belinda home," Ada said the second Adam entered the house. A strong aroma of cinnamon told him she had made his favorite cinnamon bread, which often meant her saucy ribs for dinner. A dinner he had missed, talking to Belinda—but he could always count on Mamm to keep a plate warm for him. His stomach was growling on empty, and a full meal, a hot shower, and a decent night's sleep would be the perfect ending to a long day.

"She doesn't want me walking her home," he told his mother, not bothering to hide the hurt in his voice.

"And why not?" Ada shoved one tight fist on her hip.

"She doesn't want anyone to get the wrong idea."

Mamm huffed and turned back to the stove. "Of all the stuff," she muttered, pulling leftovers out of the oven. "I raised you to treat all with respect and whatever ideas she thinks others might get, *I* expect you

to walk her home when it grows dim out."
Mamm continued mumbling but Adam
couldn't make out a thing she was saying.

"She's a smart *maedel*. with a heart for
helping others," Atlee sang from the sitting
room. His parents were being awful chipper
about his new partner. It was a little aggra-
vating, but he knew they were right. Belinda
had been kind to help, especially since she
didn't like stepping out of her comforts. And
here he'd treated her like a child, making a
fuss about everything from her clothes to
her rebellion against gloves.

"She should wear gloves, but other
than that, I like her bee outfit. Though I'm
surprised the bishop lets her wear britches."
Adam's father had a deep voice that tended
to carry fully.

Adam unlaced his boots, walked into the
sitting room, and dropped heavily into the
recliner. "Bishop Schwartz doesn't mind as
long as it's for tending to bees. I'm surprised
you saw her wearing it. The window is too
high for you to see out."

"Oh, Belinda came to see me. You know
how bored I get without company." Atlee
smiled widely.

"What am I, furniture?" Ada quipped
from the kitchen.

"*Nee*, my love, you are a permanent fixture in my heart," Daed quickly added, and
gave Adam a wink.

"She came to see you in britches?" Adam

rolled his eyes. He hoped his parents hadn't caused her too much embarrassment. He knew them enough to know they would have poked and prodded at her agreeing to help.

"I invited her in," his father explained. "She hesitated, but you know how convincing I can be." Adam did. "I so enjoy her company. She isn't a talker like some. Rambling is a waste of good air, I say." That was true enough, Adam was quickly learning. Belinda wasn't a talker, unless the subject was flowers or bees, and then she had plenty to say.

"I know you didn't like Susanne all that well, but..."

Ada stepped into the room, her apron splattered with rib sauce, shaking a fork in his direction. "I liked Susanne well enough. As a Christian we are to love all, even chatty *maedels* with no good sense or a willingness to help another." *How Christian of you*, Adam nearly responded, but he had no opening since his mother kept talking. "But a mother can't tell a lie to her *kinner*. Belinda Graber is the kind of *maedel* worthy of you. She doesn't spend her days running about with friends acting all willy-nilly. She helps her family, owns a flower business, and now she is helping you. Not to mention, she and Tabitha sent food over when your *daed* got out of the hospital. Susanne didn't even bake a pie." Mamm darted him a glare that dared him to deny it. "That one ran when things got tough. A man needs a *fraa* who isn't afraid of a little hard work." "Afraid" was usually Belinda's middle name—or so he had thought. Tonight, it seemed like she was a lot of things. *A walking contradiction.*

Adam couldn't deny Mamm's words. Susanne did run, straight into another man's arms, the moment Adam found himself solely responsible for his family. "You don't need to play matchmaker. Belinda is nice and kind," and beautiful, and surprisingly funny, "but she is just a business partner. That is all. Neither of us have an interest in courting. We like our lives just as they are."

"How would you know that? Have you ever tried talking to her before you needed her help?" Mamm's light blue eyes pierced him. "I know how you used to watch her all the time at church and gatherings, and don't think we don't know the reason Melvin had you mucking stalls three days straight." Adam's mouth fell open, his face turning crimson. Of course he had been a curious boy, and he'd long outgrown such childishness, but it was still embarrassing ten years later. Good thing they hadn't a clue about all his mischievous ventures with Tobias.

Still, Mamm's words stabbed him straight to the core. For so many years, he hadn't approached Belinda because he didn't want to scare her. Yet, he had found himself turning to her when he found himself in a jam. He swallowed hard. Guilt tasted bitter and a tad bit sharp. He had never thought himself selfish, yet he obviously was.

"I didn't dare in school, because every time I got close enough to speak to her she would hide her face and tremble. No one wants to make someone scared enough to cry. She seemed like she'd rather help the teacher grade papers than make friends."

"You know she was teased in school," Mamm said solemnly, and went back to ready his plate. "She must have seen you staring at her and thought you were making fun," she called behind her while heading into the kitchen.

"*Ach*, that birthmark," Atlee added. "*Kinner* can be cruel." He shook his head. "Well, you can't even see it anymore." Belinda's birthmark was the size of a dollar piece and had been colored deep red when they were ten, but with the passage of time, it had faded into a soft strawberry hue that was easily overlooked. Sort of. Adam was finding he rather liked seeing it. It was like a small rosy kiss on her sun-stroked cheek.

"I'm going to wash up for supper. I'm starved." He left the room and headed upstairs to the bathroom. He couldn't handle any more talk about Belinda Graber in his own home. It was bad enough that she was starting to penetrate his daily thoughts. He lathered his hands, worked the soap roughly. When he rinsed the soap away, she still remained there, a perfect picture in his mind.

Chapter Thirteen

BELINDA BRUSHED A HAND DOWN her black apron front as she stepped inside the barn Sunday morning, a shadow behind her siblings.

Mammi had wandered off to chat with Betsy, the bishop's *fraa.* This week marked the anniversary of the loss of the family's youngest. Little Joshua had been only four when he choked to death, and he'd left a gaping hole in their hearts. Belinda glanced toward Abigale, the eldest Schwartz child, herding her siblings Daniel and Karen toward their seats. Belinda counted her blessings each night she never endured the loss of a sibling as Abigale had.

Nelly rushed to her side. "Did you hear?" Nelly tugged Belinda into a corner. She was a few inches shorter than Belinda, but

Belinda always felt smaller somehow next to her friend, a mere shadow compared to Nelly's strong presence. Nelly never lacked for confidence, an open mind, and the undivided attention of Caleb Esh. Three things Belinda would never have. "Caleb told me Susanne and Jerimiah went to see the deacon."

Belinda gasped. Had Susanne been courting two men at once?

There was only one reason two people went to see the deacon: hoping for a marriage blessing.

Henry Schmidt and Nathan Byler, the two community ministers, moved past them, removing their hats and pinning both women with a warning glare. Not only was gossiping a sin, but they were going to be late taking their seats.

"That's terrible," Belinda whispered, as a clutch of older women hurried past. Belinda's heart went out to Adam. On top of all the troubles he already had to endure since his father's accident, he'd lost the woman he'd courted for the past year, and now she was marrying another so quickly. But even her sympathy had a note of disgruntlement to it. Why hadn't he told her, instead of gripe about gloves and auctions? *Because we are partners, not friends*, she reminded herself. Still, her heart ached for him. Adam had hardly said a word when she helped him Saturday with May's chicken coop. It seemed no matter what she did to help him, he remained prickly and sour. Instead they had worked in companionable silence and parted with the same.

"You think they will be published, today, here?" her voice squeaked out.

"That's what Salina thinks, and she is closer to Susanne's family," Nelly said.

"I have to tell Adam; he will be devastated and embarrassed." Belinda stepped from the corner, eyes searching through the gathering crowd filling the Lantz barn.

"I think we are too late for that." Men were already hanging their hats, women already filling the backless benches. With the exception of the two young women and a few lingering young boys who were in charge of putting horses out to pasture, everyone was assuming their places. There was no time to take Adam aside.

"We have to find a way to let him know," Belinda said in a panicky breath. He didn't deserve to find out without a warning first.

"Belinda, he is already seated. Look," Nelly pointed as they stepped closer to a bench opposite him. "Besides, it could be just gossip. Maybe nothing will happen. If we tell him and it ends up coming to nothing, he will be angry with us. He will be angry with you, which might make him unwilling to help you sell your flowers. Besides, he might not care about the news." The last thing Belinda wanted was a reason for Adam to be angry with her and no longer deliver her flowers for her. Still, the urge to do something niggled at her.

Why wouldn't he care? She considered Nelly's words as they took their seats. Caleb shared everything with Nelly. Did she know more about Adam's state of mind, courtesy of his friend, than she was willing to share?

Lowering her head as the bishop began the opening prayer, Belinda whispered one of her own. When she lifted her head, Adam's gaze was locked onto her. His brow furrowed in concern, clearly sensing her distress.

As the hymns began, she numbly sang through both songs from the *Ausbund,* the Amish hymnal book, while the elders slipped into a private area to decide who would deliver what message today. Belinda usually loved to sing the long verses, add a hint of harmony in the drab lowering bellows around her, but right now she could only watch a beekeeper across the room sing as if he wasn't about to get stung.

Through the short sermon and the scripture Deacon Gingerich delivered, Belinda wrung her hands together nervously. Across the room Adam grinned at something Tobias whispered to him. The grin made her hope it was all gossip and she was worried for nothing.

Questions swirled in her mind until Nelly jabbed her in the ribs just as the long sermon ended and the closing prayer began. Now all there was left was the final song, and if there was an announcement to be made, it would be then. Her breath caught, but her eyes remained on Adam. As voices lifted, Belinda's remained silent.

"I would like to make an announcement." All eyes fell on Bishop Schwartz. Adam's eyes collided with hers, and for a moment she wished he could read her thoughts. Instead he offered a slow smile and lowered his gaze. He hadn't a clue, until he did.

"You all are invited in two weeks' time, last Thursday in June I am told, to the home of Elmer and Kathy Zook." Belinda could hear Salina gasp beside her, watched Tobias frown as if he could sense what was coming.

Adam's jaw tightened, his fists clenched as he leaned forward, elbows on his knees. He dropped his head, refusing to watch, but forced to hear. Belinda clutched her chest, where her heart was beating half to death as she watched a man's resolve plummet in front of an audience. How many stones could be thrown at one man before leaving permanent damage, she wondered.

"Our community will witness the marriage of their daughter Susanne to Jerimiah Petersheim." Tobias patted Adam's knee. Belinda forced her gaze away, not to look at the beaming couple smiling at one another from across the room, but to take in the faces of the community she had purposely avoided most of her life. Some were smiling, some frowning. Nelly shot her an *I told you so* look. Ada Hostetler, who finally was able to attend a service now that Atlee was doing better, stared at her son with the same ache Belinda could feel. Across the room, Mica crossed both arms, watching the couple float sweet looks of affection toward one another. All remaining eyes were on Adam, who was staring at his shoes.

Adam didn't stay for the fellowship meal and Belinda didn't blame him. Ada insisting she didn't want to leave Atlee alone for long had been the perfect excuse. Belinda gathered the empty plates and headed for the kitchen where Tabitha and Salina were doing dishes. At the sound of Adam's name, she stalled in the doorway.

"I thought you and Adam were still courting. This was a surprise, but we are happy for you and Jerimiah," Salina said, in that way Belinda knew was pure Salina sarcasm.

"Adam had no idea how to treat a *fraa*. He would rather play with bugs," Susanne scoffed. Belinda's gripped tightened on the stack of plates, her thumb slipping into someone's neglected macaroni salad. Somewhere in the back of the kitchen, dishes clacked together, followed by the sounds of three women exiting the kitchen. Apparently some didn't care for the conversation being held inside any more than she did.

"Daed says he makes a fine living with

those bugs," Rachel Byler chimed in. The minister's daughter had a knack for politely reminding one not to speak ill of others. Her tolerance was limited.

"Have you and Jerimiah known each other long?" Marisa, Rachel's twin, prodded. The eighteen-year-olds mirrored their dark-haired father, but Marisa earned a few extra admiring looks thanks to her curly hair. A dozen pins couldn't hold it in place, no matter how she tried.

"We have been seeing each other for some time now," Susanne admitted, her voice slightly arrogant. Belinda couldn't stand by eavesdropping. She needed to put down the dishes and walk away before she said something she'd regret. She had never felt anger before, real anger, not like this. Susanne had courted two men at once, and Adam had lost. No wonder he was grumpy all the time. If her life had been hammered with so many sorrows so quickly, Belinda might have been just as crabby. She gingerly entered the room, skilled at mimicking shadows, staying out of the way.

"Jerimiah is sweet. He has so much to offer and wants all the same things I do," Susanne continued. It was the only thing she said worth hearing. Couples should have similar interests and hopes. Still, Belinda put Susanne in that category where she kept people like Noel Christner. *Avoid at all costs.*

"And he would never ask me to work for

him," Susanne said, and this time her gaze set on Belinda as she walked toward the sink. It was no secret that she and Adam were helping one another. "I think it's rude to ask a woman to do such meaningless work." All eyes landed on Belinda, but this time, she didn't feel the urge to reach up, cover her ugliness. Not with true ugliness staring her in the face.

"It's a sin not to help someone in need," Belinda responded, and carefully sat down the stack of plates to be washed.

"He only cares about work. Just so you know. Don't be putting your hopes on him or you will be disappointed," Susanne warned. Belinda faced her, staring her down. Mammi was right. It was what was inside a person that mattered, and Susanne's insides weren't very pretty.

Tabitha stepped forward from wrapping salad bowls. Of course her sibling would speak up for her, as she always had. Belinda turned and gave Tabitha a look that told her sister not to bother. She wasn't a child anymore, and she was too old for words to hurt.

"I don't expect anything, so how could he disappoint? He is stretched between obligations to his family while holding on to his livelihood. I find that as admirable as everyone else in this room does." Despite the bees buzzing in her belly, Belinda forced a grin. She had never been the type to speak out in front of others, but it seemed required in the full kitchen with all eyes watching her, awaiting her reaction. In the past she would have run at any sign of confrontation, but it wasn't about her now, was it? This was about Adam.

"Admirable? He wants to raise bees to support a family. It's nonsense."

"And I want a flower farm." Why had she said that? "We all have talents and things that bring us joy and fulfillment. I'm sure if Jerimiah found himself in such a place as Adam, he would do what was most important too. I'm happy you found someone who is sweet and shares similar interests with you." With that, Belinda strolled back out the kitchen door to finish her duty. There was work to be done. And she had no interest in anything else Susanne might have to say.

Chapter Fourteen

ALL THE WAY TO SHIPSHEWANA, Belinda was a basket of nerves. Once there, she shadowed Mica closely. Buggies and *Englisch* vehicles equally crowded the area, as did the people who came in them. A sea of straw hats, white *kapps*, and more bald heads than Belinda had seen in her lifetime milled about produce heaped in wagons and truck beds. A woman brushed by, her clothes barely covering more than a bathing suit would. Belinda would never understand such a need for attention that would drive a woman to dress that way. But a spark of envy defied her meekness, as she wished for unblemished skin and flawless features.

It was a whole new world and a scary adventure, coming here. Inside the auction house, crowds thickened and she quickened her steps to stay close to Mica's side. Along the walls were crates, boxes, and large containers of produce, just as Adam had described Saturday while they repaired May's chicken coop. The heat of the day had reached into the eighties, and she thought of Adam, wondered how hot and humid working in the mill all day would be, and how he was dealing with Sunday's wedding announcement.

"You want to climb into my pocket, little sister?" Mica teased over one shoulder. He stopped and looked around, as comfortable here as he was in the hay fields. Belinda wished she'd inherited such abilities, but instead, her stomach twisted. She bit her lip and yes, wished Mica had bigger pockets.

"I saw a few men carrying in Graber strawberries and knew you must be close by." The deep voice caused both siblings to turn. The dark-haired stranger looked vaguely familiar, but Belinda couldn't place him. Maybe she'd have better luck once her head stopped spinning.

Mica stepped in front of her, and the men shook hands. "Abner Lapp. It wonders me if you might be lost. Pennsylvania is that way." Mica pointed a thumb over one shoulder. Both men chuckled.

"Is this," Abner peered around Mica. "Belinda?" He quickly removed his straw hat. His dark eyes widened in disbelief before his gaze steadied and trailed the length of her. "You are not a little girl any longer."

"*Nee*, she isn't." Mica added with an equally deep timbre. "Our Belinda here raises flowers, helps run the greenhouses, and even finds time to be charitable in helping her neighbors." Belinda didn't like the grin Mica was tossing her—or the way he was talking her up as if she was a horse for market.

"You don't remember me, do you?" She dug deep. That face, those high cheekbones and eyes that looked as dark as coffee, didn't register in her memory.

"I moved away before you were a teenager." The man scratched his head. "More than ten years ago, maybe."

"Twelve," she mumbled, finally registering him. Abner's face lit up at even this soft word.

"Can I go fetch you both a water? It's standing room only," he explained to her as if he could tell she had never been here before.

"We're fine. So what brings a horse man to a produce auction?" Mica moved closer to Belinda as the crowd grew thicker. His protectiveness never swayed, and for that she loved him all the more. A few voices to her left indicated the auction was about to start. She held her hands primly in front of her, trying her best not to bite her lip again.

"My *onkel* needed help hauling in cucumbers and beans. He heard they were bringing as much as forty dollars a bushel here." He looked to Belinda again. Why did he keep doing that? "And it's on my way." He winked.

"On your way?" Mica asked.

"I'm moving back. To Havenlee." He floated Belinda a shy smile. Suddenly it was clear. Nelly was right; she was slow-minded when it came to the opposite sex. Abner Lapp, the man she barely had a memory of, was flirting. And not once had he glanced at her cheek. She couldn't help feeling validated after years of assuming her looks were less than acceptable. Adam might have made her think outside of her normal thoughts, but he was also clear that they were only partners. They certainly weren't courting. They weren't even friends who would share truths about one another—meaning she had to hear about his and Susanne's break-up from others.

"I've missed a lot since I left," Abner replied to whatever he and Mica had been prattling on about. He locked his eyes onto her again, and for a brief moment, Belinda boldly held his gaze. He was really handsome, but those eyes weren't soft or easy, and they didn't change colors. And anyway, for all she knew he had girlfriend, maybe even a family. She ducked her head.

"So you have a family, wife, *kinner*, who will be coming with you?" Mica asked, as if reading her mind.

"Just me, though I am eager to have all those things. I plan to open a leather shop. I've found the work suits me. Little need of it where I've been, but in Havenlee, might be what's best for all my hopes and dreams." His gaze trapped her again, and Belinda fought the urge to squirm.

"We should go," Mica said, taking her elbow. "I'd like to see about some seed." His whole demeanor had shifted, and Belinda wasn't the only to notice.

"I hope to see both of you soon."

Mica's gaze went from her to Abner. "*Jah*, soon. Come by for supper sometime. You know where I live."

"I will do that." Abner tipped his hat toward her and offered another smile before disappearing into the crowd. Mica urged Belinda in the opposite direction as the auctioneer's amplified voice spouted numbers so fast Belinda couldn't make out a one of them.

"Would you loosen your hold, *bruder*? I might need that arm." Mica let go.

"He was flirting with you." It wasn't a question. The disgruntled tone in his voice irked her. Wasn't he the one who encouraged her to reconsider Noah's offer to ride home after church? And wasn't he solely responsible for her helping Adam with his honey harvest?

"*Jah*. I noticed." She smiled, showing him she no longer cared what he thought.

"You didn't mind?" Mica shot her a frown.

"I'm not a baby. Most my friends are married with *bopplin*. You talk about Noah, practically pushed me on Adam..."

"I did that, I guess." He couldn't look at her. "I thought Adam was courting Susanne. I'm sorry if that made you uncomfortable, but I'm not for you falling in with Abner. I know him. You deserve better." Belinda didn't ask for details. She trusted Mica with all her heart, and would heed the warning he was trying to offer. And maybe she would forgive him for conspiring to bring about her current partnership too. Despite Adam's sharp tongue and lies, she needed him. He had been good for her business.

"*Danki*, Mica. You are the perfect *bruder*, but promise you won't meddle any more. I think I can handle being a grownup now."

His smile came slow, his green eyes smiling too. "I promise. Unless you ask." Who could want for more?

Monday morning, Adam dragged himself into the mill on two tired legs. Tobias knew he had a lot on his mind, and the friends talked about the long weekend Adam couldn't shake. "I explained everything to them, but my parents are getting the wrong idea."

"I tried telling ya." Tobias nailed another board onto the pallet frame. Adam carried over another armload for the men. They had an order to finish two hundred pallets by day's end, and it didn't seem they would reach it. A warm breeze picked up and swirled sawdust into the air. Adam had never been so tired in all his life. It felt like he was running completely on empty.

"I told them I wasn't interested in another courtship. I mean, why would I put myself through all that again? I would rather be alone than put up with betrayal. Besides, a beekeeper isn't sought-after marrying material." Adam dropped his armload and smacked his palms together.

"Well, bees aren't really manly," Tobias teased. "I'm kidding. You make more in honey than I do here. And you don't smell as bad as a dairy farmer. In fact, you smell kind of... flowery." A man in the back of the long room whistled.

"Ha ha. It's from the flower shop. Can't walk in there and not come out smelling like it." He grunted. "Belinda says I smell like sawdust."

"She does, does she?" Tobias lifted a knowing brow.

"It's not like that. We are partners. We

spend time together, but only to get our work done."

"Good! Just keep it that way. I know it's tempting, but if you thought Susanne was a mistake, try getting fresh with Belinda and see where that gets ya." Tobias snorted out a laugh.

"What does that mean?" Adam didn't see any humor in the remark.

"She has made it very clear to every fellow in the county she has no interest in romance," Tobias reminded him. It was true, Belinda had done exactly that, but a person could change their mind, couldn't they? "One word of affection would send her running."

"She isn't like that." Adam went back to nailing, helping fill in for two absent workers. "In fact, she's smart, and funny, and surprisingly witty." He hoped she was having a good time with Mica at the auction today. Part of him wished he was there to help her deal with the crowds that must be making her anxious, but Adam knew Mica was well-practiced in seeing to Belinda's needs.

Tobias lifted a sharp pointed brow dusted with sawdust. Adam regretted the words the second they left his lips.

"You're partners, like you said. She needs you and you need her for your businesses to succeed. What would happen if you start talking more, show an interest, and it doesn't work out between you?"

For a man who thought nothing of

spreading his charms over two communities, Tobias was spot-on, surprisingly so. "I am getting to know her, which has surprised me plenty, but you're right." Adam shifted, and sank to his knees to work on the concrete floor. "She already thinks she was my last choice for help, and she was. I'm just lucky she could do it." Lucky, blessed, intrigued. He didn't dare share those thoughts with his best friend.

"Would you risk all you worked for over a *maedel* who has made it clear she wants a solitary life? Heck, they all do in that house. Neither Tabitha and Mica care for a date. It could go bad, Adam." Tobias's tone held a warning.

Adam considered what his friend was trying to say. It was odd that the Graber siblings all had set aside any thought of marriage at their age, but their lives were extremely busy. He, for one, understood the strains of courting, and admired their ability to set aside their wants to help their family's prosperity grow. It was clear he was likely to follow the same path. *The safer path.* "If you don't have another person to be responsible for, you won't fail. Stick with being friends and partners, or you will be sorry." It was sound advice, even if it came from Tobias.

"I agree. Besides, the last thing I need is making any more mistakes. It was embarrassing enough dealing with all those looks on Sunday." If he couldn't satisfy a woman like Susanne Zook, he could never please one like Belinda. She required a special kind of man, as special as she was. He was not that. All he had to do was get through until his daed was back to work. The physical therapist said Atlee was doing great, and Adam had even helped him to the supper table last night. Adam just needed to keep his head straight, his heart hidden, and focus on the bees for the next few months.

And whatever he did, avoid Belinda Graber as much as possible.

Chapter Fifteen

THE FOLLOWING TUESDAY MORNING, AS was becoming routine, Adam stopped in front of the flower shop. He toted three buckets inside and was immediately greeted by Marcy. "Good morning, Adam. Oh, these look so beautiful." He set the buckets down, took a step back. Today Marcy wore bright orange, and he tried not to stare at her outlandish style.

"I wish you could convince your friend to come with you just once. I would love to meet the one responsible for such beauty." Adam wished he could convince Belinda to come to town, too. Then she could meet Marcy and Mia herself, and he wouldn't have to get the flowers every morning and drop off the buckets every night, sneaking around like a thief to avoid seeing her.

"Belinda is..." He removed his hat, ran his fingers over his hair. "Shy. She doesn't do well with others." *That's not why I have been avoiding her for over a week*, his conscience whispered. Keeping some distance was hard with the harvest upon him, but Tobias's wisdom made more sense as the days went by.

"Well, maybe she hasn't met the right people." Marcy winked a dark eye, and she lifted a bucket and sat it on a low table. "I had a cousin who was afraid of her own shadow," she went on. "She was bullied in school because she was very sick and had to bring an oxygen tank with her everywhere she went." Adam watched her usually cheerful expression darken. "Kara had leukemia, and you would think even children would have sympathy because of that, but some didn't. They called her many names and her parents ended up teaching her at home, until..." Her words fell short and she sniffed. Adam felt his chest tighten. When their eyes locked, he knew Kara was no longer alive.

"I'm sorry," was all he could offer, surprised Marcy cared to share such personal information with him.

"She spent two years, her last two years, with no friends except for a chattering cousin who couldn't see her often enough." Marcy emptied the bucket and went to retrieve a second. Adam could only watch, listen. "You see, sometimes we are our own worst enemy, letting others get into our heads. Kara deserved to have piles of friends. Instead, she was stuck in a small house alone nearly all the time. She missed so many chances to see things, do things. Oh, listen to me go on." Marcy's face flushed. Quickly they finished their dealings.

Was that how Belinda felt as a child?

All the way back home, Adam couldn't help but think about it. When he pulled into the drive, he released Honey and gave her slap on the rear at the pasture gate.

Across the road, Belinda was strolling from the gardens, heading toward the kitchen carrying a heavy basket. Her plum-colored dress drifted behind her, helpless to keep up with her strides. Mentally kicking himself for leaving her hanging for days, for his less-than-civil demeanor, he gathered her three empty flower buckets and hurried across the road to her side.

"Let me," he said, setting the buckets down and taking her basket of zucchini, beets, and radishes, without giving her time to react. She allowed him, but refused to look at him. He deserved that. "If you have time, I'd like to show you the honey house, maybe pull a few frames and get started." Her face didn't light up as he'd hoped, expected. Instead she bent to collect the empty buckets and continued to the house. Adam followed her to the back screen door, and she pointed to the step. He put the basket down as she set the buckets on the grass. She was clearly upset.

"I took the day off. What do you say? Want to get this thing started?" She studied him for the longest minute before letting out a huff.

"I'll be ready in an hour." Her empty tone cut him. Before he could think of anything else to say, she scooped the basket up with surprising ease and fled inside.

It was clear her feelings were hurt. What was less clear was what he should do about it. They had a business partnership and nothing more—was it really his problem how she felt? It wasn't as if he wanted her prying into his own personal affairs. On the contrary, he'd gone out of his way to avoid talking about them. Each morning he found her buckets of flowers on his step. Each evening he left them at her door. His personal life wasn't her concern. What could he say to her? That his life had turned over, that the future he wanted so desperately had vanished, or that he needed to keep his distance from her? What would she think of him if she knew Susanne had wounded his pride, but not his heart? In fact, there was some relief knowing he wouldn't be strapped to a woman like Susanne all his days. So he would say nothing.

An hour later, they were both dressed for inspecting hives. Adam crammed a few dry shavings from the barn into each smoker and lit them with a pocket lighter. Here, among the hives, he made few mistakes. This was his sanctuary, where everything fit, and order was obtained. Like a keeper of the planet, a shepherd tending his flock. Then again, considering ninety percent of a colony consisted of females, maybe he should start expecting the bees to become as contrary and frustrating as the other females in his life. If they did, Adam didn't like his odds for success. He shoved the musing aside.

Belinda was again wearing her homemade bee outfit, and he tried to concentrate on the bees as opposed to the denim-clad beauty beside him. One distraction might upset the balance, earning him a few deserved stings. She pumped a few puffs of smoke over the nearest hive and removed the lid with such natural ease. In spite of himself, he found he wanted to tempt her to talk to him.

"I used to ask Mica a million questions," Adam admitted. "In the beginning, when I was learning." She made a sound, listening, but not participating.

"Your flowers are selling really well," he said, trying another route to coax her into conversation. She nodded, giving him nothing. The silence was killing him. He was man enough to admit he was wrong, even if his wrong had been right. Avoiding her this past week had been as much for her benefit as it was for his. And yet now that they were

179

together, he found he just couldn't maintain his distance any longer. If an apology was what it took to break the ice, then that was what he'd do.

"I'm sorry." He stood, faced her through the confines of his veil.

"For which part?" There she went, surprising him again, and refusing to look at him.

"For staying gone, and for not starting the harvest like I should have." He wouldn't mention last Sunday's debacle. He watched her expression, noted no change.

"Don't be," she replied sharply. "We are only partners, remember. You have done your part and I will do mine." If she meant to bruise him, she succeeded.

"I've had a lot going on in my life," he tried to explain. "I'm not someone to depend on."

Her eyes jerked over to meet his. "I agree."

With which part, he wondered.

"Starting today, I will try to keep most of my focus on helping with the harvest," he concluded. She nodded and he gave up.

Just the thought of spending more time with Adam Hostetler made Belinda's stomach twist. How dare he make her think he still had a girlfriend? Tabitha was right, it was very cruel. Did he think her some desperate *maedel* who might bat lashes his way if she knew he was available? She growled inwardly. How dare he commit to start harvesting and then not show up? If he wasn't hurting, heartbroken and embarrassed, she would have addressed his failures at keeping his word.

After loading one full super into the wagon, she rode silently beside him on the buggy seat. It was one thing to know you were viewed simply as the help, but to be lied to was another thing entirely. She gnawed the inside of her cheek as they pulled up to the honey house.

The honey house wasn't a house, really, but a small barn with metal sides. Belinda jumped easily from the wagon seat, excited to finally see inside. Just because Adam was a jerk didn't mean she had to hate the whole experience.

"Let me show you the extractor first." He lifted a super from the back of the wagon and aimed for the door. Belinda shadowed his steps.

The honey house was cooler than the warm June heat outside, thanks to a thick slab of concrete underfoot. A short table sat in the center of the room with a large metal can on top. The crank on its side indicated he had made his own extractor instead of purchasing one like most did. A spigot, much like her grandfather's, sprouted out near the bottom. Next to the metal container was a large square one with a wooden board across the top, also with a spigot near the bottom. Why did he need two, she pondered. Belinda had to admit Adam's setup was nothing like she was accustomed to.

Adam lifted the first frame and sat it upright on the wooden strip of the square container. One lone bee that hadn't been shooed off by smoke flew up and searched her surroundings.

"Can you grab one of those clean buckets?" He pointed to a far corner where a stack of buckets, smelling strongly of bleach, sat upside down on a bench. She fetched one for him.

"It looks like Dawdi's, but..." she mumbled. Adam reached under the table and pulled out a strainer, and secured it between both spigots just above the clean bucket.

"This catches and strains the honey at the same time. Saves time. Instead of cranking all day and having to separate out the wax, I do this." He reached under the table again and pulled out a long knife-like object that resembled a thin spatula. "This is an uncapping knife. Here, let me show you how it works. It makes it easier to scrape the beeswax caps off. Then we can spin the frames. Mica says your dawdi didn't do that."

"*Nee*. It is very clever."

Adam began demonstrating the process. He began by slowly slicing away the beeswax from the honeycomb and letting it fall into the stainless square container he referred to as "the box." "So the honey flows here," she pointed to the spigot, "and leaves the wax behind? You can sell that to candle-makers." She was so surprised and intrigued that she forgot she was still upset with him.

"I do just that," he grinned, making it hard to stay angry with him. "I let it sit about a week or so to get as much honey as I can. When all that's left is the wax, a man over in Muncie buys all I can collect. We keep it in the cellar and he drives over in July and again in October to buy whatever I have."

"That's *wunderbaar*, Adam," she said openly. "Nothing is wasted."

"Nothing wasted," he repeated, pausing just long enough to meet her eyes. She couldn't explain what those long looks did to her.

Watching Adam Hostetler move about his labors, listening to his drawling voice as he chatted with ease, made all kinds of grownup notions come to the surface. Could her friends be right that Adam's heart might heal and find love again, or were her feelings one-sided? When he finished scraping the wax, Adam placed the frame in the extractor and went to fetch the next one to uncap.

"How many frames can you put in your

extractor at once?" Belinda rose on tiptoe, hands clenching her sides, and peered inside the metal extractor.

"Three. Here," he offered her the knife. "Want to do this one, get the hang of it?" She did. Belinda balanced the frame on the strip of wood and began moving the uncapping knife in a sawing motion, letting the wax drop down.

"Now take your time. You just have to get the hang of it," he said in a low calm tone that made her shiver. Maybe she was too excited—or maybe his nearness was affecting her more than it should. It was different when she thought he was courting another, but now everything had changed. As her heart galloped, her fingers slowed in their movements. Adam placed a hand over hers and encouraged her to move more swiftly. He still smelled of sawdust, mingled with wax combs and warm air into a mixture that intoxicated her senses. It was far too warm to be standing this close, and Adam must have agreed because he stepped away quickly. He went for another frame, fortunately.

"I can't get a day off until next Tuesday, but I can pull a few supers before work if you can manage the extractor on your own some this week," Adam said.

"I can manage, and get jars ready too," she said, still slicing gingerly away. It would be better if she worked alone anyway. Adam was freshly wounded, overwhelmed with duties, and clearly not interested in a woman like her. Yes, she would rather work alone. These feelings running through her were too new and confusing to deal with while he was near.

Belinda lifted her gaze and found him staring at her again. "What?"

"Nothing. It's just...you look like you're having fun. You're smiling."

"Why shouldn't I smile? I happen to like doing this. I can do more than grow flowers, you know." She hiked one side of her lips into a smirk.

"So I'm learning," Adam quickly replied. "I've just never seen anyone excited to help do this before." He wanted to know more about her. What was her favorite ice cream flavor? What kind of books did she like to read? It would be easy, using all the right words, asking the right questions, to get to know her better, but did he want to risk their partnership for something as meaningless as attraction? Attraction was a cruel trickster, and he wasn't about to let it toy with him again. He would be better off fending off an angry swarm than putting his heart out there ever again.

They worked side by side the whole day. Adam prodded her to talk about her flowers, the various types and uses, listening to her every word. He filled the occasional quiet with medicinal facts about honey and things he'd learned about bees over the years. How he had longed for a day such as this, sharing his passion with another. It was perfect—and he would do nothing to jeopardize it. Their partnership was working even better than he'd hoped, and he aimed to see that it stayed that way.

"You look like you had a good day," Tabitha said, stepping out from the laundry room with an armload of freshly folded linens. The kitchen smelled strongly of chicken and spices, the dish still cooking in the oven. Tabitha had also managed to make two of her favorite zucchini bread loaves earlier. She'd added nuts to one for herself, considering few in the house liked walnuts in their zucchini bread. But since she was the baker, she was content to please herself. The others had a separate, nut-free loaf they could enjoy.

She relished her days off from working at the market. Helping Mammi, baking to her heart's content, and of course, quilting. Just a few more days off and her newest creation, River's End, would be ready for backing. Tabitha always named her quilts. *Englisch* paid better when they were named.

"I did," Belinda said, setting the table, her smile astonishingly bright. Tabitha set the fresh linens on the stairs and stepped back into the kitchen to investigate further. Her sister looked more than happy. She was beaming, blue eyes sparkling. It was wonderful to see her sister blossoming after stepping away from the comforts she'd hidden in for so long. Perhaps Mica's idea hadn't been such a bad one after all.

"Adam has this knife—only it's not a knife really, more like a long spatula—and it skims over the comb and all the beeswax falls into a box. Well, it's a metal, square container, but he calls it the box," Belinda rattled on, and went to gather forks from the utensil drawer. "He has an extractor that holds three frames at once, and a setup that makes jarring the honey so easy and far less messy than Dawdi's." She shook her head. "Did you know honey cures allergies? And Ada still won't eat it." She quirked both brows comically, then halted, hand full of silverware suspended in air. "I forgot to ask if he wants me to box the jars of honey as well. You think Mica would mind lifting a few heavy supers in a day or so, so I can keep working? I don't want to have to ask

Adam after he showed me everything else. Anyway," she sucked in a deep breath, "it was a good day."

"I gathered," Tabitha chuckled. "First flower lover, now bee lover."

"Well, they kind of cross paths," Belinda tossed back.

"They do," Tabitha agreed, reining in another chuckle. Belinda was sensitive. "Is he easy to work with?"

"*Jah*, and even though he won't let me lift the heavy supers, I get to do plenty. I can extract and strain the honey and jar it during the day so he doesn't have to. He works a lot, you know. Oh, and he doesn't burn old cloth in his smoker either. Adam uses cedar shavings, says it smells better, which it certainly does." Belinda's face pinched in a grimace, recalling just how bad Dawdi's smokers used to smell. Little wonder, given that he'd used torn-up clothing or anything he had on hand.

"*Jah*," Tabitha said, studying the changes in her sister. "I know Adam works plenty." She smothered a grin. It was all so obvious what was happening to her sister. "Do you like him?" she asked, unable to help herself.

"Not like you think," Belinda replied. "He has made it more than obvious he has no interest in anyone romantically. I think he didn't tell me about Susanne because he's heartbroken." Mammi strolled into the kitchen, her *kapp* lopsided, revealing she had just stirred from a nap. Tabitha gave Belinda a wink as Mammi went toward the fridge.

"Hearts heal," Tabitha pointed out. "But he should have been honest with you. What do you both talk about?" Tabitha continued prodding as she pulled plates from the cabinet. Even if nothing happened with Adam, surely this new openness from Belinda was a good sign. If her sister was relaxing around one man, maybe there was hope for her yet, with someone else.

"We talked about the flowers. Adam thought all flowers were just seeds that grow and die. Now he knows how much work I put into them," Belinda grinned. "He doesn't think it's so strange anymore, me wanting to make a livelihood out of it."

"I knew you would set him straight," Mammi chimed in, and poured herself a glass of milk.

Belinda gathered butter and lemonade from the fridge. "He talks a lot about the buyers too. He says the florist has a son, Jackson. He asks lots of silly questions that make Adam laugh. And Mia, she's the baker. He said she talks funny." She made a face.

"I'm glad you two get along so well." Tabitha added three more glasses to the table.

"He is easy to talk to," Belinda admitted in a shy, quieter tone.

"I bet he is," Tabitha laughed. "Which makes you friends."

"He doesn't think of me like that. Weren't you listening?" Tabitha had been, even as she wished Belinda was wrong. Adam was a kind fellow and the two would have matched well together. "I'm doing what you said," Belinda added. "I'm trying." When they locked gazes, Tabitha knew her sister had overcome something that had pulled at her for a long time. Belinda was braver than she gave herself credit for, and seeing her sister finally realize that warmed Tabitha's heart.

"And you are doing a good job, sister. I'm very proud of you." And she meant it. Maybe it was time to push her sister a little harder. Belinda was such a timid soul and required a gentle man, not one who had so much responsibility. But who in Havenlee would fit that description? Who could be the perfect match for her perfect sister?

Chapter Sixteen

ADAM HADN'T COME HOME BEFORE dusk in days. By Thursday Belinda was starting to worry. Of course he was heartbroken. The woman he loved had betrayed him and publicly humiliated him. But that was no reason to work himself to death. And it meant that she was doing a lot of work on his honey without him there to supervise. She told herself that going ahead and pulling frames and harvesting his honey had been the right thing to do. Ada complimented her hard work, but would Adam think her overstepping? The bees were his livelihood and she didn't want him to feel she'd taken over. She wished she could see him, talk to him.

Each morning she cut flowers, placed them in the bucket, and left them on his porch. She did her greenhouse chores, helped Mammi where needed, and worked the honey harvest. Under the cloak of darkness each night, she found the empty buckets and an envelope of cash on her porch in return. She wished she could do something more to ease his hurt. Holding a few boards for a chicken coop and harvesting honey wasn't enough. She mentally huffed.

"Set an extra couple plates tonight. Ivan is coming for dinner," Mica said, entering the house. Belinda reached for two more plates. Maybe she should walk over, knock, and see if Adam was okay. Would that breach the boundaries of partnership?

"There's not enough food in the house to feed that man," Tabitha quipped. "He has a bottomless belly and a head too big for those feet." It seemed every time Ivan came within viewing distance, Belinda's sister got her hackles up.

Ivan often brought his little sister Katie Jo over. Belinda adored Katie Jo. The twelve-year-old talked so fast she stuttered, but Belinda loved her infectious energy and dramatic expressions.

"So you noticed how big my friend's feet are?" Mica teased, and Tabitha stuck out her tongue. "I need to start thinking about adding to the blacksmith shop. It is getting a mite tight, and his *onkel* had a good setup."

"Wouldn't be so tight if you would stop growing," Mammi Mollie added with a wink.

A knock came at the door and Belinda rushed to get it, hoping it was Adam. "I'll get it."

"I think she's shed that shell of hers," Tabitha muttered behind her.

"I heard that," Belinda yelled back, and jerked open the front door. "Ivan," she said, wincing when she realized how disappointed she sounded.

"Well, nice to see you too, Belinda. Were you expecting company?" Ivan was even taller than Mica, but Belinda had known him her whole life and he didn't intimidate her. He was like an extra brother. He teased where Mica barked. He went along when Mica took her and Tabitha swimming and fishing, and he tended to the place last year when Dawdi got sick and they all went to Kentucky for a week. Ivan was strong, which was fitting given that his construction trade required him to lift and nail all day, but Belinda found him as soft as a kitten. Why Tabitha become irritable every time he came in proximity was a mystery.

"*Nee.* No one comes to see me," she said, and stepped out of his way.

"They would if you didn't answer the door looking like you just ate a rotten pickle." He pinched her cheek playfully before heading into the kitchen. Belinda rolled her eyes and followed.

"I smell meatloaf." Ivan's deep voice echoed through the house.

"And you can only have your fair share. I'm not starving myself just because you can eat your weight in meatloaf," Tabitha quipped. Ivan laughed and sat down next to Mica. "If that doesn't suit, have Claire Beiler make one special just for you." Belinda was glad to know Ivan was courting. He had courted one of Tabitha's friends a few years ago, but they really didn't suit. Claire Beiler worked at the local bakery and was a kind, quiet woman. She hoped Ivan found what he was looking for in Claire. Everyone deserved happiness, she thought.

"Hers doesn't taste as filling as yours," Ivan winked, earning him one of Tabitha's sharp glares.

"Our Tabitha is the finest cook in the county," Mammi slipped in. A horn sounded and all heads shot up. "That's my driver. You four try not to make a mess of things until I return." Mammi straightened her *kapp* and fetched her purse off the coat hook by the door.

"Have fun with Edith. I know how you two say you have sewing to do, but I'm still sure you end up swapping gossip."

"Edith doesn't gossip." Mammi grinned slyly toward Tabitha before waddling out the door.

"Where's Katie Jo?," Tabitha asked, looking perturbed. "I had a new pattern I wanted to work on with her." Ivan stared at her for a moment as if unable to follow the question.

"She is having a sleepover at Mary's. Rachel said she had five girls and one more didn't matter." Belinda thought her sister almost looked disappointed in that. Tabitha would make a wonderful mother. If her manner while spending time with Ivan's little sister was any indication, she had the patience for teaching and a softness for *kinner* rarely shown toward adults. Katie Jo had no *mamm* of her own, Ivan and Katie Jo having lost her years ago, but the little girl seemed rarely affected by it. Being raised by a busy *bruder* and brokenhearted father surely had to be hard on a little girl. Belinda felt herself blessed to never have known such a life.

"Rachel's, huh?" Tabitha sounded wounded.

"So, you want to redesign the whole thing or just improve it?" Ivan asked Mica, ignoring the way Tabitha slapped a glass of lemonade down in front of him as if it had personally offended her.

Tabitha was not very polite to men, seeing as she thought they were all smelly and lazy and lacked common sense, but Ivan Shetler brought out the worst in her. They were like two bees deciding who would sting first. Belinda couldn't understand it. Aside from Mica, Ivan was the kindest man she knew. He never teased her about her shyness or looked at her face too long. He had even played cards and Pictionary with her when she was younger, when Mica thought games were stupid. Daed thought he hung the moon and Mudder always made sure to bake extra if he was coming. Still, Tabitha pinched her lips and spoke with a growl every time he came around.

"I need better air flow for warm weather, but don't want to freeze my fingers off come winter. That old shed will be the death of me one day," Mica admitted.

"I suspect it's getting tight moving around in there. The forge is no place to be if you ain't got room enough to move." Ivan settled back in his chair. "I still have that house for the Lykins family over in Mesa, but we can squeeze some work on your shop in, if you plan on picking up a hammer too." Ivan winked.

"I use a bigger hammer than you most of the time," Mica shot back playfully, his green eyes dancing with humor.

"Only half the year. The rest of the time, you grow vegetables and little potted plants," Ivan countered. They could do this for hours, this brotherly banter. Belinda rolled her eyes.

"It's good Adam lives next door. He might like working closer to home. I figure he might get more sleep this way, too," Ivan added, as Belinda and Tabitha finished setting the table and took seats. When Mica lowered his head for the silent prayer, so did the rest of them. After a few moments, Mica scooted his chair and heads lifted again.

"So how does a beekeeper work all day

at a mill, help me build porches and houses, and still find time to harvest honey?" The question was aimed at Mica, but Belinda felt her sister's eyes turn to her. "I saw Ada delivering a fresh batch of jars this morning to the market. I unloaded the boxes for her. Those things are heavy." Ivan scoped a healthy portion of meatloaf on his plate. His eyes locked with Tabitha's, who was watching him like a hawk. Those two were funny.

"Belinda has been harvesting the honey for him." Tabitha took the spoon from his hand, indicating he'd had his share.

"Belinda, I didn't know you had an interest in...honey." Ivan lifted a brow, a grin begging to be let loose. Belinda felt her face warm.

"Stop teasing, Ivan. Atlee won't be working for months yet, and Belinda is near and isn't afraid of those bees. It's what a decent Christian should do." Tabitha defense of her made Belinda sit a little taller in her seat, as did the reminder that she didn't fear bees while many others did. It was nice to not be afraid of everything. She had never thought about it before.

"Sorry. I was just teasing," Ivan said to Belinda, then turned his attention on Tabitha. "A good Christian puts in his neighbor's hay for free too." He was fishing for a compliment, since Tabitha was gifting them.

"You eat more than you work," Tabitha

replied, and shoved the butter and pan of rolls his way. "Maybe Claire will feed your ego, but I won't."

Ivan surrendered and focused on Belinda again. "I heard your flowers are growing." Lifting a roll, he began to slather it in butter.

"Smart one. Imagine that, noticing that flowers grow," Tabitha sassed under her breath.

"Woman, Belinda knows what I mean." Ivan shot Tabitha a look, but there was nothing unkind in it.

"You two are funny," Belinda giggled. "*Jah*. And they are. Adam sells more to the florist than Tabitha does at the market. It is good business." She took a bite of meatloaf, let the spicy flavors satisfy her.

"So you help him with the hives and he is selling flowers for you. That's good. Maybe you should try feeding him too. Fellow looks to have lost a few pounds lately." Belinda flinched. Was she making Adam's life harder? "Some women can wreak havoc on the heart." Ivan shook his head.

"That was a shock, I agree. Best to not give in to such foolishness, and it won't make a fool out of you," Mica added, pointing his fork across the table at Ivan.

"He just chose the *wrong* woman," Tabitha defended, and speared a green bean. "Men tend to chase after what's on the surface and forget to find out what makes a *maedel* worth having. That one has never lifted a hand to help another in her life. Adam should be grateful he won't have to spend the rest of his life with a *fraa* like her." Belinda bit her lip. Did Tabitha really believe Adam was better off? He was heartbroken, wasn't he?

"It's a partnership. We made an agreement, but now..." Belinda muttered. "Maybe I should—"

"What?" Mica had ears that could hear a bird's wings cut through air. She wrangled her tongue.

"Never mind." She filled her mouth with potatoes next. If she sold her own flowers, maybe Adam wouldn't have to get up so early. But no. She couldn't bring herself to do that. So what else could she do to cheer him up?

The rest of meal was a blur as Belinda pondered ways to make Adam's life easier, or at least make him smile. *Life is better with a smile.* She mentally giggled at Atlee's words.

"Let's work off this meal with a game." Ivan rubbed his middle as the table was being cleared.

"Can it be a manly one? I'm tired of board games," Mica said, exasperatedly dropping both elbows on the table.

"Baseball," Tabitha, of all people, suggested. Belinda loved baseball. She set aside her current thoughts and hurried to clean the kitchen.

"A woman after my own heart," Ivan

perked, resulting in a sharp reply from Tabitha, who assumed she was being mocked. If Ivan would stop teasing, maybe her sister would stop being so harsh to him. Then again, what did she know about anything?

Chapter Seventeen

ADAM YAWNED WIDE ENOUGH TO upset his balance and then shivered from head to toe. He'd survived another arduous day stacking pallets, filling orders, and loading trucks, and still managed three hours for Ivan framing a small shed while his crew worked elsewhere. It was enough to work up an appetite, yet, for once, the need for food came second to sleep. A hot shower and a pillow, that's what he desired most.

He put Honey out to pasture, but before heading to the house, Adam stepped inside the honey house. The air smelled of summer heat and beeswax. Upon closer inspection he realized Belinda had been harvesting a lot of honey. He removed his hat, ran his fingers through his hair, and frowned. He hadn't meant for her to have to do all the work alone, and without his assistance. It wasn't her job to see to the whole harvest. Was he taking her away from her dream, claiming all her time so that she had none to give to her flowers? She wanted so little, and his situation was interfering with that. He wanted things too, but was smart enough to know he would never have all the things he wanted. He would help more, finish the harvest and free her from their partnership. One of them should have the future they wanted.

His mind was crowded, but only one thought surged to the forefront. It was Belinda, Belinda humming and buzzing in his head. Imagining her here, working on his honey by his side, helped him endure long days. Even now, it felt wrong not seeing her standing to his left. How quickly that had happened, her becoming something of a fixture in his life. The quiet girl next door was becoming the woman he couldn't ignore.

Adam closed the door and strolled along the yard. Since when had *Mudder* planted a flower bed in front of the house? He really did like the flowers, and now that he was learning a few things about the different kinds, Adam could name most of them staring at him right now. There were marigolds, irises, lilies, coneflowers, and foxgloves. He struggled to recall the name of the large leafy plant boarding one side. "Hosta," he said aloud, pleased with himself. He strolled back to the porch, shaking his head. Since when did a man concern himself with the names of flowers? Yeah, lack of sleep was messing with his thinking.

"Sit with me, *sohn*. It's a nice evening." Atlee said from a shadowy corner. Daed was getting around well with the crutches. A nurse had been coming twice a week for therapy and Adam could see it was doing his father good.

"It's hot." Adam replied, but took a seat next to him as the sun began its final descent. June had proven itself hotter than usual and the rising humidity was making the evening even more dismal.

He let his gaze fall on the new flower bed again. "Mamm must have taken all day planting that."

"Your little bee charmer did that so I could see them from the window. She thinks I need some colors to admire to heal faster." Atlee leaned closer. "I didn't have the heart to tell her I couldn't see them unless standing or outside, but your *mamm* is real happy." Adam bet she was. He couldn't help but smile as he looked down. Zinnias were in there too in various hued blooms, along with small red and white candy cane blooms, and bold violet blues on long stems he had no name for. Like their giver, they brought color to his life, a respite from the drudgery of the day to day.

Laughter rose from across the street. He

narrowed his focus. Belinda and her family were playing a game of baseball. They did that a lot, he thought, sinking deeper in his seat. For once he had nowhere to be, and sitting here with his daed, watching her, was just fine by him.

Adam leaned back, listened, and held his gaze on the woman who liked bees and flowers and quiet. Her dress looked to be a richer purple than any he could recall her wearing before. He liked that, the bold color against the tan of her arms. He missed catching glimpses of her freckles, her bare feet in the grass, the way her lips curved when she tried on a grin.

Ivan pitched the ball and Belinda swung the heavy wooden bat. A firm crack split the air, indicating she had made contact. He lifted a brow, watching the woman, not the ball sailing into the air. She ran like the wind. She had always been athletic, winning races and outplaying most girls her age. That was before the nicknames came, before the age of self-awareness marred her childish innocence. Why hadn't he been a better friend back then when she'd needed him?

Adam smiled as Mica threatened Belinda with the ball, chasing her around the yard as she crossed imaginary bases. Mica would never catch her, light on her feet as she was. Her laughter echoed across the road and settled warm in his chest. She had strong powers, that one, and he wasn't sure how long he could hold his defenses against them. Beautiful, inside and out, that's what she was. A man would be a fool not to see it, to want it for his own.

"They are a happy bunch." Atlee said. "Makes me miss when you were little and we played ball and chase." Adam hated that his parents weren't blessed with more *kinner*, but when he was born, Mamm was told she should never have more. It wasn't spoken of, but he knew there were times over the years when his father had sat on this very porch watching the Grabers run about, wishing they could have that, too.

"This time next year you might be starting a family of your own," Atlee said, as if such was a possibility. "It would be good to have *kinner* around again."

"We broke up. She's marrying another," Adam said bluntly. "You know this." The whole community now knew this. He scowled, recalling all the faces staring at him like he'd just committed a crime. Belinda was right: Being stared at was unsettling.

"You think me forgetful?" Atlee scoffed. "You two weren't a good match. The split was bound to happen."

"You never said anything." Adam gave his father a sidelong look. "A warning would have been nice."

"Not a father's job to tell his grown *sohn* such. It's not as if you would have listened. You were too eager, then. Wanting something so bad you were willing to settle for it." Adam sighed. His father was right. Adam didn't want to be Tobias, forever courting, never settling, so he had in fact settled. Susanne had been the only girl to ask for his attention. "But I will say this. I think your match is closer than you think." Atlee looked out across the road, smiled with both his lips and his eyes. Adam followed his gaze easily.

"I'm not interested in trying my hand again," Adam said firmly, knowing he would always be a bystander to her. He would do well to put all such ridiculous thoughts out of his mind. No one wanted a beekeeper, a man full of responsibilities, unable to offer more than a future of hard work and responsibilities. His burdens were too heavy to ask another to share them. Even his bones were too tired to cooperate in keeping him vertical this evening.

"Your pride is hurt, that's all." His father didn't mention his heart, and Adam reflected on that for a moment. He had been so ready to make the life he wanted that he had missed realizing he was making it with the wrong person. He'd thought he loved Susanne, but deep down, despite the bruising to his ego, he had to admit Susanne had been right. He cared more about his bees than her, and no marriage could stand strong on such a feeble foundation. He didn't even miss her.

"She deserves someone better, and certainly not a bee farmer," Adam murmured.

"You're more than a bee farmer," Atlee retorted, reading where Adam's thoughts rested. "I think she's the only one who can decide what she deserves, but I'll say that *you* deserve a faithful *fraa* capable of charming bees, or mending old chicken coops. She might even let you win at baseball," Atlee chuckled. "Your mamm could always outrun me. I think that's one of the many reasons I married her." Adam turned to him. "What man doesn't like to chase, to pursue? It's who we are. You just haven't found one worthy of pursuing yet...or have you?" He winked. Adam didn't have time to chase, or pursue, but he couldn't help but recall how often Belinda left him tempted, forcing him to rush to catch up just to hear a whisper from her.

"She talks a lot more than she used to, but I don't think she is interested in anyone. Belinda loves her life the way it is, and it's too busy to add anything to it."

"But she made room for the honey—and the chicken coop and this garden for us, ain't so? She made room for you and you made room for her."

"All I'm giving is twenty minutes a day toting flowers. That was the deal. Can't build much on twenty minutes," Adam replied. "What kind of woman wants a man who only gives twenty minutes?"

"A woman who can appreciate twenty minutes," Atlee said. "She isn't so shy, really. I think she was just paranoid about her face after getting teased as a girl. Years of hiding simply made her accustomed to being alone. Doesn't mean it's what she wants, who she really is." That was true. Many people weren't who they seemed on the outside.

"I think she wants more, but I think she likes things as they are too," Adam said. He had never had such an in-depth talk with his father before. It was nice, this man-to-man time. It also felt surprisingly good to talk his thoughts out loud without fear of judgment or being teased. His friends were good men, but Tobias was not the one to seek for a serious conversation.

"Have you even asked what she wants?" Daed lifted both brows challengingly.

"I can't," Adam replied flatly. She wanted a flower farm, that he knew, but that wasn't what his father was asking.

"You can. Love built on faith and friendship, on hard times, is something unbreakable."

Adam choked on the word. "Who said anything about love?"

"My legs might not work so well these days, but my eyes are perfect." Atlee chuckled before struggling to his feet. "Now let's go inside before the skeeters eat me alive."

Adam helped his father through the front door and glanced out across the road.

Belinda stood under the failing sunlight, looking at him. She waved; she had never waved at him before. A better man would walk over, apologize for avoiding her and their partnership the last couple of days.

A better man he obviously wasn't, he decided. He waved back, then closed the door behind him.

Belinda finished the last twist of her nightly braid and secured it with a thin band before crawling into bed. What could she do to cheer Adam up? It was clear something special was needed. He looked tired. Even at that distance she could see it in the slump of his shoulders and the way his head rested on his hand while he and Atlee sat on the porch. What could she give him to make him smile? She bowed her head, whispered a prayer for Dawdi, her parents, and for the man across the road who found a way into her every thought, and maybe even her heart.

Chapter Eighteen

ADAM TOOK FRIDAY OFF WORK to help with the honey harvest. After delivering Belinda's flowers, he pulled into his drive. There she sat, her face in a book that Adam couldn't imagine her capable of seeing, much less reading, considering the sun was barely peeking through a dreary dark sky. She was dressed in her homemade bee suit. She must have had no trouble finding his note this morning. Adam had debated where to leave it, and concluded the flower garden was the best place, so he had secured it to the hoe handle he knew she worked with daily.

"You shouldn't be doing that," he said, approaching. She quickly tucked the book behind her back as if she'd just been caught stealing. He stifled a grin at how adorable she looked. "Not enough light. You could hurt your eyes."

"Oh," she relaxed. "I was almost finished last night and fell asleep. I hate starting something and not finishing it," she shrugged, getting to her feet before brushing her pants nervously to wipe away any imaginary dirt. "I found your note." Her cheeks warmed to a soft rose shade. "I can help the whole day. Mica says he has everything covered." She bit her lip and asked nervously, "How have you been?"

"Fine," he replied. She cradled her book, lowered her gaze to her feet. *Gott* had a way with things that often made Adam wonder if he was pointing a finger or encasing a portrait. Right now, He seemed to be doing both as the sun peeked through two darkened clouds, hitting Belinda in a kiss of light. She seemed to embody sunshine itself, and though Adam knew better than to stare into the sun, he couldn't turn away from her.

"What?" She nervously checked her clothing to see if he was gawking at something amiss, then ran a delicate hand over her kerchief and honey gold hair.

"Your hair looks just like the honey." He shouldn't have thought so loudly. He clamped his lips shut.

"Tabitha's is more strawberry. Even Mica has auburn hair like my parents. Daed says I was hatched." It was plain to see she

211

was rattled by the comparison. Adam was just pleased he could rattle her so easily.

"I got a bit of both my parents." He reached the porch and saw his bee suit and veil sitting nearby.

"*Jah*, your daed has green eyes and Ada's are blue. Are you ready?" She bounded off the steps as light as a feather, leaving a sweet flowery waft of breeze behind her. His heart did a little leap right with her. This was going to be a long day.

"I already put the tools in the wagon," he said. "Go ahead and get in while I tell Mamm we're leaving."

"And sneak some breakfast. Take your time." She waved him off. "I know you haven't eaten. Besides, the light is better now." She lifted her book with begging eyes. How could he ever say no to her? "Only three pages left. I really need to read the end or I will be in suspense all day." Well, there was no harm in letting her finish her book.

"Okay then. Let's not leave you in suspense." He slipped inside, feeling like his life was in suspense and every corner held something new to endure or ponder over. Adam didn't dare tell her that Mia had given him two pastries covered with icing, filled with cherries and cream cheese. He would give Belinda a few minutes to finish her book. After all, he did appreciate a person who finished what they started.

Belinda pumped the smoker across the top of the hive as Adam pried the lid off with his hiving tool. The flat crowbar had a hook at one end that served many purposes, including prying loose sticky frames before lifting them. Once the lid was removed, she pumped more smoke as he extracted the first frame.

"It looks like your queen is overdoing it. You might have to put in a queen extractor or she will lay it full of eggs and you won't have honey this fall."

He looked at her with his mouth open, shocked. Every time he thought he had a grasp on who Belinda was, she would surprise him more. Still, she didn't know everything.

"But if I block her in below, the workers will try to squeeze through the extractor and risk damaging their wings. Plus she might swarm, if she thinks it's too crowded. I already lost two hives."

"True, but a virtuous queen shouldn't be so selfish. She should leave room for everyone to work," she returned. Adam eased the frame back down and placed the lid back on top. He moved on to the next hive.

"I'm not using the slotted extractor to trap my queen," he said firmly, putting an end to her thinking. "How many hives have you robbed so far?"

"Nine. I can average three a day myself, but no more—it's peak season for our greenhouse plants and vegetables."

Adam pulled the first frame from the super with the hiving tool.

"This one is really full," he said, carefully sliding the frame back into place. Handing her the tool, he lifted the full super and carried it to the wagon. Belinda pried the top from the next one and began lifting it.

"Whoa now." Adam hurried to her. "I told you I will do the heavy lifting." She gave up the weight and moved to the next super, clearly biting her tongue to keep from protesting his orders. She pried the next super free from the one below it and soon they had a solid rhythm going.

"Mia said she wanted to talk to you about some lavender, and something else. I can't remember," Adam grunted as he loaded the last super into the wagon.

"Can't she just tell you?"

Removing his veil, he wiped the sweat from his brow. A few bees danced about but they seemed more concerned with hurrying into another workday than they were about being robbed.

"You really should meet her. Mia is very nice. I think you two would have a lot to talk about. She has been asking if Mamm has a recipe for rhubarb. I know you and Tabitha make the best rhubarb pie in Havenlee." His frown lifted slightly. "But don't tell Mamm I said that." He winked.

He shouldn't wink at her like that, but he couldn't seem to help himself. Unfortunately, Belinda didn't seem at all moved by it. "That wasn't part of our partnership," she argued. "We shook hands. You agreed to deal with customers if I took care of things here."

"I keep my promises. I just thought I should mention it. It won't happen again." He shot her a glare and she stubbornly held it there with one of her own. Clearly, he had touched some wild nerve.

"You know your passion here is no less important than mine, over there." She pointed in the direction of home, a full mile away.

Her vehemence baffled him. When had he said her work was unimportant? Or was she saying that *his* was? "I protect bees, use what they make to earn a living, and it's not easy work," Adam said.

"I do too, and you have no idea what it takes to raise a thousand flowers for your bees to forage through," she retorted.

"And my bees do love that sunflower field, but sunflowers don't need constant watching over," he argued. "You dig in the ground, drop seeds, and walk away."

"How dare you! Your bees need my flowers."

"And your flowers need my bees."

Belinda opened her mouth to deliver

another sharp remark, but changed course. "You have no idea how to talk to others."

"That's funny, coming from you," he shot back. He watched her recoil, saw the look of total devastation in her eyes. Why was he being so hard on the one person in his life who least deserved it?

"I'm sorry your life is so busy and complicated," she said. "I'm sorry Susanne left you for another and Atlee was hurt, but I did nothing but help you. You don't have to be so sour—all you seem to do is stand there and growl hurtful things, and..." She sucked in a breath and tears pooled in her eyes.

"Stop," Adam said quickly, and reached out to her. Belinda jerked back. "Please, don't cry," he said, head hung in shame. "This is not like either of us. You aren't cruel and I shouldn't be, either. Let's just stop now before we say something we will regret. I'm sorry. You're right. Tell me."

"Tell you what?" Belinda still held on to a harsh tone.

"Tell me about what it takes to grow a thousand flowers from seed. Teach me." He hoped that she could tell he was sincere, trying to make right after the heated exchange. "Distract me from everything else."

"Not all flowers come from seeds," she began, starting slow but gradually warming to the topic. "Some come back year after year, and some are bulbs that must be dug in the late fall and stored in the cellar until spring."

"See, I know nothing," he admitted. "I'm truly sorry. Can we put it behind us, forget what a fool I have been today and every day before it?"

"That would take a lot of forgiveness," she answered all too quickly.

"But you're capable, as you are with everything," he complimented. How had he got so lucky to find a woman like her—as a business partner, that is? She was quick to forgive, quick to move on. He listened to her describe soil and care, amazed by the attention she gave to every detail. Even the trees and vines around her family's property were used to sell in arrangements. She was unaware she had let her guard down, and as she prattled on about lilies and roses, Adam let himself be mesmerized by the beautiful woman who had already put aside his harshness as if nothing had transpired between them.

"So is lavender edible too?"

"*Jah.*" She blew out a breath.

"Huh, I thought it was just to make you smell good."

"I make lavender lemonade. It's *wunder-baar* good."

"I would like to try that sometime." She stared at him, watched him load another super in the wagon.

"I can give the recipe to Ada." Did partners make each other lemonade? She would have to ask Tabitha about that.

"She would like that, and it's okay if you don't want me to try yours." But even as he said it would be okay, he sounded wounded, gave her a slow look, and then moved to the next hive. She let loose her lip, the soreness growing there, and brushed a few loose hairs from her face.

"So you can eat daisies, dandelions, pansies, and lavender?" Adam asked as he loaded the last two supers into his wagon.

"And violets, lilacs, and hibiscus," Belinda added, as she bent to retrieve the smoker, still warm with a slight stream of smoke escaping its tip. She liked that he seemed so interested in learning about her flowers.

"Ouch!" Adam jerked. "That's the second time today," he said angrily. He turned to face her and Belinda couldn't mask her amusement.

"You don't even wear gloves, and yet you never get stung. I don't get it. Ouch," he yelled again, swatting at his backside. Before they knew it, more than a dozen bees found Adam's rear end to be a perfect place to sit a spell. "Smoke it. Smoke me!" his voice cried out.

Between uncontrollable laughter, Belinda tried pumping cedar-infused puffs of smoke toward his rear. It was a chicken dance. His high steps and deep growls, and her trying to rescue him between giggles.

Adam was literally on fire, and not in a place he could tend to easily. When the bees finally lost interest, they both stood, laughing.

There was that rare sparkle in his eyes, birthed from laughter. It was purely appealing. "I must have sat in a whole pie by the way they attacked!" He winced, rubbing his rear end. "How do you never get stung, and I do under two layers of clothes?"

"Well, I am the queen," Belinda said, and spewed out a rare cackle. "And you smell like Ada's blackberry jam. I can smell it from here." She couldn't remember ever feeling so happy, so playful.

"You smell like a flower patch." He said it too quickly, both brows lifted.

"That wasn't a compliment, was it?" She cocked her head to one side and smirked.

"*Nee*. Bees love flowers; you should be screaming right now. It wonders me how you never get stung." He smiled, showing her he was kidding.

"You're getting circles under your *green* eyes today. Maybe you should let me finish here. I can get everything done, boxed, and ready before you wake."

"This is our last day to work together for a while. I want to be here." His gaze held hers for a moment, a sheepish smile on his lips.

She didn't respond, only gave him a half-hearted smile.

Chapter Nineteen

ADAM PULLED HIS BUGGY UP to the barn. Five days had elapsed since he and Belinda had last worked together. The five days since had been spent depending on another person to see his work done. But there was no spare time to be had each day, no matter how many clocks he owned.

A door across the road slammed shut. Belinda strolled across her yard and headed his way, carrying something in her hand while keeping her eyes trained on her feet. He jumped down and began unharnessing Honey. She said nothing as he went through the motions before turning Honey out to pasture. She just stood there, waiting, with that stoic patience he respected.

"Hi," Adam said as he walked up to her.

She was dressed in a brown faded chore dress that made her eyes brighter. Adam couldn't help but smile. She could wear a feed sack and still make his heart skip a beat. "Do you need me to carry your flower buckets over?"

"*Nee,*" she muttered, and chewed on her bottom lip, a habit he'd noticed she tended to fall into when nervous or scared. He couldn't have her feeling either with him.

"Okay," he said. "What do you have there?" He eyed the plate in her hands.

"I brought you something. They're Mica's favorite, but he was so busy he barely ate any." She lifted a plate full of soft brown *kichlin.* Adam reached over and snatched one. He hadn't had much of an appetite these days, but it wasn't every day a man got homemade cookies from Belinda Graber.

"That is delicious, Belinda. So delicious I don't mind eating Mica's favorite," he teased, swallowing the rest in one bite. She lifted the plate again. He wasn't one for turning down free cookies, but he had a sneaking suspicion she was softening him up for something.

"Have you been talking to my *mamm?*" he asked. "She thinks I'm getting thin."

She shook her head again, still chewing her lip. Something was certainly troubling her. At last, she spoke. "Don't be mad, but I did something," she confessed.

He had been *mad* when Susanne had

dumped him, and was tired of being angry. No way was Belinda capable of making it worse.

"So you figure to sweeten me up first." She lifted the plate again. He couldn't help but chuckle at her antics. "These honey *kichlin* might work." He wished she would smile. Instead she looked about ready to cry. "Come on, it can't be that bad," he assured her.

"It is." She winced. "Follow me." Like a child sent to fetch their own whooping stick, she walked as slow and sluggish as a body could. It was adorable.

"Whatever it is, I promise not to be mad." The very thought she had worked herself up over the idea of his anger made his heart ache. Had she truly baked those cookies for Mica, or him? He had his suspicions, and they warmed his heart. When they rounded the house and neared the hives, she stopped, head down as low as it could get without snapping off her shoulders.

"Belinda, you're worrying me." Adam reached out and touched her shoulder. She pointed beyond him and when Adam focused his gaze on the hives, three had been decorated with drawings of the prettiest flowers he had ever seen. Adam strolled over for a closer look but she didn't follow.

"Bee, these are..."

"I know. Mica said it wasn't right to do it without talking to you first. He came over to help carry two supers today and saw the drawings. I wanted to mark them so you would know they were finished..." She hung her head. Adam nearly broke into a laugh. She truly was innocence and goodness. He could never be good enough for someone so perfect.

Adam went to her and wrapped her in his arms. He probably smelled like sawdust and sweat and nothing she'd want anywhere near her, but he *had* to hold her. "*Nee,* I like them." She fit right there, head and heart connected, and smelled like heaven. He lifted his eyes to the sky, prayed for strength. "I must say I'm surprised, but I like them."

She looked up with those big blue eyes, and it was all he could do to not kiss her. He quickly let go. "Sorry." But she didn't look at him as if he was someone who had crossed a line. It was enough to make him wish he hadn't let go.

"Mamm calls me that sometimes," she murmured.

"Huh?"

"You called me Bee."

"Bee Graber." He reached out and tucked a loose lock of her hair behind her ear. "Queen of the apiary. It suits you." One corner of her lips lifted. She really had beautiful lips. He took another defensive step back.

"So you're not mad at me?"

"About *drawings*? No. And there is nothing I can think of you could ever do to

224

make me angry with you." That was, unless she finally decided to take skinny Noel Christner up on his offer.

"So the *kichlin* really *were* to sweeten me up," he added with a wink, making her cheeks flush. "I've never had honey *kichlin* before." She lifted the plate again, but this time offered a soft smile.

Adam reached in his back pocket and pulled out the paper. "Here's your flower order for tomorrow. I want to help you fill your next order and anything else you need before we finish the orchard hives and maybe get a start here."

She stared at the paper. "I still can't believe you haven't eaten honey *kichlin*. Susanne should have..." She threw a hand over her mouth. "I'm sorry, I shouldn't have mentioned her."

"I made a horrible mistake with her, ignoring what was important. A mistake I won't repeat."

"What was important?" Adam just shook his head.

He could tell her that their friendship was important. That being around someone who enjoyed the same things as him was important. That he'd had no idea was love was, before. Real love, he was learning, was far easier, more fulfilling, scarier. Wanting more for another than yourself was important. But he couldn't tell Belinda any of that.

By the following afternoon, Belinda couldn't
feel her arms. Lifting supers, cranking the
extractor, and spinning frames all week had
left her spent. But her legs, like her mind,
were restless. Today most of the community
had gathered for Susanne and Jerimiah's
wedding, but Belinda couldn't bring herself to attend. She spent the day like any
other, tending the greenhouses, hoeing the
vegetable gardens. It wasn't the crowd that
deterred her, just the man whom she knew
was hurting. Susanne had chosen another,
and Belinda knew what being second felt
like. So she wouldn't attend, in silent support for a friend.

   After washing off the dirt of the day and
putting on a fresh dress, she wandered out
to her flower rows. The sunflowers were in
full bloom and she wandered into the small
patch to walk among them. The earth felt
soft under her bare feet, despite the lack of
rain. A whippoorwill called, testing the silence, spurring a few cicadas into song. She
loved the evening air, anticipating moonlight
on her flowers, and the sound of humming
of a few thousand worker bees heading back
inside so they could start early.

"Did you just get back from the wedding?" His voice jerked her to attention. "I'm sorry. I didn't mean to startle you. I thought you saw me walk over." Adam was there, standing at the edge of her sunflower dream, as if summoned by her thoughts. His damp hair told her he had just recently showered. He looked tired, a shadow of the man she had spoken with just days ago.

"I'm not much for such events." She looked away, trying not to let the fresh look of him bother her. Who was she kidding? Adam bothered her no matter how he looked. But this was business, their time together, nothing more.

"Who has time for such things?" he said, offering a good-humored grin.

"Not you, obviously," she countered with equal playfulness. She liked it when they could be civil, tease without bruising. "So why are you not resting? You wouldn't be so tired all the time if you took advantage of your time off." She waded back out of the sunflower patch, toward him.

"Too much dust in the attic," he pointed to his noggin. "You?" Adam reached out, brushed a lone sunflower, rough fingers tracing the edges tenderly. Was he melancholic, feeling a fresh tear in his heart knowing his one-time intended was marrying another? She took out her scissors, clipped a few near blooms, gathered them into a small bouquet.

"Not so much dust, but a little fresh air

227

does save on dusting." *Because you keep getting in my thoughts.* Belinda lifted the bouquet, and smiled.

"Nice," he said, then lifted his eyes to her again.

"Nice," she repeated. "Nice is kittens and marshmallows in your cocoa. These are beautiful." She said it wistfully.

"*Jah*, they are." But his eyes did not turn to see what she was holding, just her. "Well, want to take a wal,k then? Listen to the bees and watch that big old moon rise?" He pointed toward his side of the road.

A walk with Adam Hostetler in moonlight, listening to the hums of nature. Was she dreaming? "*Jah*. I would like that." They walked in silence across her yard and when they reached the road, Belinda ran across the warm pavement.

"So why don't you ever go to the singings or volleyball games?"

"Gatherings are for friends. They're for one to meet a potential husband or wife." She fingered the flowers' stems delicately as they walked side by side toward the hill, glad to have her hands full.

"You don't want friends or a husband?" She pondered her answer as she listened to the evening's buzz of life. Ribbons of chicory blooms swayed in a breeze. Adam carelessly snipped a few wild daisies, chicory blooms, and black-eyed Susans growing free throughout the pasture, offered them up to add to her bouquet of tamed blossoms.

"You know why I don't go. Please talk about something else." She sucked in her emotions. This was supposed to be a perfect night. She didn't want it ruined with a reminder that she was just Belinda, no one's first choice.

"I *don't* know. That's why I asked. I don't understand why you, of all people, don't go. I know you're good at athletics. I have seen you play baseball, remember?" he bumped her shoulder with his.

"I'm not without ability, but I know I'm different from the other *maedels*. No sense pretending to be something I am not."

"I agree, but I don't think we're talking about the same thing. Your differences are what are most attractive about you." She drew in a breath. "Besides, lots of people are shy. They work through it, just as you have. You talk to me all the time."

"*Attractive?* I'm ugly," she said bluntly. Adam reached out, gripped her hand, and brought her to a stop.

"You're crazy."

"So, I'm shy, ugly, and crazy. See why I don't go?" She jerked her hand free and began walking again.

"Belinda," he stopped her with a tender hand on her shoulder. She felt the same tremble and surprise as she had when he placed his hand over hers in the honey house. *Butterflies.* There were so many but-terflies darting about in her stomach right now.

"I don't think you see yourself clearly." He relieved her of the flowers in her hands, giving her nothing to hold onto for sup-port. "You're beautiful, inside and out. You do so much for everyone. And how many people can charm both beast and insect?" He looked serious, sincere. Did he truly not see her flaws? Had they spent so many days together he was immune, like her family?

She blinked. Did he find her capable of charming *him*? She blinked again, certain she heard him wrong. "You don't think me ugly?"

"*Nee.*" Adam was stepping into deeper water. He needed to tread lightly. Tobias was right. He wasn't supposed to mix business with pleasure. Just because he found her beauti-ful didn't mean he should risk his harvest to tell her—unless she cried. He had a moral obligation to say anything that might soothe her if tears were present.

"Look at me, Adam." She raised her voice and moonlight revealed tears daring an es-cape. He had to stop this now. He *had* looked at her; for weeks he had looked at her; for years, even. He wasn't stupid. Right now, he had to do everything *but* look at her.

He started walking again. "I have looked at you, and that little strawberry kiss on your cheek isn't ugly. It's all in your head." Adam did a mental slap to his forehead. "And vanity is a sin, Belinda," he added, just to put the cherry on top of his current screw-up.

Belinda opened her mouth, and then quickly closed it again. "I know," she whispered, and hung her head.

"I didn't say that to hurt your feelings. I don't understand how you could let something so small keep you from enjoying life." She was hostage to a past that had marred her confidence. How could he convince her that what she saw as a fatal flaw didn't matter to anyone but her?

"That's what I do, isn't it? Tabitha says such. I just have felt this way so long, I guess..."

"You let it become who you are," he quickly added. "You are more than a little girl who got her feelings hurt because of a few harsh words."

"But growing up hasn't changed things. Not really. They still stare at me."

"They do," Adam agreed. "But the birth-mark is *not* why they look at you."

The strawberry moon grew overhead.

They walked to a clearing and looked up. "Are we friends?"

Adam paused, letting the words soak through him. "*Jah*, Belinda, we are."

"Good. Now it's your turn." She looked to the moon again.

"My turn at what?"

"I told you something private, something I don't speak of outside of my family. It's your turn. It's what friends do." She strolled up higher and found a place to plant her bare feet.

"That's not part of our partnership," he tried to argue, fisting the bouquet a little tighter.

"It *is* our friendship." Her chin tilted upward, challenging him. "Or is your idea of friendship that I show my weakness, my vulnerability, while you get to remain un-blemished?"

She had him stumped and trapped at the same time. Adam couldn't risk opening up to her, but when those blue eyes danced in moonlight, he couldn't resist either. She tapped her foot, crossed her arms, awaiting his answer. Rolling his eyes, he let out a deep groan. "Fine." He sat down and stretched out his legs, knowing she would follow. "What do you want to know?"

"Why didn't you tell me about Susanne, in the beginning? You made me think..."

"I didn't want you to get the wrong idea." He answered too quickly. "I needed help. I didn't want you to think I was trying to get to know you, you know, like that." Honesty was not always the best method between friends.

"Like a potential girlfriend," she quipped. "You think me desperate, that I'd hound you if I knew you were single? You're not the first man to knock on my door." Her sharp words slapped him.

"Everyone else was getting the wrong idea about us, our partnership. I didn't want you to, as well." He flinched. "Wait. Who's been knocking on your door?"

"That's none of your business. And I'm not some silly *maedel* needing attention from a grumpy man who doesn't even know how to talk without growling." She got to her feet again.

"*Nee*, starved for attention, you are not," he agreed, and hurried to his feet. "I mean that as a compliment, Bee. You are nothing like the others, and that's a good thing. If circumstances were different..." His words brought her to a halt.

"We would still be strangers," she finished. She clearly saw him as nothing more than the grump next door. At least that's what he thought until he noticed the slight tremble in her hands. Something she did when she tried being firm and bold, for neither came to her naturally.

"I'm glad we aren't." Adam offered an extended hand. "I'm glad we needed each other and became friends as a result."

Belinda couldn't stop staring at him, hand out, waiting. His brow lifted, encouraging her to trust him.

"Let's go home before it gets too dark," Belinda said, accepting his hand and his offer to walk her home. He told himself that he was grateful for her friendship—that he *had* to be, since it was all he could ever ask of her.

They walked in silence, neither letting go of the other's hand. Home lights burned in the distance, a coyote called out and was joined by friends. But she didn't look afraid. He wondered if that meant she felt safe with him guiding her home.

When they reached her porch, Belinda turned to look up at him. Adam let her hand go, tucking his safely inside his pocket.

"You confuse and surprise me both," she announced.

"You've surprised me plenty," he said, eyes holding hers. "I wish things could be different." He cleared his throat. "Susanne was right." He had nothing to offer her, nothing to offer any woman. So why did this woman make him want to drop to his knees and hand her his heart? He fought the urge back.

"What *maedel* wants a bee farmer?" He shrugged.

Belinda thought about that for a moment, then smiled. "One who doesn't want a farmer who smells like he mucked stalls all day," she quipped playfully. Adam laughed. She reached out. "My flowers," she said, "before you squash the stems, please. I like to put them on the table for Mammi to see first thing in the morn."

Adam handed over the mix of wild and tame blooms, his gaze narrowing on her. "Not a one limp or bruised," he assured. "It might surprise you, considering my behavior of late, but I do know how to handle delicate things." They held each other's gaze for longer than what seemed proper for friends who had declared no romantic interest.

"She was wrong, you know. She chose a lesser man." His shoulders lifted and his gaze grew more intense. Sun and moon both played with the shadows. "And what kind of man would want to marry a *maedel* like that?" A cautious smile flitted across her face, taunting him. She seemed to be getting a hang of this flirting thing.

"Not me." He returned her smile. "*Gut nacht*, Belinda Graber, and *danki* for letting me walk you home again." He tipped his imaginary hat before strolling off into the night. There was no mistaking what was growing between them.

His father's favorite saying came to mind. Life *was* sweeter when you smiled.

Chapter Twenty

AFTER DELIVERING FLOWERS, ADAM HAD a half hour to waste before work. He stared at all the paint tubes splayed out on the shelf in the local hardware store and brushed a hand over the sunflower yellow, such a powerful likeness to the ones growing in her garden—such a reminder of the drawings now decorating his hives.

It wasn't that his hives looked better with drawings, though they did, or that Belinda had another secret talent he'd never known about, it was that she gifted him a little joy in his life when joy seemed so far away. How had she not known it would put a smile on his face? She had given him a reason to smile, and he had the urge to do something in return.

It was a struggle to decide between buying paint for Belinda to capture her flower drawings in fullness, and walking out, putting the whole crazy idea out of his mind. Madness won. He wouldn't overdo it, he decided, even though part of him wanted to buy every tube of paint in sight. But that would look desperate and might give her the wrong idea. So he selected colorful hues he thought might please her, along with a few brushes of different sizes, and made his way to the counter. Once he paid, he stepped outside into the cloudy day and looked up. "It's just a thank you," he mentally said. One purchase didn't mean he would concede, open his heart to the idea of love or romance. All they had was friendship. And friends should find reasons to make the other smile, he reasoned.

He crossed the street to where his buggy was parked. Belinda wasn't the kind of *maedel* who required constant attention; in fact, she preferred the opposite, but she had a way of wearing a stubborn man down. That's all it was. She had wormed her way into his world and they had become friends. *Partners and friends.*

"Adam," he heard from behind him. He closed his eyes and cringed, safely out of sight where she couldn't see it. The voice made the hairs on his arms stand to attention. Slowly he turned. Barely a newlywed, and she looked no different than she had on her porch months ago when she told him he wasn't worthy of her.

"How are you?" Susanne forced a weak smile. In a soft lavender dress and with her sorrowful blue eyes, Adam wondered just what he'd ever found appealing in her.

"I'm fine." And looking at her, he realized he was. "Congratulations."

"You weren't there," Susanne muttered.

"*Nee.*" He owed her no explanation for his absence. Who cared what she thought? Adam only cared what one woman thought. *Where did that come from?*

"I'm sorry," Susanne said, lowering her gaze. Adam saw the regret, noted the sag of her shoulders. It was a new look for her. And with that, at last, he was no longer angry. Adam pitied her. She wanted a life of ease, of romantic notions and everyday bliss. Maybe she'd found that with Jerimiah. Probably not. Some people were never satisfied with what *Gott* gave them. Standing here with her now, he knew. Adam was not going to let one gift, not one moment, pass by without grabbing it.

"Don't be. Be happy, Susanne. I know I will." He walked away, paints in hand, a new hope in his heart.

Humidity had declared war on Havenlee, and Belinda felt every inch of herself soaked, clean through her thin chore dress. After finishing another hive and picking beans most of the day, she went to the greenhouse to get some more work done. Tabitha had been selling twice as many hanging baskets as usual. Any spare minutes to be found were needed here, readying extra baskets for tomorrow.

She gingerly traced the geraniums with her fingertips. She loved geraniums, the soft petals and hardiness making them an ironic mixture. Tomorrow three hundred chrysanthemum seedlings would arrive and would need to be potted quickly. It was knee-aching and backbreaking work, but necessary.

Don't worry about tomorrow. Baskets first, she mentally whispered, and continued working. She had made baskets with million bells, allium, and verbena. Tropical sunrise was *Mamm's* favorite: five petals streaked with blushing pinks and sunflower yellow. But who could forget the daisy, all simple and perfect? Whether in field or greenhouse, old seed or new stock, their beauty lasted and endured summer heat and storms. She brushed her finger over a red Shasta daisy, and smiled. Stability lay in the traditional, familiar—and yet, this newer plant represented how, with a little altering, something already strong could be improved. Her thoughts drifted to Adam again. She'd cher-

ished her quiet routine for so long, and yet...
Could she ever be more, worthy of more?
Worthy of him?

She began humming, woolgathering
about a man who made her see more color,
made her itchy for new views. Memories of
his hand in hers contrasted with the look on
his face when he confessed he had no intentions of marrying. Did she dare challenge
his plans? Could he find happiness with her,
looking beyond the mark on her face? Faith
had taught her looks didn't matter, but Belinda had spent too many years absolutely
certain of the opposite. So she tamped down
fanciful hopes; she should learn to appreciate the few rare moments of happiness that
being around him gave her. She allowed
herself to save each and every one, for rainy
days and lonely afternoons in the future.

She got to her feet, knees sore from
being on them so long, and lifted the last
basket by its plastic hook. She held it high,
aiming for the pipe overhead that Daed used
to store the baskets to keep from overcrowding the floors, but the dip in the matted
floor made it impossible for her to reach the
one empty spot left. Stretching as far as her
body would allow achieved nothing. The pipe
was still too far out of reach. *Like life*, she
mentally grumbled.

Suddenly a strong hand wrapped
around steadied her back, while another
lifted the basket from her fingers and se-

cured it to the pipe. Belinda gasped, nearly letting out a cry, but the strong whiff of sawdust, man, and summer heat quieted her. She closed her eyes, inhaled. His scent was distinct, familiar, and slightly intoxicating.

"You're shorter than you look." Adam's deep voice so close to her sent a shiver up her spine. Belinda turned sharply but he didn't step back, only let his hand drop from holding her steady. For a moment Adam just stared down at her with those pale—currently green—eyes lacking something she couldn't put a finger on. He looked tired, ever so, just as he always did these days. The barometer inside the greenhouse rose a few degrees. She took a step back.

"And you're as tall as you look," she said, brushing her apron free of potting soil.

"Comes in handy." He looked around the greenhouse. "I've never been in here before," he said. "How is your dawdi today?" She liked how he often asked about her grandfather even though he had never met him. It was sweet.

"*Mamm* called this morning, said he felt up to attending church Sunday. And I can't believe you have lived so close by all your life and never been here. You should get out more," she teased, recalling his comments about May's orchard. "Are you just getting home?" She moved toward the open doors.

"*Jah*," he followed. "We finished pouring a foundation for a house this evening. Tobias and Caleb were both absent today so I had to pick up the slack at the mill."

"You should rest more."

Adam rubbed his neck, the stiffness hard work had pressed on him. "I feel old," he confessed.

"You're looking it too," she smiled over one shoulder. "It's been a long hot day for everyone and I know just what you need. Come."

Fireflies lit up the evening as a threat of rain hung heavy in the humid air. Adam sipped his lavender lemonade as Tabitha and Ivan, seated nearby, tossed snarky comments back and forth. Had Belinda ever sat with a man on the porch before? He thought not, by the warmth building on her cheeks. He knew he should stop staring, so he focused on the others.

Mica was sprawled out in a chair that didn't look sturdy enough for a man that size. Katie Jo, Ivan's little sister, lay on the wooden porch floor, flipping through a book. And Adam was indulging in Belinda's special lemonade, his second glass already, and chatting with friends. For a moment, life was giving him a glimpse of just what he would be missing if he held firm to his stubbornness about living his life alone.

"I have *kichlin* I made this morning," Belinda announced, and went inside. When had she found the time to make cookies? Adam sure hoped they were her honey cookies, having developed a fondness for them. She had a gift for anything to do with honey. As for his bees...four more hives and their time was over. Maybe he would ask for her help in August, the next harvest. When she returned, she offered the plate to him first, and he wasn't shy about taking one.

"I heard you're about done over there. Do you intend to keep selling flowers for Belinda?" Tabitha never shirked a chance to speak her mind, say what others wouldn't.

"I do. We made a deal and I intend on keeping it." He sat up straight. "I was hoping she would help come late August too." Adam looked straight at Mica, knowing he was the one who would have a say in the absence of their father. "Daed is doing great, but he won't be working that soon. It's a smaller harvest, less honey is taken so the bees have plenty for winter, but help would be welcomed."

"Atlee must be miserable. I would be, limited to a chair," Ivan said.

"You would not. Having a *fraa* waiting on you hand and foot, you would be in bliss," Tabitha smarted off, earning a few laughs. "If you can find one to put up with ya, that is." It was no secret Ivan had dated four local *maedels* in the last two years, and none had held his interest for long.

"Ivan doesn't like chairs; he prefers the couch," Katie Jo jested, her baby blue eyes looking up from her book. An hour had flown by and Adam knew he should head back to his side of the road, get an early night. He never got an answer to whether Belinda would help him again in the fall, but there would be other chances to ask.

Belinda looked at him, and catching him staring, she tried—and failed—to hide a grin. She was less nervous, here among family and familiar faces. Maybe he could coax her into meeting Marcy. He could take her himself. Just the thought of riding with her to town made his palms sweat.

"Well, I should go." Adam stood. "Walk with me, please?" he said to Belinda.

"Of course." Belinda handed her sister her half-full glass and followed him down the steps and across the yard.

"So there is only a day left to finish out the hives. I have a lot of work to do," he began, as they walked toward the road.

"You're afraid I can't handle the last of the harvest alone, and yet, I have been doing it all along."

"*Jah*," he said, running his hat in circles through his fingers. "But I feel like I have taken advantage of your kindness." Adam turned to face her, and she stopped and looked up to meet his eyes. He knew Mica was watching, his hawk-like gaze stalking Adam's every move. He smiled slowly. Belinda smiled bashfully in return, moonlight glinting in her eyes, glowing over her delicate tanned features.

"I too feel like I've taken advantage," she countered. "All your duties and you still deliver my flowers. Did you really mean what you said? You will still do that for me, even after the honey harvest is done?"

"I don't say things I don't mean," he replied. "Belinda," he began, heart pounding in his chest. "I have more obligations than most, right now." Belinda deserved all the affection and time Susanne had begged for. In fact, she deserved more, and he wished he could give her the world—but instead, he had so sadly little to offer.

"You do." Did she understand he was no longer talking about flowers or honey? Her body slightly trembled and he yearned to take her hand, explain the things going through his heart, his head. If they didn't have an audience, he would have. "We are partners, and friends," she continued. "I love helping you." Long lashes swept down over her eyes before she slowly looked up to him again.

"Help me with the next harvest, then," he blurted out. "This temporary partnership mostly benefited one of us. I will keep delivering your orders if you will help come

August." Getting to know her more, spending more time together, Belinda might see him as more than he was right now.

"I would like that." Relief washed over her features. She had clearly been thinking he might leave her to fend for herself once he no longer needed her. Adam was finding himself struggling to leave her right now.

"Something else," he paused as her family slowly retreated inside, leaving them alone. For once Adam praised *Gott's* decision to create mosquitoes. "Go with me into town to deliver the flowers, at least once. Let me introduce you to Marcy, or Mia. You choose." She took a step back, her brows quickly gathered into a worried look.

"Is that your part of the deal?" Her voice squeaked out.

"*Nee*," he said quickly, and moved to her. "That is me asking you to trust me. See your flowers in a store window. Know how much they are appreciated. I want to show you that."

"I don't know," she stuttered.

"Think on it? I'm not rushing you to decide, just encouraging you to try. If you agree, I promise I won't leave your side. It's the least I can do—I don't pay you nearly enough for all you've done for me," he grinned, generating a soft laugh from her.

"I'll find a way for you to make it up to me." She took a step back and turned to walk away. "*Gut nacht*, Adam Hostetler."

He watched her stroll back to the house, to her family and all her comforts. "*Gut nacht*, Belinda Graber," he whispered.

Belinda leaned on the door after closing it, releasing a pinned-up breath. Touching the mark on her face—a strawberry kiss Adam had called it—she couldn't help but smile, her heart so giddy. Love had taken root. She would do well now to cut it, before it bloomed, before it grew deeper, before it died. Loving a man like Adam certainly would end in sadness. He might never love her back. Still she smiled. Losing was at least participating, and she never wanted the tingling to stop.

Chapter Twenty-One

LATE-JUNE HEAT HAD BORNE DOWN relentlessly on the backs of men laboring all day. Adam secured the last nail into the outer wall frame. He stood and stretched out his sore back. The heatwave that had dogged Havenlee for the last couple of weeks was showing no signs of abating. He tugged on his shirt where his skin was begging for a breath.

"Here, can't have you passing out now, can I?" Ivan offered him a bottle of water. "Lunch break," Ivan called out to the crew of a dozen men, before turning back to Adam. "Sit with me over here. Tab made an extra meatloaf last night and I saw fit to get her worked up enough to give it to me," he said with a devilish grin.

"I got lavender lemonade and honey

kichlin." Adam tossed him a smile. It seemed they both had become smitten with the most beautiful women in Havenlee.

"Oh, those honey *kichlin.*" Ivan rubbed his belly. "My *mamm* used to make them. Belinda's talents in the kitchen equal those of her sister, with less snarling and snapping." Did anything taste as satisfactory as Belinda's cookies? Adam thought not.

"So, I know you need the money, but it wonders me why you insist on working two jobs and running a business, as well. I know the harvest is over for now, but I also heard you can be seen in the wee hours of the morning in a certain sunflower patch."

Adam grinned. He enjoyed catching a few early morning minutes with Belinda in her gardens. They watched the sun rise, drank coffee, talked about flowers and hives and what they wanted to do with them. She had painted a glorious spoken portrait of her flower farm. Adam no longer saw it as silly, marveled that he ever had. Both of them wanted to grow what had started out as a hobby into something sustaining. There was nothing less silly than that.

"It doesn't seem smart, and you look about ready to drop lately. You know the community has funds to help with Atlee's medical bills. We take care of our own." Ivan pulled out a long plastic container and opened it. He cut the meatloaf in half, placed one half on the lid, and offered it to Adam.

"*Danki*," Adam said. Tabitha's meatloaf looked a whole lot more filling than the ham and mustard sandwich he had brought.

"Extra fork is in the cooler next to the two containers of cobbler," Ivan pointed toward the cooler.

"Peach?"

"Of course. Is there any other?" Ivan chuckled.

"I kind of have a liking for blackberry. And I know what you're saying, but Daed doesn't like to put a strain on the community. Not when there are others in greater need. He is getting around rather well thanks to that therapist. If it gets to be too much, I'll let the bishop know. I've put a fair dent in the medical bills so far." And he had, keeping only enough for himself to barely get by. He didn't regret giving up most of his savings to cut the medical bill in half. At the time, building a home of his own, starting a family, had been far from his thoughts. But his thoughts were changing.

"I don't believe you." Ivan grinned. "Stubbornness and pride are close kin."

Adam took a bit of meatloaf, savored the spicy flavors on his tongue.

"I heard you and Belinda will be working together come August again. She is quite the bee charmer these days."

"She has always been a bee charmer," Adam said with his mouth full. "I feel bad she worked so hard helping me when all I do is deliver flowers for her." Adam forked another mouthful of meatloaf in. Tabitha made really good meatloaf.

"It's good she does more than stay home, even if your hives are just across the road. Mica says she still looks after the bees."

"She checks them every couple of days like clockwork. She even takes Daed on a walk after lunch so Mamm can have a few minutes to herself." The thought of her kindness, her charitable heart, made him smile.

Ivan bumped his shoulder. "She is a sweet one. I think of her like a *sister*." Ivan said it so flatly Adam felt his already-warm body heat a few degrees hotter. "I hope you don't take advantage of that sweetness." It seemed Ivan was looking after her too. Not that Mica needed any help with his brotherly role.

"I would never do that. I would never do anything to upset Belinda or make her feel taken advantage of." Adam looked his friend square in the eye, emphasizing his sincerity.

"I don't believe you would. You know you both make a pair. Her flowers, your honey. It's kind of like two sides of one business." It wasn't the first time Adam had considered that. *The oldest romance*, Mollie Bender had called it. Images of Belinda in the garden just this morning flashed before him. She had a way of making a man dream of coming home to eyes like that, beaming with love. Could he ever give Belinda the life she deserved? The moon and stars would only be a start on what she deserved—and he barely had enough in both pockets for a pack of gum. Plus, he still owed a few thousand dollars to the hospital. Paying it all off could take a couple more years.

"Ivan, I know what people must think, us spending time together. You can tell Mica I have been kind and respectful."

"So you read minds as well as your other many talents. *You* can tell Mica if it's important." Ivan filled his mouth with the last of his share of meatloaf.

"I figured he put you up to asking." Adam forked up some peach cobbler.

"Told you, I love her like a *sister*. I didn't need to be put up to anything. I only want what's best for her." Ivan shifted to face him. "And why would you care what Mica thinks anyway?"

"Same as you. He is protective." The fact couldn't go unnoticed.

"He only acted that way when you were *kinner* because she came home crying every day because you or some other little *bu* with no good sense was always staring at her face."

"She had a pretty face even then. Not all of us meant it in a bad way," Adam confessed, and it felt freeing to say the words out loud.

"You've had eyes for our Belinda since school?" Ivan's voice rose.

Adam shrugged. It was silly thing to admit, but the words were already out there now. "She deserves better than a bee farmer. Belinda deserves somebody who doesn't push and who values her kind heart."

"You're not just a bee farmer, and no one believes you to be the kind of man who would push her into anything that would truly upset her. You underestimate yourself. Do you still like her?"

"I'm not sure how to answer that." He felt it would be wise to tread lightly.

"It's not a trick question." Ivan was not the kind of man who asked many questions, but when he did, answers were expected. Adam swallowed the lump in his throat. He hadn't truly admitted even to himself what he felt for Belinda, though he knew well enough, felt it with every fiber of his being.

"I do. She's beautiful, funny, works harder than any woman I've ever known, and has a voice like an angel. What's not to like?" he said casually, as if it was obvious and inevitable.

"Do you love her?" Adam's mouth went dry. Did he? Ivan chuckled.

"I ruined one *maedel's* plans. What makes you think I need to try doing that to another?" Adam retorted.

"That one ruined her own plans—and anyway, that was months ago, over and done with. Now back to the question. Can you see

253

Belinda in your life?" Ivan would make a fine father someday, his patience unfailing.

"She *is* in my life," Adam said.

"All right then, can you see her *not* in it?" That Adam hadn't considered, and didn't want to imagine.

"I don't want to see that," Adam muttered. At the very idea, his appetite vanished.

"Then I guess you have your answer." Ivan stood. "Better go do something about that before someone else gets there first. You're not the only man in Havenlee who has taken an interest." Adam narrowed his eyes. "Now, let's build a house, what do ya say?" Ivan continued. "Then maybe you can leave early and stop by the general store for something sweet for your pretty neighbor."

"I already bought paints," Adam said gruffly. What other men was Ivan talking about? Had someone said something to him? Was it Noel? Belinda would never take a liking to Noel, he was nearly certain.

"Did you now?" Ivan laughed. "And what is the paint for?"

"She drew these flowers on a couple of the hives and I thought she might want to paint them, make them permanent. I'm not sure if I should give them to her. A gift from me might make her run off screaming. But I want her to have them, to keep her from thinking she doesn't matter, or that I only want her around because I needed her help. I want her to feel like I put her first, and right now, I haven't given her a reason to feel that way. She's been so open with me, I can't think of ruining that because I...care for her. I've always cared for her. I'm such an idiot." Adam slapped his forehead as it all became perfectly clear. "All these years she sat right across the road and I was too afraid of making her uncomfortable to go over and talk to her."

Ivan gripped his shoulder, forcing Adam to look up. "Take her the paint. You won't know how she'll react if you don't try. And your hives will look better for it. Time's a wasting, and we get so few chances at the real thing."

"You should take your own advice," Adam retorted, snorting when Ivan lifted a brow, confused. "I saw how you and Tabitha stare at one another," Adam added with a glint of humor. "You have courted a half dozen *maedels* and not one has stuck. Has to mean something."

"It's not like that. She's my best friend's sister. I come with an extra. You know my daed isn't present half the time. Tab doesn't need that, and I promise you if I did try, she'd laugh me right out the door."

Adam put the conversation aside as all the men gathered to lift the south wall of the house in progress. Adam bent, felt the sting of hard weeks of labor, and took a deep breath. At least talking to Ivan had helped him sort out his feelings. For too long he'd thought too much about his neighbor, even arrived earlier each morning to help her cut flowers and learn their names, and lingered in the evenings after returning her buckets and pay, chatting to her about everything he could think of until he ran out of things to say.

Some of the men behind him had long poles beside them to help raise the wall. Ivan called out the count. "One. Two. Three." Everyone lifted.

Adam felt like he was singlehandedly lifting the whole house. Lightheadedness fogged his sight and he closed his eyes in the hopes of steadying himself. His muscles strained, but he pushed through the weight bearing down on him, cursing gravity for unbalancing the score. He heard a thump next to him, and then raised voices. Adam opened his eyes, looked right at Chris Schaffer, who was nearest to him at the base of the wall. Suddenly the wall grew heavier, Chris's face redder, and a vein protruded in the center of his forehead. More yelling. It was coming down. All Adam had to do was let go and move left or right, but a tired body didn't always respond as quickly as it should.

The wall came down. Surprisingly enough, it wasn't as brutal an impact as he'd expected. It was just a few boards, just heavy enough to leave a few bruises, but the impact, coupled with fatigue, shut out the world, and everything went dark.

Ivan stood in the Graber kitchen, hat in hand, talking to Belinda's sister and grandmother.

Mammi was the first to notice her standing in the laundry room doorway. "Oh, Belinda," Mammi sniffed and walked toward her. "*Danki* for getting the linens hung for me. Would you mind checking for fresh eggs?" The long, sorrowful faces of Ivan, Tabitha, and Mammi told her some ominous secret was being hidden from her. Her first thought was of Dawdi. Had he succumbed to his disease? Why would they keep something like that from her? She wasn't a child and was tired of being treated as one.

"I already gathered eggs this morning, like every morning. What's going on? Is it Dawdi?" She moved past her grandmother farther into the kitchen.

"*Nee*, my love. Saul is faring well. Please go gather the eggs like I asked." But Belinda didn't move. She wasn't leaving until she knew what they were hiding. She crossed her arms stubbornly and locked gazes with her sister.

It only took a full minute and Belinda wore her sister down. "Tell her," Tabitha said, looking at Ivan. Belinda watched him gulp visibly. Whatever news he was withholding wasn't good.

"Is Mica okay? Where is he?" Belinda felt her breaths began to labor. Had something terrible happened to her brother?

"Adam got hurt today," Ivan began, not beating around the bush any longer. Belinda gasped, bringing both hands to her mouth.

"Not like *that*, Ivan. Men are such idiots." Tabitha led Belinda to the table, and pushed her into a chair.

"They were framing the house and the wall fell when someone's pole slipped. He is okay—don't panic. But Adam did hit the ground hard enough to be sent to the hospital. He should be coming home soon. Maybe two days. He will be fine." From Tabitha's careful tone, Belinda knew there was a lot her sister wasn't telling her. Tears immediately burst forth. Ivan stepped forward, knelt by her side.

"I came from there to here. Ada asked that I stop by and tell you—and see if you would look after Atlee for a time." Ivan lowered his head and ran his hands through his hair and growled. "I should have sent him home before this even happened. It was obvious he is overworked. The man never slows down, and now..."

Tabitha reached over and placed a

hand over his. "It's not your fault. It was an accident. And he will be fine, he just needs some rest. Adam is a strong man." Belinda watched her sister soften toward Ivan, the man who made her blood boil.

"What are his injuries?" Belinda could barely get the words out between sobs. She felt Mammi's arms drape over her shoulders.

"He has four broken ribs. He will be down for some time. They said he has a concussion and was severely dehydrated too. I heard the doctor mention it. I keep water on hand and take it to him when he forgets— but he's been forgetting a lot lately, and I don't always notice. He just works right along and even forgets to eat most days. I should have... I'm sorry, Belinda. I know what this means to your partnership." Ivan looked pale and ghastly. "He wants you to know how terrible he feels about it too."

"You expect me to be worried about my flowers? You think that matters now?" She didn't mean to sound so harsh. Taken aback, each of them looked at her in total surprise.

"Let me fix us some tea," Mammi quickly suggested.

"I know you all think I'm fragile and need to be coddled, but I don't." Belinda got to her feet and wiped her damp face along her sleeve. "I will be glad to see to Atlee," she said to Ivan, lifting her chin in a take-charge motion. Ivan looked stunned, though she couldn't say whether it was her boldness that startled him or residual shock from the horrible day. "I would appreciate if you and Mica would load the buggy in the morning for me with about a dozen boxes from Adam's honey house."

"Why?" Tabitha quickly asked.

"They will have more medical expenses now, and I will need to do all I can to earn more money for them." Belinda turned to Mammi, who was pouring boiling water over fresh tea leaves. "Also, we should bake a casserole or two. Atlee likes spicy foods. Ada will be tending to both her men, but not alone. We are neighbors, and it's our job to care for each other."

Tabitha looked to Ivan, and then turned back to her sister. "I can help too. Mica has to take beans to the auction, so I can go see Atlee now and then help prepare a few meals. When is the next harvest?"

"I have a couple more hives to rob now, but then not until August. I would appreciate it if you could help me with the vegetables for the next few weeks. I will have my hands full selling flowers and honey." Her declaration earned her more shocked looks. Mammi, on the other hand was smiling from ear to ear.

"I can get Mary to watch over our stand a couple days at market and help with the picking. We can pick the gardens before breakfast and handle cleaning both houses in the afternoon," Tabitha added.

"I can manage keeping up some of their canning. The Hostetlers' vegetable garden isn't that big," Mammi offered.

"And I will talk to some of the men. We can all spare a few bucks to help. Maybe pay a visit to the bishop. Atlee and Adam are both stubborn, but now it isn't just charity. It's necessity." Belinda couldn't agree more with Ivan's words.

Belinda's eyes stung with joy. Her family was going to help her see that Adam and his family didn't have a worry in the world.

"Ivan," she collected herself. "I want to see him."

"I will see what I can do," Ivan nodded. With that, Belinda busied herself with supper and preparing casseroles.

All the while, Adam never left her thoughts. She needed to see him, care for him. Belinda worked numbly though her tasks as she awaited Ivan's return. She missed Adam. Missed him for reasons even she couldn't explain. For so long she had kept to the shadows, avoiding any eyes that made their way to hers. She had never thought beyond the life she had, but right now, standing there trying not to cry, Belinda wanted to think about what tomorrow might bring. She could take care of both their businesses, with her family's help. At least until Adam and Atlee were both set to rights again. She straightened her shoulders, blew out a pinned breath, and smiled.

Adam deserved all the help she could give, even if that meant facing her fears. And she needed to find out just what she had been missing. She wanted more than the quiet, isolated life she used to have. She wasn't sure how much more she could handle, but she was ready to find out. It was scary—terrifying, really—but she wanted it nonetheless.

Chapter Twenty-Two

THAT NIGHT, BELINDA BARELY SLEPT a wink, thinking of Adam hurting and in pain. When the morning light woke her, she put that all aside and got to work. She loaded her fresh-cut flowers into the buggy—bold red cannas, purple dahlias, Dusty Miller, and sunflowers. Mica had loaded five boxes of honey, jarred and labeled. In her pocket was the list of stores she needed to visit to deliver the honey. It was now or never. She hated that she was so afraid, but Tabitha was right. She would never get over her fears if she didn't face them. Adam had said she needed adventure, had begged her to meet Marcy and Mia and a little boy with eager curiosities. This might not be his idea of adventure, but she was stepping out of her shell, for him. That had to count for something.

The first stop was Zimmerman's, the Amish general store. Belinda had been inside more times than she could count, and knew Marcus and Katie Zimmerman well. Just because she was alone shouldn't mean a thing. She could do this.

She pulled the buggy up to the hitching station and hitched Benny, her mother's horse, to the pole. She retrieved one box of honey out of the back seat, and headed to the storefront. She sucked in a deep breath before stepping inside. The light was much dimmer inside the store and she stood still momentarily to allow her eyes to adjust.

"Belinda?" Katie Zimmerman called out. "How *wunderbaar* to see you. Is Tabitha with you?"

"*Nee*, just me." The little flicker in Katie's eyes when Belinda said that didn't go unnoticed. They were close to the same age, had grown up and gone to school together, so Katie knew full well how out of character this was for her. "I'm sure you've heard about the accident. Adam's unable to deliver his honey today, so I told Ada and Atlee I would bring it to you since I was coming to town." She hoped the tremble in her voice wasn't recognized.

"He has the best honey. I think it's all those flowers of yours." Katie winked and hefted the box of honey from Belinda's arms to the counter. Belinda's heart swelled at the simple compliment. "How is he?"

"He sleeps a lot, Ada says. The medication does that. I haven't spoken with him, but they say he will get to come home tomorrow." And then she would get to see him, talk to him.

"I hope she can keep him in bed. That one needs rest more than any other. He is always busy working. I heard he suffered a bout of heat stroke too."

"Dehydrated," Belinda replied. "*Jah*. He does a lot." Belinda smiled proudly. It felt strange having a conversation about Adam in public, but she was glad others had also noticed how hard he worked.

"Well, you are such a special friend to help. Do you want his pay for the honey?" Katie offered a stack of bills from the register.

"Oh *nee*, just hold it until he or Ada comes by. I'm just delivering." Belinda quickly said her goodbyes and strolled back to the buggy. That wasn't as bad as she had feared. Next stop, the florist.

Marcy Swift was a round woman in her late thirties, and had no concept for matching colors. Belinda felt as if she already knew her and her strange fashion choices from all Adam had told her, but he hadn't mentioned she had one eye that liked to wander off slightly. It was terribly distracting, more than wearing stripes and polka dots in one outfit.

Marcy brightened up when she met Belinda and ushered her into the store. "Oh, peonies. I'm so glad you thought of those. I didn't put them on the list because I wasn't sure you had any left. The stems are so hard to work with, but they are worth the extra effort." Marcy swooned over the selection.

Belinda set the other bucket down and let her eyes scan over the little shop. The open room smelled glorious. It was like standing in the middle of her garden, only without the sun burning freckles into her skin. "I also have dahlias and hibiscus. I think them *schee* in an arrangement."

"You have a talented eye. I'm just so happy to finally meet the woman who grows the prettiest flowers around. Not every florist is lucky to have such a skilled gardener nearby. And these sunflowers won't sit in here long. People just love sunflowers, no matter the season."

"Hey," a little voice said. Belinda turned to find a little sandy-haired boy licking on a sucker and wearing a fair bit of it, smeared and sticky, all over his hands and face.

"Hello. You must be Jackson." His brown eyes widened at her knowing his name.

"You Adam's girlfriend?"

Belinda chuckled. "*Nee*. I mean," she cleared her throat. "No. I just help him with his bees. And he helps me with my flowers."

"He said he has no girlfriend, but mom says he's not being truthful. Mom says he smiles too much talking about the flower lady." Jackson pinned her with a serious look. "And boys don't like flowers. That's girls' stuff. Lying is against the law, you know?"

"It is." Belinda couldn't help but giggle before looking to Marcy again, who blushed with embarrassment over what her son had revealed. Belinda knew how she felt. Did Adam really smile a lot when they talked about her flowers? When they talked about *her*?

"Adam thinks a lot of the work you do. He also says you're a very good cook." Marcy grinned knowingly.

Belinda ducked her head. The air conditioning in the little flower shop did little to help the rush of warmth running over her. "I have another bucket outside. Let me go fetch it." She hurried out before her joy was noticeable. Was Adam only trying to help her sell her flowers, tossing compliments out so freely?

Back inside, Jackson was still standing in the center of the floor, working hard to eat more sucker than wear it. Marcy was on the phone writing down an order, so Belinda wandered about. Baby's breath, carnations, and roses of every color sat in narrow containers and tucked inside lighted coolers. She bent for a closer look, admiring each bloom and petal.

"You like flowers?" Jackson shadowed her.

"I grow them, so yes. I like flowers." She glanced over her shoulder, offering him a smile.

"Do you always wear that hat thing?" He cocked his head, his deep blue eyes searching. A curious one for sure and certain, he was.

Belinda chuckled and stood upright, giving the little questioner a fuller study. His tan shorts portrayed a scatter of pictures of kites, his shirt, a deep blue, had two patches of what Belinda believed was his uneaten breakfast. "It's called a prayer *kapp*, and yes, I always wear it."

"So you pray a lot then." He worked his blue sucker again, still staring at her intently. Mere weeks ago, she would have turned her body, lifted a shoulder to conceal her mark, but Belinda felt no threat of harshness waiting to be revealed. Just a little boy with questions, and a healthy appetite for suckers.

"I do." Why had she been so afraid to meet Marcy and a little boy?

"Mommy says we should pray a lot. Did you know *hinkel* is Amish for chicken?"

Belinda leaned forward, placing both hands on her knees to meet him at eye level. "Did you know *gaul* means horse?" His face lit up.

"Gaul?" Jackson repeated the word.

"Yes. Next time I visit, I will teach you another word." Because there had to be a next time. Belinda looked forward to it, surprisingly so.

"Sorry about that. Here is your weekly pay." Marcy handed her an envelope. "I hope you come again. I know you are very busy and I really like Adam—he is such a sweet fellow—but I must admit, I really wanted to put a face to the flower lady," she winked.

Belinda left the florist carrying an empty bucket with one hand and clutching an envelope of money to her chest with the other. Her chin lifted a little higher and her smile wasn't forced. The next two stops were the local grocery store, where she picked up a few things for home and delivered Adam's honey, and the Amish bakery. The longer she interacted with the shopkeepers, the easier it got. Finally, she reached her last stop, the foreign-talking baker Adam had told her about.

Mia Gwinn was in her late forties, spoke in high-pitched tones, and used her hands to emphasize every word out of her mouth. For a woman who spent her life baking, Belinda figured she must not eat her own sweets, as skinny as she was. *Mamm* would call that a sign of a poor cook, but by the lingering customers filling her shop, she seemed an exception to that rule. Her dark hair was pulled tight into a bun. Her long white apron was smeared with a pink frosting.

The bakery smelled heavenly. There were scones and frosted donuts with sprinkles. Pies of every fashion, and frosting piped on cakes, muffins, and even sugar cookie tops.

After Mia had exchanged a few pleasantries with Belinda, she said, "Your sweet boyfriend thought I was silly to buy flowers for cakes, but after a slice of my lavender citrus cake, he changed his thinking."

"Adam is just a neighbor," Belinda corrected, but she couldn't hold back the flush at the baker's assumption.

"Oh. I thought... Never mind." Mia waved off the comment. "You want to see what those violets of yours look like when I use them?" Belinda did, so she followed Mia into the back of the bakery.

"Oh my," Belinda said as she stared at the wedding cake. Four stacks high, white frosting spread so perfectly it looked to be painted on. In the blossom of white squiggly lines over the top lay sugared violets in clusters. Mia had arranged them so that they looked like they dripped down one side of the cake. It was the most beautiful dessert Belinda had even seen.

"I knew what you wanted based on pictures I saw in a magazine, but I must say I never imagined how pretty it would look. It is beautiful," Belinda complimented.

"It is a small wedding. If you had come last week you would have seen the one with the pansies and daisies and lilac. It was eight tiers." Belinda's brows gathered. "That means eight stacks high. I even had a water fountain on it. Many customers want water-falls these days." The little baker rolled her eyes comically.

Amish weddings were simple, basic. Belinda couldn't imagine how one made a waterfall on a cake, but simply nodded. She was impressed. Mia gave her a quick tour of the bakery and with the promise to return with her *mamm*'s lemon blueberry cake recipe, Belinda picked up her little bucket and readied herself to leave.

"I should go," she explained. "My sister works at the market, and I want to stop and see her for lunch before heading home."

"Here," Mia reached into a glass case and pulled out a variety of muffins, and began putting them into a blue box. "My treat. You are my favorite supplier now. I am happy to finally meet you, Belinda Graber. You remember that lemon blueberry cake recipe for your next visit." Belinda smiled and nodded. She wouldn't forget it. "Oh, and tell that...you tell Adam I hope he feels bet-ter soon. We all heard about his accident and have been praying for his healing." Mia clasped her fist around a small necklace with a cross. Belinda's heart warmed at the kindness and showing of faith. She hadn't thought the *Englisch* held the same rever-ence for prayers, but they did. It seemed the only strangers there really were in this world were just friends she hadn't meet yet.

Mia handed over the box. "There are four for you and your sister to share, but the one with the lemon on top is for someone who isn't feeling so good right now." Mia leaned over the counter and whispered. "It is his favorite." The baker winked as the doorbell rang, signaling more customers.

Adam wanted to kick the wall.

"Stop pouting. You're too grown up for that," Ada scolded.

"I can't work for at least six weeks," he said. "How will we get by with me lying here doing nothing for that long?" He worried a loose thread on the thin quilt. His mother looked down on him on the bed, a sorrowful expression on her face. How she had managed to not age at all since he was a boy was beyond him. With the exception of one thin line across her forehead, she was timeless. The same could not be said of him. With ribs bound so tight he could barely take a full breath and a head still throbbing days later, Adam felt old. Every muscle, every limb ached.

"Just like we always have, before you

knew what work was. Now stop pulling that apart or I will be bringing a needle and thread in for you to fix it yourself." He let the thread go, wishing he had something else to pull apart. *Like my life has been.*

"I guess I could take up quilting while I'm lying here doing nothing." Adam tried on a deep sigh but found it only caused more pain than it was worth.

Ada ignored his self-pity and the way he growled in frustration just as he had as a *bu*. "The bishop came by while you were sleeping yesterday. They are seeing to the medical bills, so get that out of your worries. Your daed and I feel terrible you have worked yourself to exhaustion for us. We should have said something sooner, but you were so determined and always claimed that you had easy jobs that did little to tire you." Her eyes glistened and Adam hoped she wasn't about to cry. It wasn't her fault. He could only blame his stubbornness, or maybe his slowness, not getting clear of the falling wall fast enough.

"I didn't want you to worry and I knew Daed wouldn't accept anything from the community funds." Adam tightened his fist at his own stupidity. He had just added to his family's burdens when all he'd wanted to do was lessen them.

"He's the one who called the bishop," his mother informed him. Adam's eyes snapped up to meet hers as she lay a tray over his lap. "Well, had me call him, but you know what I mean. Now eat some lunch so you can get to feeling better."

"I won't ever feel better again." He looked down resentfully at the tray with a sandwich, a spoonful of *Mamm*'s potato salad and a bowl of cobbler. "Is that blackberry?"

"Belinda makes the best cobblers," Ada smiled wittily.

"Belinda?" His anger vanished instantly. Had she been to see him? He wanted to ask but didn't dare. *Mamm* would assume he was inquiring because he was worried about his bees, not because he thought about little else but their neighbor.

"She came by a couple times, but you were resting." *Mamm* was a smart woman.

"Those pills make me sleepy and dizzy. She's probably upset with me, getting myself hurt and all. I've let a lot of people down," he muttered.

"You have done no such thing. And why would you think that of our sweet Belinda?" *Mamm*'s sharp blue eyes narrowed in disappointment.

"I cannot deliver her flowers like this," Adam slapped the bed and winced. He could barely take an able breath and here he was getting riled, which would only set him back.

Ada grinned and used her apron to wipe his bedside stand clear of dust. "So much dust in here. I think you best worry about healing and not flowers or honey. Belinda has everything under control."

"What do you mean?" Adam studied her smirk, suspicion blossoming inside him.

"I just mean you need not worry. She has been working hard since she heard about the accident."

Adam closed his eyes and clenched his jaw so hard his teeth ached. "Please tell me she isn't letting someone else help her sell her flowers." The thought that someone else—another man perhaps—was helping her only fueled his rotten temper.

"Trust that all is well, and rest." She bent toward him. "Where is my *sohn*'s faith? Is it here?" She lifted the sheet over his feet.

"Funny," Adam said. "You haven't answered my question."

"You finish your meal and rest and I might answer one question. Now drink all that water and don't let that cobbler go to waste." She was clever and not one to cave when he wanted. Adam looked down at the cobbler, Belinda's cobbler, and shook his head in surrender.

"Never." Adam pushed the sandwich aside and dug straight into the purple sugary delight. He had no choice but to trust and it infuriated him, but blackberry cobbler did have a strangely uplifting effect on a man's mood.

Chapter Twenty-Three

HOW HAD SHE MANAGED TO live all her years and not come to the Amish market before? It all seemed so silly, so immature, now that she stood in the midst of it. Adam was right, the only thing holding her back was herself. Cradling the blue box from the bakery, she peered across the aisle of tables and booths just ahead. There were a few dozen souls milling about, but none seemed to care she was here among them.

Tabitha had spoken of her view near the courthouse clock, the same one Adam had mentioned weeks ago. She lifted her gaze and searched out the brick tower, then aimed herself toward it.

She was barely four booths into the maze of chaos when she found her heart melting at the sight of four fuzzy puppies. Just as Adam had told her. She lowered herself, gave all four a pat on their fluffy little heads. To her left were the two food trucks he had also described. A strong scent of grease mingled with the hot summer air. Not a very pleasant scent, she discovered, but still interesting and new. Looking right, there was the Amish man from the next district selling chairs and other outdoor furniture. Beside him were the secluded tables under three tall oaks, all crowded with lunchers at this noontime hour. Adam had mapped out every detail, which left her feeling strangely at home. She moved on, knowing Tabitha's stand wasn't far now.

"Belinda Graber," a voice called out, causing Belinda to turn abruptly. Her surprise kicked up her heart rate as a tall, dark figure stepped out of the crowd. Recognizing Abner Lapp, she felt a rock drop into the pit of her stomach. He jogged toward her, and she struggled against the urge to run and hide. She had confronted a lot this day, and one man wasn't about to make her become that frightened little girl again.

"I thought that was you. I've been hoping to see you again. I saw Tabitha this morning," he told her. He looked darker than she remembered, hair and thick brows the color of night. His face was darkly tanned, as if he stood in the sun for hours and hours a day. He was tall and practical. A nice-looking man, if she was being honest. And yet, she felt uneasy with him, struggling to forge a welcoming smile.

"You look nice today," he complimented, eyes once more trailing the length of her. "I planned to come out and see Mica soon, once I'm settled." He removed his hat, ran his fingers through damp dark hair, and then placed it back on his head.

"He would like that," she replied, and took a step back.

"Are you here to see your sister?" Abner asked, his wandering gaze attempting to hold her still.

"I was hoping to share a treat with her, *jah*. It's good to see you, but I must be going." Belinda started walking.

"Well, your family's table is over this way," he pointed out. "Right next to my cousin Joshua's. Let me walk you." Before she could decline, Abner had gripped her elbow and began weaving her through the crowd that had suddenly doubled in size. She let Abner guide her, keeping her head down.

"It's not so crowded today, Joshua says, but I'm glad to see how much the market has grown since I lived here before. I should do well selling my goods here. Here she is." Abner lifted an arm, finally releasing his captive. At least that was how the last full minute had felt. Adam never made her feel so uncomfortable when he offered her a hand.

"Belinda. What are you doing here?" Tabitha's green eyes went wide in surprise. She rounded the table and wrapped Belinda into a tight hold. It was the milestone of Belinda coming out here by herself that Tabitha was pleased with, but Belinda hoped her sister didn't address it in front of Abner. She pulled away.

"I brought a treat." She lifted the box, gave a shrug.

"Well," Abner said, "I'll let you two have your lunch. It was really nice to see you again, Belinda. Maybe when you're done, I can walk you back to your buggy?" He looked hopeful. *Absolutely not.* She couldn't let Abner, a man she barely remembered, walk her anywhere. Were all men this pushy?

"This is so kind of you, Abner." Tabitha turned to Belinda. "Belinda, isn't that kind that Abner doesn't want you walking all the way back alone?" Belinda felt her tongue thicken. She lowered her head.

"It is," she muttered. "*Danki.*" Abner smiled like someone had just handed him a whole cake. Why hadn't she just spoken up, said no? Why did her sister insist on pushing her toward things that made her uncomfortable? Wasn't being here enough to please her for now?

Tabitha led her behind the table. "I'm

almost sold out. Just beans and potatoes left. Your flowers are selling even better than I expected." Belinda noticed only a few limp sunflowers remained. "So what did you bring?"

"Muffins, or cupcakes, the baker calls them." Belinda lifted the lid.

"They look too pretty to eat. Is that one lemon?" Tabitha poked a long, delicate finger toward it.

"That one is for someone else. Mia said so." Her voice hitched possessively. She might not have been able to stop her sister from pushing Abner on her, but Tabitha certainly wasn't going to eat Adam's special dessert. "But you can pick any of the others, or all. I don't mind."

"Do I look like I need three cupcakes? I'll try the one with green icing."

"Matches your eyes," Belinda said affectionately. Tabitha collected her recent quilting project, and set it aside to clear a spot for Belinda to sit.

They sat under the green Graber's Greenhouse canopy as the noonday sun bore down hot and heavy. Belinda shared her morning with her sister as they each had a cupcake and split another one that tasted like strawberry angel food cake.

"I should go. I've had enough adventure for one day, and need to help Mammi with the laundry." Belinda got to her feet.

"I'm so happy you came. I know this

wasn't easy for you, especially going alone to the stores. I hope you can come and work a day with me here soon. We always made a good team." Tabitha smiled.

"Perhaps I will." Belinda hugged her sister farewell and turned to leave. Before she knew it, Abner was by her side, as if he had been waiting for the moment she stood. Had he been watching her and her sister for the past hour, invading their privacy? She was glad she'd come, experienced everything firsthand, but she couldn't get back home and away from this man soon enough to suit her.

"Ready to go?" He put both hands in his pockets, indicating he would at least be proper and not touch her arm again. The look of joy and satisfaction on Tabitha's face made walking with Abner tolerable. It wasn't far to her buggy and Tabitha's approval meant a lot, especially since she was the one who often reported the daily comings and goings back to *Mamm*. Still, a growing swarm gathered in Belinda's belly as Abner led her forward. She should have never have eaten so many sweets in this July heat.

"I hope you don't mind, but I asked around about you." If he had, then why did he insist on walking her to her buggy? "I hear you sell flowers all over town. I always knew you had a green thumb like your parents. I still can't see Mica potting daisies and petunias." Abner chuckled.

"He does, and does it well," she argued. "What do you do again?" They turned the corner by the food stands. Abner steered her toward the outer grasses to avoid the crowd lined up to place their orders.

"I raise horses and work with leather." He sounded proud of that. She didn't know if working leather meant making saddles and harnesses or maybe those tourist keychains, but she didn't dare inquire further. The smell of grease and French fries grew heavier in the air.

"Like I mentioned before, at the auction, I came home to start my own shop here. I hope to do well with it." She picked up her pace now that they had reached the large parking area.

"I pray you do."

"Do you come to the market often?" He leaned closer, flirting. Even she recognized it.

"*Nee*. I don't have time." She hoped maybe she would share a lunch with her sister again after visiting the shops as she had today, but he didn't need to know that.

"There is a gathering tomorrow. I haven't been to one in years, but if *you're* going, I really would consider attending." Belinda flinched. Was Abner asking her to join him, at a gathering?

"I don't go to gatherings." This was not being brave, but at the moment, she couldn't bring herself to care.

"What do you usually do, then?" She

picked up her pace and refused to answer him. Where was Benny? She searched the long rectangular lot, now full with a mix of vehicles and buggies. "I know you're not dating anyone," he continued. "I would really like to see you again, Belinda." He was as straightforward as Adam, but unlike Adam's harsh honesty about having no plans to marry, Abner was laying his intentions out there in invitation.

"Here's Benny, my horse." She patted the horse's head and quickly moved toward the buggy. "*Danki* for walking me over." Belinda awkwardly scrambling up into the seat, dropping the cupcake box onto the floor-board beside her.

Abner unleashed Benny from the post. Belinda gave herself a mental slap for forgetting she needed the lines to drive home. His smirk wasn't masked under his hat and she felt a shiver skid up her spine as he handed over the reins. She reached to accept them and he closed his hand over hers and held tight. "I know you never liked crowds. A walk perhaps? Mica and I are old friends and he will invite me to dinner. If I came, would you take a walk with me, Belinda?" She could see her reflection in those dark eyes, her wide eyes looking back at her. His smile improved what was already a handsome face, but she didn't have that ease about him.

"I don't know," she stuttered as fear began wreaking havoc on her nerves. Just when she thought she had overcome her childishness, here it was, returned in full force. She jerked her hand and the reins free.

"I think I also remember you being fond of fishing." He ducked his head and gave her a wry grin. Fishing meant they would be alone with not a soul in sight.

"I really must go." She didn't want to upset him, but the "No" sitting there on the tip of her tongue was literally stuck. She had tackled enough for one day.

He grinned. "I will see you soon, Belinda Graber," he said with an irritating confidence, and slowly backed away.

Belinda sorted out her belly full of bees as the distance grew between her and the market. Eventually, she decided that she would simply speak to Mica, tell him about today's encounter, and he would see to it that Abner didn't make a pest of himself. With that thought, she relaxed. She could always depend on Mica. *Except once*, she recalled and smiled. When he sent their neighbor to seek her out for help.

She'd had a huge day and here it was not even two o'clock. She had accomplished meeting her customers and going to the market. Adam would be happy for her. A milestone—that's what today felt like. She had to tell him all about it. He'd told her to have an adventure, and she had. He was right. Nothing was so scary that she couldn't overcome it, and no one had stared at her cheek. If he was sleeping again, she would go back again tomorrow, but after three days apart, she really hoped he wasn't this time.

When Belinda reached the farm, she observed the familiar white truck pulling in across the road. She climbed down from the buggy, tethered the horse, and then went to greet Steve, who was currently making his way toward the Hostetlers' front door.

"Can I help you?" Belinda hurried toward him. If Adam was sleeping, then the bee inspector's knocking might wake him. Adam needed all the rest he could get. Besides, she was sure she could answer any questions the inspector had, even if she felt a little foolish, running toward him like a crazy person. That was obviously the reason for the goofy smile that greeted her.

"Hey there, darlin'," Steve said. Belinda came to a halt, collecting a few breaths. He looked different in shorts and a shirt with no clutch of pens in his pocket.

"I came to speak to Adam about a few things. Is he home?" He turned and looked at the Hostetlers' front door.

"I can help you. He can't be bothered

right now." Steve grinned and stepped down from the porch.

"I need to do a quick inspection, have another look at Adam's hives. Seems we have a mite problem in the area. It's the worst I've ever seen. I'm hoping Adam got lucky, but I have to check. Is he at work?"

Belinda explained about the accident and led the inspector to all three apiaries. Luckily Adam's twice-a-year application of Apiguard had done its job. "I've never seen someone work around bees like that without some form of protection." Steve sounded in awe, not like Adam had sounded at all. Adam hated when she went without protective wear, but needs must, especially since she had just returned home when the inspector arrived.

"I've worked around them for years, tending my gardens." Belinda pointed across the road as they descended the hill behind Adam's property.

"I don't want to offend you by offering advice you didn't ask for. But if he's laid up for a spell, I'll pass on anything I can to help. I'm not sure what all you know about keeping healthy hives and all, but I recommend monthly checks of all the hives. And soon, you should see to housekeeping and bee stores," Stephen said.

"Housekeeping?"

"This time of year, things are slowing down. We've had a dry summer, less to forage on. Most beekeepers clean away any dead bees that haven't been carried off. They can sometimes collect in the bottom of hives. You also need to check for overcrowding. This is a time when you have to decide whether to help feed them if they can't find plenty for themselves. If they don't have enough stored up for winter, a hive won't make it. Adam has a lot of hives here, and that takes a lot of food."

"I know that part. Actually, we are doing so well thanks to my family's farm over there, which is mainly plants and flowers. I plan to do a small harvest mid-August."

"That's good."

"What do I do for overcrowding?" Belinda asked, noting that this might be an issue even if mites weren't.

"Add more supers." Sounded easy enough. "I know the hives here near the house have plenty of water sources, but that spot with the apple trees, not so much."

"Can I just place water beside them without buying those fancy bottles you see in beekeeping books?"

Steven laughed. "Yes. As long as you keep water in them; maybe add some sugar," he winked. "Don't want unhappy bees swarming off."

"A swarm in July ain't worth a fly," Belinda spouted absentmindedly. "My dawdi, my grandfather, used to say that."

"Exactly. I tell that one to the newbies

all the time." Steve laughed. "You know, July is also a good time to split colonies, since broods are bigger."

"Split colonies?" Belinda knew nothing about that, and immediately bit her bottom lip.

"Oh yeah. Watch your step," Steve pointed to a dip in the earth as they crested the hill. "Adam could add more profit selling nucs."

"Nucs?"

Stephen chuckled. "Nucleous hives. Lots of people want to take up beekeeping and you can ship them practically anywhere in the world." Belinda couldn't imagine the mail service would be happy about handling bees, packaged or not. "I don't offer this advice to many, but you two have the makings of the best apiary I have ever seen. Everything is well-maintained, your bees are healthy, even when those close by have problems. I think this would be a good next step for Adam to consider."

When they reached his truck, Belinda replied, "I will mention it to him." She needed to talk to Mica, ask how hard splitting colonies would be, how much profit it could generate. She imagined that the income would help Adam's family tremendously.

"I have some information here in the truck, pamphlets and such." He sifted through a small box in the back seat until he had a good selection.

"Here, read these over, show them to him when he is feeling better. I have to be out this way in a couple weeks to check on a couple places not faring as well as Adam's. I can print off some more literature for you two to look over." He slipped into the front seat, then eyed the darkening sky. "Looks like we might get that rain they keep teasing us with." Rain would be a blessing right now, as dry as it had been lately.

"Oh, here is my card too." He offered it to her. "You can call anytime you have questions or worries."

"Thank you, Steve." Belinda felt better taking care of Adam's livelihood with Steve a phone call away.

"You know, I can ask a woman I know when she plans on separating colonies and perhaps if the timing is right and Adam is able to travel, I could take you two to see her."

"That would be *wunderbaar*. Hands on is better than reading." Even as she spoke, she surprised herself with how easy the words came. Before Adam, books were as close to stepping out of her comforts as she got, and now she was selling flowers and honey and talking to state inspectors and contemplating a trip to visit a perfect stranger. She never would have thought she was capable of any of this until Adam had showed her what she could do. She could never repay him for seeing more in her than she did herself.

"I agree. You tell him it's been another five-star review. He knows what it means."

"*Danki* for all your help."

"You're welcome. You take care of that fellow and those hives."

"I will. Goodbye, Steve." He drove away as the first drops begin to fall.

Chapter Twenty-Four

"A DAM!" BELINDA RUSHED INTO HIS bedroom, breathless. Adam jerked awake and rolled over, shirtless, and what little breath she had vanished. Hadn't Ada said he was awake and eager to see her? Belinda gripped the doorframe to keep from toppling over at the sight of his bare torso. Even under the tight wrapping around his four broken ribs, those muscles his clothes had hinted at before hadn't been exaggerated one bit. She quickly turned away as any respectful *maedel* would do. Today was certainly one for the books.

"I'm sorry. Ada said I could come in. I'll come back," She made a motion to leave.

"Bee, wait," Adam quickly said, bringing her to a halt. She could hear the strain in

his voice. She chided herself for her carelessness in startling him. "Don't go."

She stilled. *Bee*, he'd called her again.
She liked when he called her that. Like she
was important, as important to him as his
bees. But maybe it was simply easier than
her given name, she reminded herself. He
slipped into a shirt, folded neatly at the end
of his bed. "All right."

Belinda turned cautiously, her cheeks
flaming. No way would Susanne Zook ever
have broken Adam's heart if she had seen
where he kept it.

Adam chuckled, making her redden even
more. "You look embarrassed."

"I shouldn't have barged in. This is your
room." A fact that she was now becoming too aware of. What kind of woman just
barged into a man's personal space? "I just
was so excited and Ada said..." Adam held up
a hand.

"It's all right, Belinda. You have a brother.
And I know he and Ivan have taken you and
Tabitha swimming a time or two. There's no
sense in getting embarrassed."

True...but Ivan didn't make her heart do
backflips.

She stepped into his room and worked
to control her breathing. "Did startling you
jostle your injuries? Are you in pain?" She
winced. She didn't dare glance at his upper
torso a second time. No need with such a

vivid picture already stained into her mind's eye.

"It's going to hurt no matter what. Not your fault." She could see pain etched on his face. Adam slowly moved himself into a sitting position. Guilt ravaged her for causing him further pain.

Belinda turned to take in the room, his personal space. The floors resembled butterscotch candy, smooth and polished. There was a five-drawer dresser, a hook where he hung his Sunday best, and one simple chest in the corner. Did he keep his secrets in there, she wondered, staring at its cherry-tinted wood. She and Tabitha had hope chests of their own, filled with linens, birthday cards, and books that Belinda found so wonderful, she purchased them to keep instead or returning to the local bookmobile. She bit her lip, clenching her dress nervously. She was standing in his room and couldn't remember a single reason she had come in the first place.

"Did you come to check up on me, Belinda?" His tone remained steady, only flustering her more.

"I've come before, but you were sleeping. I have something to tell you." She regained her composure and beamed a smile. "I've had such a day, and I couldn't go home before telling you about it."

"You look...like sunshine. I feel better already," he teased. At least she thought him to be teasing until something in his eyes flickered. "Mammi always said sunshine was the best medicine. She was right." He shifted slightly, a boyish smile playing on his lips. "Did something happen today?"

"Something did," she finally remembered. Adam smiling like that made it hard to concentrate. "After dropping off all the honey and making flower deliveries, I..."

"You did what?" That deep voice she found she rather liked more and more suddenly shifted into a growl. "Was this what *Mamm* was keeping from me?" His body jerked angrily and he let out another groan. It was obvious she was causing more distress than he needed. Had he not known she was making deliveries? The tight binding around his middle seemed to not be holding everything together right now.

"Adam, please," Belinda begged, moving nearer. "I didn't mean to upset you. I will go." She sucked in a sob. "The last thing I meant to do was cause you to hurt yourself."

"Don't go," he said between bated breaths. "Finish, please."

Belinda bit her lip and stared at him with sorrowful blue eyes. "You're clearly in pain, and I caused it." He closed his eyes, took a slow breath, and opened them again.

"It's not so bad, I promise," he assured her. "Now tell me everything," he urged. She didn't believe him one bit.

"I made the deliveries," she repeated.

"We can't stay in business if I don't," she explained when his lips tightened into a firm line. He clearly didn't like that she had done that.

"I'm sorry I got hurt, Belinda. You should never have had to go alone."

"*Nee*, it was fine," she quickly assured him. So he wasn't upset at her, just at himself, again. How did he not see that he alone couldn't do everything? "I should have done it long ago, Adam. We both know that." She pinned him with a serious look. "I took flowers to the florist and Marcy was as nice as you said she would be. She said I am her best supplier and that she hopes we have a long relationship working together. And Jackson," she smiled. "Jackson is as curious as you said too."

"You see now that there was nothing to fear. I'm happy to see you happy." His stiff frown lifted slightly. "And as I warned you, Jackson asks lots of questions."

"*Jah*, he does." She cocked a hip and waved a long delicate finger toward him. "He thinks you have a girlfriend. You should not lie to *kinner*." She watched him swallow hard, a nervous grin playing on his lips.

Belinda stepped slowly around the bed to the window and looked out. "I went to the bakery. I got to see my flowers on a big wedding cake. They were so beautiful." She turned to him again, a blush flirting with her skin. Her freckles were multiplying from summer's time with her and he found he adored each one. She touched her cheek. "Sorry. I'm just..."

"Exhilarated," he muttered. "I like this side of you."

"You do?" She really hadn't a clue just how beautiful and amazing she was, and that made him love her all the more. He startled at the thought, glad that she started talking again before noticing the shock of his own thoughts hitting him.

When she finished telling him about her visit with Marcy and Jackson, Adam hoped she wasn't ready to leave. "What else? Tell me what you did next." *Nice save, Adam.*

"Well, Mia is *wunderbaar*, like you said. She talks differently and I've never met anyone who uses their hands so much when speaking, but I really liked it. The way she says things is so, so, enchanting. She gave me four large cupcakes and...oh, wait." She ran out of the room and before he could exhale fully, she returned with a blue box. She sat down on the side of his bed gingerly, so as not to disturb him, a breath away. He could smell the flowers, the bakery, and sunshine waft off her. God, how he'd missed her.

She lifted the box's lid. "Mia said it was your favorite." She tilted the box so he could peek inside.

"She thinks she has to feed me every time I walk in there. I think she's using me to test her recipes." He winked. She smiled and he quickly lifted the muffin out and bit into it greedily. It was that, or kiss her. He assumed she hadn't been kissed before and imagined she was not yet ready, but still, it was tempting to try to steal at least one. Lying in bed for days with so little to fill his time, thoughts of kissing Belinda had played in his head a lot.

"I went to the market to share my treat with Tabitha." Her shoulders straightened. She was proud of all her accomplishments today, and so was he.

"You *have* been busy today." Maybe they could deliver flowers together next Saturday. He hoped he would be up to it by then. The doctor had said six weeks without working. Riding in a buggy with the most beautiful woman in the district didn't count as work. Pure pleasure, that would be.

"I ran into Abner Lapp today." Her voice lost all its excitement and he heard the shift clearly. "Well, I met him at the produce auction when Mica took me first, but I ran into him again today at the market." Adam lifted a brow as she fingered a thread loosening from his quilt. "Tabitha sort of pushed me to be nice and now Abner wants to take me fishing, or walking, or something." Her face scrunched adorably, but all Adam registered was that Abner Lapp was back in Havenlee and asking Belinda on a date. Had this been the extra interest Ivan had been hinting at?

"He did, huh?" Adam frowned, shoved another bite into his mouth. "I didn't know he moved back." He set the rest of the muffin back into the box, appetite spoiled.

"He says he is opening a leather shop." To his ears, she didn't sound impressed—but that might be wishful thinking on his part. "I don't want to go," she whispered. Those big blue eyes and soft-spoken words were trampling all over his heart. If he just leaned forward a bit, he could make her forget all about Abner Lapp. Her scent covered him completely and he leaned into that waft of air more for himself than for her.

"Then don't," he said in a grave tone. The urge to pull her closer filled him. It would be worth whatever pain four broken ribs cost him. Then again, *Mamm* would probably have a conniption if she caught sight of that under her roof. They were close enough now, it would be worth risking. Belinda's eyes widened. She felt it too.

298

After overcoming so many obstacles today, she might as well tell Adam how she felt while she was still riding this cloud of bravery. He had to know she had no interest in Mica's old friend, and that she was having some feelings she wanted to explore further, with him. Before she could open her mouth and let the words fly carelessly into the air, Adam leaned slightly closer, his eyes on her lips, and she panicked.

How many nights had she thought about that kiss, her first? Belinda jumped to her feet, as if only now realizing she was in his room, on his bed, and near enough to be kissed. What would Ada think if she walked in—and was she even ready to kissed?

"You were right." She brushed her hands down her apron and nervously tidied her *kapp*. "No one all day even looked at my ugly mark."

"Strawberry kiss," he corrected, not taking his eyes off her. She backed away farther.

"So you need not worry about me selling flowers or honey, or going to town on my own." She lifted her chin and struggled mightily not to take the bottom lip between her teeth.

"I'm proud of you for that, though I wish it wasn't because I got hurt. But Belinda, that's not what I'm worried about." His words were so direct, his gaze arrowed onto her.

How did one respond to that? Head

spinning, the only thing Belinda could do was leave. She needed air, and time to think. "Well...uh...you just heal and rest. The bees are happy, the flowers are selling, and everyone has been helping, so I don't have to it all alone. The inspector came by. Apparently, there is an outbreak of mites in the area, but we checked everything and your hives are safe. He said he gave them a five-star review." Each word came out in a nervous stutter. Despite the urge to run, put some distance between them, she couldn't leave without thanking him for all he'd done to help her. "I have some things to discuss with you about the hives, but that can wait." She needed to get away from him before she did something more stupid, like fall harder for him. Adam didn't want a wife, he wanted a hundred hives and a busy, solitary life.

"Today I had an adventure and it's all because of you, Adam."

"Yeah, I'm a keeper," he said, leaning back against his stack of pillows.

"I'll come back tomorrow and we can talk more...about the hives." She stepped to the doorway. "If there is anything I can do to show my appreciation, just say it. I could never have gone to town without you encouraging me."

Adam stared at her for the longest moment, and then grinned. "Anything?"

She swallowed hard, noting his eyes had traveled down to her lips again. "Anything," she boldly replied. She should tell him now. Tell him she wished *he* had asked to take her fishing, not Abner Lapp, that he was the only person she wanted to walk under the moonlight with—but she had missed that opportunity, letting too many thoughts run through her head, just as she might have missed her only chance at a kiss.

"Let me think on it and get back to you."

Chapter Twenty-Five

ADAM TOOK A BREATH, GLAD to be out of the house and into the sun. Late-July heat bore down on him, but he didn't mind. He needed to see Belinda, talk to her. He walked cautiously across the road, mindful of his steps. Mica was at another auction, Tabitha at the market, so Belinda would be alone today, aside from her grandmother, and Adam was fairly certain Mollie Bender had taken a liking to him. That last casserole alone was signature Mollie, and the chocolate cake made especially for him was like permission to proceed.

When he didn't find Belinda in the greenhouses as Mollie suggested, Adam knew where to find her. He'd spotted her earlier, dressed in jeans and carrying her veil. She had to be at his mammi's, checking the hives for the last harvest coming in just a few more weeks. It amazed him how much one woman could accomplish throughout a day. It was a long walk, but he would take his time. His ribs were still sensitive, but he was healing well and *Mamm* agreed it would lift his mood to go see her. Funny how he didn't have to tell his mother where he was going, but she knew all the same.

At the base of the hill, he heard it. It sounded like a madman with a bat. Surely those town boys hadn't returned. Adam picked up his pace just as another clash resounded through the air. With some effort, he reached the crest of the hill where fence separated pasture and parcel, and came to a sudden halt at the scene splayed out before him. Adam knuckled both eyes clear of dust.

Not a madman, but a madwoman, with two large pots, pounding them together as if trying to wake the dead. If this was some adventure of sorts Belinda had bravely talked herself into, some new experience to add to her newfound independence, he wasn't impressed. In fact, he half wished he hadn't tried coaxing her at all.

"What in the world are you doing?" he yelled toward her, and began slowly making his way over. Belinda shot up an arm.

"Stop there!" He did, though he hadn't a clue why. "I found them," she said, and pointed to a section of fencing. Adam looked—and that's when he realized Mammi's back gate was no longer a faded rust red peeling with age, but dark, a thousand honey bees dark. *His lost swarms.*

In this slow-moving summer, he had almost forgotten about the bees that had swarmed off months ago. What were the chances? He shook his head and watched Belinda bang pots together again. She quickly fetched an empty super she must have carried up here, along with the two large pots. The woman truly was stronger than she looked. She nudged the wooden box closer to the gate in deft movements.

"Bee, you can't think to..." But his words fell on deaf ears. He all but raced to reach her, to stop her from this exercise in blatant stupidity, but by the time Adam drew near, he was gasping in pain, soaked in sweat, and scared to death that the most important person in his life was about to do something terribly stupid while he had no way of stopping her.

"Don't come any closer. They aren't very pleased right now." Adam was none too happy with her either.

"Neither will I be, if you think you are going to capture them. Bee, you're not even wearing a veil." He took another slow breath to rein in his nausea.

"I dropped it," she replied, and then the woman dared to wink at him. Oddly, instead of anger, in that wink, Adam felt the earth move. Spellbound and speechless, and hoping not about to pass out from exertion, he watched her scoop up bees by the handful and lower them into the super. Defenseless to do anything, unable to talk sense into her, he could only watch from twenty feet away, a bystander to her recklessness. How could someone afraid of so much be so fearless?

Halfway through her task, Belinda paused. "Hear that?" she called out to him.

He bent an ear her way, wary and alert. An even hum rose, and soon the rest of the gate became visible as the remaining bees, like obedient soldiers, went straight into the super without any nudging or forcing. It was the most amazing thing Adam had ever witnessed in all his days.

"I got the queen." Belinda smiled proudly, her eyes glittering in triumph. Suddenly Adam wasn't thinking of his lost queens, just the most important one, the brave woman capturing them right along with his heart.

Later that evening, as frog song filled the warm air, Belinda went to check the answering machine at the phone shanty. Barefoot, she kept to the grass cradling both sides of the pavement before slipping inside the cramped space. One message from Mia, the baker, panicked as she asked if Belinda could deliver daisies by tomorrow for a rushed retirement event, and another from Daed. Belinda missed her father's voice and was lulled by its familiar sound as he gave Dawdi's most recent update. It seemed not taking all those treatments had sparked a bit of life back into Saul Graber, but cancer was not something that simply disappeared. Belinda brushed a tear from her cheek, knowing time was still running out.

When the telephone rang, Belinda let out a squeak of surprise before answering. "Hello," she said.

"Belinda. How nice to hear your voice," Mudder said on the other end of the line. Belinda felt her pinned-up emotions deflate. How she wanted to tell her mother everything that has transpired since her leaving. They chatted for a moment about the market stand and then about the vegetable garden. "Has Mammi finished canning beans and started the corn? Saul has a bit of a garden, but not enough to press on me. The neighbors here have kept us in food for days with their charitable gifts." She sounded tired, but happy. How would she react if Belinda told her about Adam, about her strong and growing feelings? Would she be happy Belinda was making deliveries for herself and for Adam, all alone? Suddenly the wooden shanty door swung open and there he was, the topic of her thoughts. Belinda held up a finger, indicating for Adam to keep silent.

"Mammi just finished the last three runs of beans and the house is full of tomatoes and corn lining all the counters," Belinda said into the receiver. Adam leaned stiffly on the doorframe, neither stepping forward, nor away to give her some privacy. He shouldn't be out again, overdoing it. He should be resting. She gave him a narrow look which only earned her a mischievous smile.

"I'm sorry, what?" Belinda tried ignoring her distracting neighbor as *Mudder* went on about Pleasants, Kentucky, and its tight-knit Old Order Amish community. When Adam opened his mouth fully, as if threatening a holler, Belinda swatted at him playfully. She placed her hand over the receiver. "Would you give me a minute?" she asked him. To her surprise, he shook his head back and forth, indicating he absolutely would not, and simply stared at her. Wasn't it enough that those eyes had a way of making her breaths labored when he was doing nothing at all? Did he have to tease her too?

"*Nee*, I have been helping. We finished the harvest but it's near time to start again." Belinda held his gaze as her mother poured out more questions. "He can be a bit moody and awfully bossy, but I think he is learning that I know plenty about what I'm doing." Belinda grinned, earning her one of Adam's more challenging looks. It was the kind the made her knees feel like jelly.

"I hated to hear about his accident," her mother continued. "Such a sweet boy he always was, and a dutiful son. Do you find him handsome, a good man?"

Belinda's cheeks blushed. Good thing Adam couldn't hear a thing *Mamm* was saying. "*Jah*. I mean, sort of." She couldn't confess, not with him standing there.

"Mica says he is a hard worker." Adam was more than that. He was the kind of man who put everything aside for others. The kind who kept his word. But not one who followed his doctor's orders so well.

"He does work hard, but I'm not sure he knows how to rest so he can heal properly." Adam narrowed his gaze. Something warm washed over her. He knew the conversation had shifted from canning to him. "Mamm, I should go. Is there anything else you want me to tell Tabitha, Mica or Mammi?"

"*Nee*, I will call again. Oh, Bee, my dear. One more thing."

"Just one." She smiled at her mother's "Just one more thing" ritual. Adam's gaze grew concentrated, deep. She swallowed hard in the face of it. "Don't ignore what *Gott* is placing before you. I know about Abner returning to Havenlee. May be best you stop spending so much time at our neighbor's and see if you and he have things in common." Belinda bit her lip.

Sensing the conversation had become too serious, Adam reached out and poked at her ribs playfully. She jerked, slapped away his next attempt, and suppressed a giggle.

"I don't have time for that, and I'm not sure I would want to even if I did," Belinda replied to her mother.

"Okay. We'll see. I love you, Belinda. Tell everyone I will call tomorrow." When she finally hung up, Adam burst into laughter.

"You should have seen your face."

"Did you want Mamm to hear you?" She flushed and nervously began tidying herself.

"What would she have heard?" he said. "You laughing? She might have liked that. You don't do it enough."

"Adam." She tried to charge by him through the doorway. He didn't budge.

"You have a nice laugh." He stepped back, let her through. "You should bring it with you to supper tomorrow night. Mamm insists." He closed the shanty door before she could respond.

All the way home, Belinda pondered it. His teasing and the invitation to supper, Mamm's words, and that lingering smell of sawdust that Adam somehow still carried even though he hadn't been to the mill in weeks. She shook her head. *Silly thoughts.* First thing she was going to do when she got into the house was ask Mica how to keep a stubborn man down so he could heal.

She turned just as she reached the adjoining mailboxes and veered right. Home.

Chapter Twenty-Six

G OING TO TOWN WAS GETTING easier, but why Tabitha insisted on Belinda going today with so much to do at home was beyond her. At least she had the treat of running into Nelly, who was working at Zimmerman's. Spending time with Adam and keeping up her regular duties, Belinda had failed in recent weeks to connect with her closest friends.

"So, we are going to be published in a couple weeks," Nelly continued, after announcing Caleb had proposed.

"I'm so happy for you." Belinda hugged her. "How did he ask?"

"Not like in one of your books," Nelly laughed. "But he did take both my hands in his and asked me to sit. Then he kneeled in front of me," Nelly said dreamily. "It was so perfect. I am the luckiest woman in the world."

"I agree. You two will have the greatest life together."

"I want you and Salina to stand with me." Nelly gripped her hand. "I know you don't like such things, but please say you will try. You are my best friend, and I want you standing beside me on the happiest day of my life." The old Belinda would have cringed at such a request.

"I will be right beside you. I promise." The sound of the bell ringing overhead alerted the two that a customer had entered the store. Belinda walked with Nelly toward the front. Once the woman had paid for her purchase of chocolate chips and a bag of oatmeal, Belinda followed Nelly back to the aisle where she had been stocking shelves.

"I notice Abner Lapp is back in town," Nelly said.

"I know."

"You should know that he told Caleb he's hoping to court you once he gets your parents' permission," Nelly informed her, as she stacked coffee on a shelf.

"He already asked if I would go fishing or walking with him. I'm not sure how to tell him no. I don't want to be rude, but I also don't want to spend time with him. My parents can't decide that for me." It was a particular bee farmer who had already consumed her heart. He was the only man

Belinda wished to spend her time with. In the last week alone, they had shared several meals together and played more card games than she thought had existed. Belinda couldn't help but wonder about his recent fascination with soils and plants, but chalked it up to boredom. Adam was stuck with so little he could do until he was fully healed.

"Oh, Belinda. He is handsome, opening his own leather shop, and wants to spend time with you. You might have a proposal by the end of the week." A sly look came into her eyes. "Unless you have changed your thoughts about a particular handsome man who happens to sell honey for a living."

Belinda couldn't help but grin. Of course Nelly knew Belinda was in love with Adam, but Nelly also knew Adam would never change his thoughts about marriage after suffering such a heartbreak. Nelly nudged Belinda's shoulder, and just as Belinda was ready to share the account of her recent visits with Adam, a familiar voice intruded.

"Hello, Belinda." She spun around to find Abner walking their way down the dimly lit aisle.

Nelly giggled. "Hiya, Abner. We were just talking about you." Why hadn't they heard the bell ring? Belinda bristled.

"Is that so?" Abner's dark eyes danced with delight. He was handsome and possessed many fine qualities, but he made Be-

313

linda's skin so itchy with discomfort that it was hard not to scratch. "I thought I might find you here." Had he been looking for her?

"I should go. I'm already behind today and just needed to pick up everything for Tabitha's chicken dish tonight." Belinda scooted past him until she was in the open area again, Nelly close behind.

"Could I give you a lift home?" Abner urged. "I have nothing else to do right now."

"I have a buggy, but *danki*." Belinda looked to Nelly, hoping for help out of this awkward conversation. She was not a fan of this kind of attention, at least not from Abner. She thought of Adam. The way he leaned toward her the other day, close enough to kiss. If she hadn't panicked, she might have gotten her first kiss.

The bell over the door jingled and all eyes lifted to see who had just entered. Lynn Christner, Noel's mother. Too many people were running into Belinda today, kicking her nerves up a notch. Could it get any worse?

Lynn gave a wry smile as she studied the three standing in the aisle. Surely Lynn would be displeased Belinda was talking with Abner and not her precious Noel.

"Excuse me," Belinda offered politely. "I need to go." She went to move past Abner, but he sidestepped into her path. She clutched the bags closer to her chest.

"Let me help you to your buggy?" Abner reached out to take her bags.

"Nelly, it's not polite to make customers wait. Your *onkel* won't like you ignoring paying customers. I am in a hurry," Lynn called from the front of the store. Nelly offered a sympathetic look, but it was clear Belinda would have to deal with Abner alone. All the confidence and self-assurance she had worked for all summer vanished as she stood between Abner Lapp and her mother's dear friend Lynn, both blocking her only exit.

"I...I..." Her head was spinning, her heart pounding, and she was fairly certain breathing was something a person could actually forget how to do. She clenched the bag of spices and butter to her chest and took one step to the left.

"Maybe we could stop by the diner for pie, before you head home?" Abner grinned that cocky smile of his. His confidence bothered her. Belinda didn't like cocky, any more than she liked the newly arrived customers being drawn to the scene.

"Excuse me," she said, before fleeing into the little backroom she and Nelly used to use to play board games in when they were little and their mothers chatted in the store for hours.

"I will be right here when you get out," Abner yelled after her.

That's what she was afraid of. Breath quickening, she turned the corner. Once out of sight, Belinda veered right. The supply room was small, but no one would come looking for her in here. She closed the door, quickly secured the lock, and let out a pinned-up breath. Once her breathing slowed, she realized the consequences of her actions. There was only one door and now she felt as trapped as a wounded animal. Nelly would have customers to tend to, and her family was too far away to offer any assistance in the mess she had gotten herself into. She was on her own, alone.

Dropping her face into her hands, tears spilled out. Why did her sister send her to town today? She wanted to be home, with her flowers and buzzing bees. Her heartbeat began pounding in panic again. What was wrong with her? *Apparently everything*, she decided, and wept harder.

Adam thought things were going swell. He was still a bit stiff, but healing. Spending these extra weeks with his parents had reminded him of the simple joys his busy life had suffocated. And then there was Belinda. His heart had no doubts what he wanted any longer. Spending time with her these past days, unrushed, had given them the chance to grow even closer. But leave it to his best friend to stop by today and spread the latest gossip, pouring a cup of vinegar straight into Adam's happy little basket of hope.

He knocked on the Grabers' front door. No matter how many conversations Belinda and he had about her willingness to handle delivery days on her own, he had seen apprehension in her eyes. Belinda did what needed to be done. It was that simple. But she clearly wasn't fully comfortable going to town alone so often.

She had also expressed that she had no interest in Abner Lapp, who was inviting himself to supper at the Grabers' house tonight, according to Tobias. Adam wasn't the kind of man who marked territory or staked claims, but he wasn't having Abner step into what he had finally admitted he wanted.

The door swung open. "Is Belinda home?"

Tabitha motioned him inside. "She isn't." Why did Tabitha look so ill?

"Is everything all right? Has something happened with your dawdi?" Adam removed his hat and stepped inside the doorway. If Saul Graber had passed, Belinda would be heartbroken. She spoke so often about her grandfather that Adam felt he knew him himself.

"*Nee*, that's not it. Mica is right. I shouldn't have meddled. I just wanted her to see she wasn't the ugly duckling she always thought she was. And Abner is such a good

man and seemed interested. He talks about
her all the time, comes to the market daily
and asks me what kind of things she likes,"
Tabitha blurted out defensively.

"I'm sorry. I'm not sure what you're
saying." But even as he spoke, understanding settled in. Tabitha had played a hand
in Abner's supper invitation this evening.
Heat rose up inside him. Why couldn't Belinda's family just let her be herself? She
was content at home, in her gardens, around
the greenhouses and hives, in her mother's
kitchen. And there was not one thing wrong
with it. In fact, it was those qualities that
made her perfect for him, and him for her.
Adam knew what he wanted, what she
needed, and couldn't stand by and let others
try and alter that.

"I'm a horrible sister. I told Mamm about
Abner and how Belinda let him walk her to
her buggy. How he asks about her all the
time. Mamm said I should give her a little
push. So I sent Belinda to buy a few things
and made sure Abner knew where she would
be." Tabitha sighed. "And I invited him for
supper without asking her first. I did that,
to her, and I feel horrible about it now. What
kind of sister am I?" *Indeed*, Adam wished
to say.

"Belinda loves you. She knows you mean
well." He wanted to believe his words were
true, even as he knew *he* wouldn't be so
forgiving in Belinda's shoes. Tabitha had no

right to push her sister into a situation that would make her uncomfortable.

"But is it really okay that she is shy and timid and doesn't want to be courted?" Painful regret racked her voice.

"*Jah*, it is. She is Belinda. That is who she is. She doesn't need pushed or altered, just loved for herself." Adam said. *Where was Mollie?* Adam looked around the kitchen and into the sitting room. Belinda's grandmother would have never allowed Tabitha to play matchmaker in this intrusive way. When Adam faced Tabitha again, she was staring at him with wide green eyes.

"*Ach*, no. I hurt you too, I see. She said you didn't like her like that." She shot him a sideways glance. "But that isn't true, is it?"

"No, it isn't. I love her," he said with utmost sincerity.

"Oh Adam, I'm so sorry." She looked about to cry. Adam stepped forward and placed an arm around her. "What have I done?"

"You didn't know, and neither does she, yet. I hope to tell her soon. So, when will she be back?" he pulled away.

"I don't know. She should have come home hours ago." She lowered her head in shame.

"Hours?" He tensed.

"Mica said leave her be, that she was happier helping you than she has been since she was a child. I should see if Mica will go look for her."

"*Jah*, I can handle that." He aimed for the door. "I'll see she gets home safe."

"What about your injuries?" Tabitha gave him a doubtful look.

"I can handle a buggy just fine. Now where exactly did she go?" Adam placed his hat back on his head, determination swirling in his gut.

"Zimmerman's. I just sent her for a few things. What if something..." Tabitha's hand flew to her mouth.

"I will find her, bring her home. Trust all is well." Adam went to the door, giving himself a reminder to trust, too. If Belinda was sharing a ride or walk with Abner, he didn't know what he would do.

"*Danki*."

"No thanks needed. But I do intend on having a talk with her. So don't expect to see us anytime soon." He winked. Tabitha nodded, understanding his meaning as he slipped back out the door.

Adam hurried to get the buggy ready. The simple task was tedious, but at least he could breathe without feeling like needles were being jabbed into him. When he got to Zimmerman's, he carefully got down from the buggy seat, cautiously took the steps, and strolled inside. Tabitha said this was the only place Belinda planned to go today, and Mica's horse and buggy outside was evidence that she was still here. A quick scan told him plenty. Abner was staring at a quilt hanging on the back wall, looking bored. Bee, on the other hand, was nowhere in sight. Nelly finished ringing up an older man and he went to the counter as casually as he could manage.

"Where is she?"

Nelly looked about to burst. "How did you know?" Adam shrugged. "She's hiding in the storeroom. She won't come out. I was about to call Mica and leave a message on their machine," Nelly whispered. "I wanted to try to talk to her, but customers have been like flies on buttermilk and I haven't even left the counter. Abner showed up and insisted on taking her home and she panicked." Nelly sniffled. "I should have run him out of the store, but customers started pouring in and Lynn Christner was giving her that look. You know the one." Adam did. The woman could scald the wool off sheep with her deep-set frowns and piercing glares.

"It's all right. She knows you would have helped if you were able. I came to take her home," Adam said.

"She won't come out. Not with him here." Nelly looked over his shoulder toward Abner still lingering in the arched opening in the back. "Mica usually handles these matters," Nelly said.

"Then I need to get him out of the way first," he said matter-of-factly. "I *will* be taking her home to her family." He scanned the store. "Is there another way out of the storeroom? She will be embarrassed coming out if you get another rush of customers." The bell overhead jingled again, proving he was right to worry.

"*Nee*, but the shipping room has a back door. What have you got in mind?" Nelly asked, seemingly impressed Adam had no plans of leaving without Belinda.

"Run him off and simply take her home," he said, as if it were going to be as easy as that. Nelly's eyes went wide at his bold statement.

"I see why she won't give Abner the time of day now." Nelly grinned, lifting his spirits. "I think she feels the same, in case you want to know." Nelly winked. His heart lifted, grounding him deeper in his pursuit.

With purposeful strides, Adam marched through an aisle of canned goods to the back of the store.

"Hello, Abner," Adam greeted him.

"Adam Hostetler." Abner offered a hand. "Heard about the accident. You look to be getting around well enough."

"*Jah*, just a few bruises left. I think Mamm's soup and Belinda's special lemonade was all I needed." Abner bristled at the mention of Belinda's name, and Adam redirected the conversation. "How long have you been back in Havenlee?" He already knew the answer, but thought a more cordial approach would save him a few bruises. Adam was never a fan of taking the low road. He suspected Abner felt much the same. It was not their way, being physical and quarrelsome. But if it came to that, he would do whatever was necessary. One way or another, Adam was taking Belinda home.

"A few weeks now." Abner shifted his body toward the back room. "I'm opening a shop. Just about got everything ready. I was hoping to work on getting the rest of my plans in order." The man clearly wasn't leaving easily. "I wasn't aware you and Belinda were...friends."

"More than friends," Adam put in.

"I was told by a few that she wasn't dating." Abner lifted a thick, challenging brow. "I would think you too busy caring for your family to have time for...friends. Are you throwing your hat into the ring?" he said between clenched teeth.

"I don't need to. My hat is the only hat in it." Abner took one step forward to object, but Adam held up a hand to keep him at bay. "Courting is private." It wasn't a lie. "And I won't step aside. My mind is set on it." Adam lifted his chin and smiled.

Chapter Twenty-Seven

T HE DOOR FLEW OPEN AND Belinda jumped up from the box she had been perched on. There stood Adam, a set of keys dangling in his hands, and a sheepish smile spread across his handsome face. She was horrified, him seeing her in such an embarrassing position. How could she prove herself worthy if she couldn't handle a quick trip into town without needing assistance?

He cleared his throat and slipped inside the little room, closing the door behind him. "Thought I might find you here," he said. He looked red-faced and sweaty. He shouldn't be here, not in his condition. Why wasn't he home resting?

"How?" she managed, trying not to cry again.

"Oh, well, ya know." He shrugged and

leaned against the door. Books hadn't prepared her for how the damsel felt when the
hero came to her rescue. Despite her embarrassment, she immediately felt calm, safe.
Adam was near; all was well.

"Did he say something to cause this?" He
leaned forward, winced, and then brushed a
tear from her cheek.

"*Nee*. I'm such a baby." She dropped her
head into her hands again and the flood
resumed. "Tabitha said I had to go and then
Nelly said Abner wants to court me and
that I could be proposed to by the end of the
week, and I thought I was getting sick right
then but then Lynn gave me that scary look
and Abner persisted so I ran in here and
hid."

She looked up to him and saw him
watching her as if his heart would break.
When she blinked back the tears, he spoke.
"But you don't want to be here, do you?"

"*Nee*. I don't want to be here." She bit her
lip.

He lowered his head, fidgeted with the
keys in his hand.

"I want to go home. Even the hot greenhouse has more air than this little room."
She tried for a grin, but failed.

Adam reached out for her hand. "Bee,
my queen," he smiled gently. "Come with me."
She was awestruck and relieved. "My horse
is behind the store. Let's slip out of here and
I can drive you home. Nelly and Caleb will

see your buggy is returned." He had come for her. She couldn't hide what that did to her.

"What if someone sees us?"

"Are you embarrassed to be seen with me, Belinda Graber?" he teased, as she wiped her face with her sleeve.

"You should be more worried that I will embarrass *you*. No one wants to be seen with a crybaby."

"I'll risk it." He laughed, and she couldn't help but feel herself yield to his overwhelming charms.

"All that matters is what you want. If you want to stay in this smelly supply room all night, I'll walk out right now. Or," his thumb made a small circle over her hand, "you can let me sneak you out of here and drive you home. It could be quite an adventure. Bee, the queen of masterful escapes." An unexpected laugh escaped her. Not only had he come for her, but Adam wasn't about to let her hide herself in a closet.

"I don't know how I put up with you, or how you put up with me," she said, after taking in a shaky breath.

"We are quite the pair, aren't we?" He gave her hand a kiss and reached for the door handle. He always knew how to distract her. It wasn't fair, the effect he had on her. He had made it clear, time and time again, he had no interest beyond friendship. Still, despite the future heartbreak that seemed

certain, she knew she would follow him anywhere.

No one saw them sneak out the back. Belinda sat in the buggy seat beside him, hands
primly on her lap. "I feel bad. Abner said he
would wait." Belinda nibbled at her lip.

"He left. He knew I was taking you home.
But if you want to go back..." Adam began.

"I don't," she quickly shot back. "And
how does he know that I'm with you?" She
glanced over and watched his lips curve up
in a smile. His hair had grown a lot and he
was in need of another cut. She had never
known a man who could grow hair faster
than grass in summer. Belinda focused on
one curl at the nape of his neck.

"Because I told him," Adam said and
smiled at her, locking gazes until he pulled
away to focus on the road.

"You must think me a coward too. What
kind of person can't even walk or ride in a
buggy with another without wanting to
cry? Tabitha will be upset with me. She's
going to tell *Mudder* and I will never hear
the end of it." She blew out an exasperated
breath.

"Tabitha is upset with herself. She told

me where you were. She knew you didn't want to go, and felt bad for letting Abner know you would be shopping today."

"She did that?" Belinda's voice hitched in surprise. Though it shouldn't surprise her how far her sister would go.

"She meant well," Adam said, "but I also made her promise me it won't happen again." Her mouth opened, then closed again. "Bee, there is nothing wrong with being timid. In fact, some people enjoy your quiet nature. And I think you are brave."

"I am not," she puffed out.

"How many people would willingly surround themselves with thousands of bees without a suit? I watched you scoop them up like grain in a bucket. You own your own business and help with two others—both mine and your family's." She hadn't thought about that. "And you *are* riding in a buggy, with a man, at nightfall as stars are about to come out, without your sister."

"I am, aren't I?" Her shoulders lifted. She looked at him and smiled, her heart galloping in her chest. Belinda was riding with a man, and she couldn't imagine doing so with any other. She loved him—his patience, his fortitude, his dedication to those he cared for. He cared enough for her to seek her out, sensing her fear from miles away. Could she be brave enough to tell him how she felt?

"Want to make it a double adventure? Add ice cream to our adventurous evening?"

"You want to take me for ice cream?" *Like a date?* He smiled, his green-blue gaze tenderly observing her, cautiously waiting for her to say yes. How strange to be wanted, by him. Nothing in life would ever be the same after this moment, and she knew it.

"I do hear it's the best cure for sadness," he continued, trying to tempt her. She was no longer sad, but didn't want to go home, end this time together. She had been craving more of it, praying for opportunities, and here Adam was, beside her in the buggy seat, smiling at her.

"As much as ice cream with you sounds *wunderbaar*, I don't think I can eat a thing with my stomach in knots. But I'm in no hurry to get home. We could take our time." She smiled bashfully.

"I have all the time in the world, for you." Adam felt his pulse rise as she sat beside him on the buggy seat, smiling timidly at him. The paint Adam had purchased was still in his room. How he wished he had brought it. It would have cheered her up considerably.

Havenlee had many back roads, all slithering into the next, weaving in and out chaotically. Adam veered down Buchannan Road. Traffic was light here and the new bridge was just at the other end. After showing Belinda the bridge, he went down Penny Patch, where most homes were Amish and farms stretched as far as the eye could see.

"The Planks have more than a dozen baby goats running around in the field. We can drive by there, and if you're feeling like real adventure, we can watch the fireflies on the lake. And you don't have to say a word if you don't want to."

"I haven't been to the lake in over a year. Let's do that," Belinda said giddily. She looked as eager as a child, wanting more, hanging on his every word. Adam had never held someone's attention so fully, had never wanted it so strongly. Since May, that moment he cornered her in her garden, needing her help, he had been captivated by her. He knew then, despite railing against it, that she was more than the shy quiet girl of his childhood. He looked over, studied her profile. Like a flower in a harsh summer wind, she seemed fragile, but Belinda was far from weak. Her roots were as strong as her will to grow, and he wanted to grow with her, feed her curiosities, and embrace her insecurities. There was still the need of her, working together to build on what they both loved, but above and beyond all practical concerns, Adam wanted her—as his wife, his life's partner, his future. She was first, above all.

She was as beautiful in evening light as she was in the morning. The little mark, the reason she had held herself back for so long, tiptoed through life, now held his attention. That blessed mark she hated had become her most beautiful feature.

After stopping along the road to pet a dozen dairy goats, Adam pulled up beside the lake. They sat in the buggy, watching fireflies dance over fields, flicker between trees, and encase the water's edge with their twinkle. "So you want to tell me what happened back at the store, or would you rather we just sit here in the quiet and not say anything?"

There was a pause as she collected her thoughts. And then, she spoke. "I don't want to be made to do things I'm not comfortable with. I don't see why I can't just be me. I don't like the attention my face gives me. People still stare." She looked up to him. "And you're staring at me now. I just want to hide under my pillow and never come out." Belinda reached up to hide her mark.

Adam shifted to face her. Slowly he pulled her hand free and held it. It fit so perfectly there, belonging in his. How could he tell her he loved her, had loved her all their lives, and not scare her? How could he not?

He brushed a finger over her mark, watched her eyes widen into large blue orbs. "We all stare because this quiet woman, who barely says three words to anyone, has walked into our lives with her sunshine and her kindness and has left us all wondering where she has been all our lives. You have the biggest heart I know and there is nothing you wouldn't do to help others. You don't gossip or put things on others that you can do yourself. And don't think I don't know about what you said to Susanne months ago." He laughed. She opened her mouth, but he placed a finger against her lips to hush her. "You are the most amazing person I have ever known, and I will never even be worthy of being your friend." Though friendship was the furthest thing from his thoughts now.

"Why are you saying all of this?" She stared down to where their fingers linked. As his thumb traced her hand, Adam turned it over, grazed from her palm to her dainty wrist, felt her pulse. Her easy acceptance of his touch did all kinds of things to him. She wasn't afraid, not of him—never of him. He'd known that from day one. But her pulse was quickening, and her nearness made him respond in turn.

"Because, the morning of my accident, a good friend reminded me of something very important. He asked me if I wanted you to be part of my life." She looked up at him, met his eyes. So striking, those violet blues.

"I am. We are business partners, and friends." Adam chuckled at her innocence, or was there a soft hint of flirtation in there too? God, he loved this woman. He struggled for control, to keep a clear head. Not kissing her right then was harder than he thought it would be. But he knew she deserved the proper time, the right moment.

She also deserved a better man than the one sitting beside her now, but he wasn't going to let that deter him.

"He also asked me how I would feel if you *weren't* in my life." He swallowed, battling nerves.

"And?" There she was, the woman who captured bees barehanded, faced her fears, and still preferred a simple, quiet life. She was a walking contradiction. A life with her would never be dull. Adam lifted a hand, brushed his thumb along her raised brow. He was done. Lowering his hand, he cradled her face, felt her give. Nothing in life would ever be this rewarding, he thought. She loved him too. He knew it without the confession, without the words. It was there in her compliance, her trust. Trust he had earned.

He leaned forward, smiled as her eyes roamed his lips. Joy filled his heart. Belinda was his and he was hers.

"Bee, I'm going to kiss you now."

She exhaled, then smiled. "Okay," she whispered.

Chapter Twenty-Eight

JUST AS TABITHA TURNED OFF the burner, Ivan attempted to snatch a strip of bacon from the plate beside her. Tabitha gave his knuckles a good rap with the gravy spoon. "Ouch."

"You're big enough to eat hay, Ivan Shetler. Get outside and tell Mica breakfast is ready, instead of hoovering like a starved *hund*." Tabitha waved a spoon to direct him to the door.

Belinda giggled and continued pouring herself a cup of *kaffi*. She hadn't gotten a wink of sleep all night thinking about the first kiss Adam had given her, or the second. Who knew such a simple thing could burn the flesh and muddy the mind? Who knew someone so handsome, strong, and devoted would want to kiss her? She sipped her coffee and smiled to herself, holding on to her exhilaration.

"If you weren't Mica's sister…" Ivan's threat was weak. His eyes narrowed and his lips tweaked into a mischievous smile. Belinda wondered just how long the two were going to keep ignoring their feelings for each other. She hoped it wouldn't be for much longer. For if it was one thing she knew for sure and for certain, guarding your heart out of fear made for a wasted existence. Some risks were worth taking.

"You would still be outside. No woman will put up with a bacon thief," Tabitha quickly shot back. Now that she had a better understanding of love, years of her sister's harsh words toward men, especially this one, made a lot more sense. It seemed to her that Tabitha was even more afraid than she had been. Or was it that her sister only had eyes for Ivan? Belinda giggled again, making a mental note to share her thoughts with Mammi soon. It was no wonder every *maedel* Ivan courted didn't last beyond a month. It was a clear as rainwater the two were perfect for each other.

Ivan shoved his hat back on his head, but the look of affection remained as he tipped his hat to each lady. "You two have a good day." He reached for the door handle, pulled, and then turned back. "You should wear green more often," he said simply to Tabitha, before slipping back outside.

"You two are funny," Belinda couldn't help but say, though she'd said it before.

"The man is a pest. No better than a barn full of gnats and muck," Tabitha said sharply, wrapping a dishcloth around the cast iron pan of gravy and removing it from the stove. She still looked flushed and it was clear to Belinda that the heat of the warm August morning kitchen had nothing to do with it.

"If Mamm was here, Ivan wouldn't be snooping around in the kitchen." Tabitha blew out an agitated breath. "I wish they were home, but I know Dawdi needs them more."

Belinda had missed her parents too. "Mamm said he sleeps a lot now," Belinda sighed. "She says we shouldn't worry, that he is comfortable. I guess I should be grateful for that."

"He lived a happy life," Tabitha started. "I don't think I ever saw Dawdi frown once." Belinda thought on that and concluded she hadn't either. "He built a beautiful home and raised a family. And..." she pinned Belinda with a soft look, "he had the love of his life." The sisters simply stared at each other. It was reassuring, for the most part, that Saul Graber was spending his last days surrounded by some of his children. And Tabitha was right. He loved their Mammi Graber very much. She hoped she was half as blessed as they had been.

"So I noticed Adam drove you home last night. *Late* last night." Tabitha pinned her with a knowing look. Belinda flinched instinctively, but the giddy feelings inside could not be tamped down for long.

"*Jah.*" She grinned, teasing her sister by saying nothing else.

"Belinda, stop keeping me in suspense," Tabitha begged, and leaned on the counter beside her. The previous night, Tabitha had apologized more times than necessary for tricking her into going to Zimmerman's and Belinda had forgiven her. Not only because it was the right thing to do, but because she could see her sister truly meant well. And while the trip hadn't gone quite as Tabitha had planned, it *had* worked out for the best in the end. In fact, if not for Tabitha's meddling, Adam would have never had to find her, which meant he wouldn't have felt compelled to drive her home, and without that drive, who knew how much longer she would have had to wait for her first kiss?

"I think I love him," Belinda muttered, then laid her cup down. "No, I know I do. It's crazy, and *wunderbaar*, and," she took a breath as she tried to gather her thoughts and speak clearly. She loved Adam Hostetler. The man next door. She loved his grouchy moods and his strong constitution. She loved his protective nature, now seeing how it was reflected in his awareness of her, and attentive way of always making her feel included.

She loved how her name rolled off his lips, even—or maybe especially—when he shortened it. Belinda touched her cheek, smiled as she remembered the tingling that went through her when he pressed his lips just there. She loved her strawberry kiss, because he loved it too. He made her stronger, braver, and made her feel...appreciated. *Mammi was right about that.*

"I'm so happy for you." Tabitha embraced her, a laugh on her breath. "Mudder is going to be so pleased." Tabitha pulled away. "And no two people were more meant to be." Belinda felt a sting of tears.

"I can talk to him about anything. I don't even remember when it started. He is so patient. And last night when I freaked out and hid in the storage room..."

"You hid in a storage room?" Tabitha's voice hitched in horror.

"I know it was stupid, but Abner just wouldn't go away." Belinda explained the rest of the details and how the back of Zimmerman's store had seemed her only refuge at the time. "But Adam came," she said dreamily. "Like he knew right where I was and that I needed him right then. He didn't get upset when I drew flowers on his hives and he thinks my birthmark is a strawberry kiss."

Tabitha smiled and gave the birthmark a slight brush with her fingers. "It does sort of look cute when you think of it like that."

"He thinks I'm beautiful, and admitted that he used to stare at me all those years back when we were in school because he thought so then too. Who would have guessed he cared for me all these years, and I was too stupid to notice?" She looked to her sister again. "Tabitha, I didn't know love could feel like this. Like, I'm bigger or something." Her voice rose. Tabitha laughed at her sister's wide eyes and sudden awareness.

"I never heard love described quite that way before," her sister teased. "It's sweet. I'm almost envious."

A knock came at the door. "I'll get it. Adam said he wanted to show me something special today." Belinda couldn't conceal the joy in her voice.

"Oh, I've got to see this." Tabitha followed her, just as enthralled in her sister's current state of bliss as she was. Belinda opened the door, but no one was there.

"I guess I imagined it." Belinda took a step back to close the door.

"Wait. Look," Tabitha said, before stepping out on the porch. Belinda watched her sister bend over and retrieve something. "It's...paint." Tabitha stood up with a small green tube with a yellow ribbon and handed it to Belinda.

"Green paint?" Belinda hiked her brows, perplexed. "Why would someone leave this? How did it get there?"

"Look," Tabitha pointed to the walkway

at the bottom of the steps. Another tube lay there, also tied with a yellow ribbon.

"Blue." Belinda picked it up, shot her sister a surprised look. "I don't understand."

"I think he is leaving you a trail to follow," Tabitha grinned.

"For sure?"

"For sure." Tabitha's softened expression told that her sister knew more than she was revealing.

"Did you know about this?"

"I know everything, little sister," Tabitha said. "Now come. Let's see where it ends." Tabitha cupped Belinda's arm and they both searched for the next tube. "Or begins. Depends on how you look at it."

Next they found a sign with an arrow, so they crossed the road and followed the path. "This is so exciting, like a scavenger hunt," Belinda said, with a hint of thrill in her voice.

"I must admit, I never thought Adam would prove to be such a romantic."

"Oh, but he is. He even told me he was going to kiss me like a real gentleman before he did it. So I could say no if I didn't want him to. That is the kind of man he is." She was the luckiest *maedel* in all of Havenlee. As her eyes were searching for the next tube, Tabitha gripped her arm and brought her to a halt.

"And what did you say?" Belinda's

cheeks warmed. "Bee, did you and Adam kiss?"

"It's not proper to talk of such things. Courting is private." Belinda smirked and resumed walking. They had kissed for what felt like hours, but no one needed to know that.

Along the fencerow, through pasture grasses freshly cut, Belinda gathered more tubes of paint, nine in all.

When they reached the rise above May Fisher's orchard, Belinda spotted Adam in the meadow to the north where trees outlined the property's borders. He wasn't alone. Mica, Ivan, and Tobias were with him. Ivan drove stakes in the ground while Mica and Adam held a measuring tape stretched out between them. Tobias was carrying what looked like a huge rock. It was a strange sight for men who were supposed to be building Mica's blacksmith shop on the Graber property. Tabitha's hand tightened on her arm.

"Why are they all out here? Tabitha?"

"You're not getting nervous and running this time, sister," Tabitha warned. "Let's go see what they are doing." Confused though she was, running was certainly the last thing on Belinda's mind. With nine tubes of paint in her apron, Belinda walked along with her sister until they reached the others. She noted the sly smiles, even on Mica, the small collection of rocks Tobias was adding to, most likely gathered from the field, and there in the forefront of it all was the man who had captured her heart. He was dressed in a crisp blue shirt she suspected he wore only for church on Sundays. Nothing made sense, but for once the unknown, that knot of nerves twisting in her belly, didn't scare her. They excited her.

Adam looked up and was aware everyone's gaze was currently aimed behind him. That meant that she had arrived. He closed his eyes and whispered a mental prayer. He could do this, he reminded himself. Like that first walk down the streets of Havenlee with a bouquet of flowers, he could step out of his comfort zone and give Belinda the proposal Nelly had sworn she dreamed of.

He turned to find her standing there, Tabitha at her side, with her apron gathered in one delicate hand, most likely securing her paints. When their eyes locked, he felt that same jolt of lightning he had the first time she looked up at him from her garden. It had been a cool May evening, and a shy *maedel* with violet-blue eyes had, with her promise of help, stopped his world from spinning out of control. Now as August heat burned down on them, he shivered. Ivan was so right—Daed too. How could he imagine a life without her?

"Hey," Adam said as Belinda and her sister approached. It wasn't normal for a man to be so romantic, so public. Private and simple was the Amish way of life, but Belinda deserved more than simple. She should have something just shy of embarrassing, and overflowing with a love worthy of her. Something she could look back on in years to come and smile about. *Something storybook and unforgettable.*

"Hey. I found the paints." Her sweet lips curled into a grin and a second chill overcame him. He wanted to kiss those lips forever, every second of every minute of every hour of every day. What a life they would have.

"I hope I got every color you will need," Adam said, closing the distance until there was barely a foot left between them. Tabitha moved away and joined the audience he knew would be mocking him for the rest of his life after today.

"Need?" Belinda's face scrunched adorably. Adam turned back to her, and couldn't help but smile.

"To paint all the hives," he said, and watched her eyes light up in that way that always made him grateful for *Gotts* creations.

"You want me to paint *all* of them?" Belinda glanced around; trying to understand what was going on. What were they all doing out here in the middle of nowhere, and did he really want all the hives painted? She would do it, of course, but why?

"We are partners. What is mine is yours. So paint away, my dear." His pearly smile reached inside and made her heart pound a little faster.

"Partners?" Belinda regained a little composure and met his smile. Partners didn't kiss for hours at a time. Partners didn't look at each other like they were right now. No, they had crossed over that connection and the newness of that "more" they were building together made her cheeks flush.

"In everything, I hope." His words melted her heart. Before she could respond, Adam dropped to one knee. Her hands shot to her mouth. Paint spilled to the ground, but she barely noticed. She scoured the faces of her siblings and friends, all smiling, except Tabitha, who was crying into her apron front.

"Adam?" She looked back to the man kneeling before her. Kneeling the way she had always imagined a man would. But despite all the stories she'd devoured, no fictional book had prepared her for what was coming.

"You snuck up on me, when things were the hardest. I thought I didn't have room in my life for love, but you showed me I was wrong—because *everything* in my life is better when you're a part of it. I love you, Belinda Graber."

Tears made their way out, and one blink was all it took to set them free-falling onto her cheeks. Adam only deepened his smile.

"I'm pretty sure I have since you were, like, eight," he said and chuckled. Was this really happening? If her hands weren't trembling so badly, Belinda would pinch herself awake right now. Adam took one hand, squeezed it gently. "I want you as my forever partner. I don't want a life without you in it."

He was asking...asking to marry her. Her heart felt like it was about to gallop out of her chest, and tears, those pesky embarrassing tears, made a full out spectacle of her.

"But I can't even keep a house like Ada," she stupidly muttered.

"I don't have allergies, so that's no problem." Adam grinned, sensing her nervousness.

"I hate shopping for anything, much less groceries." She started to back away, but his grip prevented it. Had he thought this through?

"Good thing you're a wonderful gardener

345

then," Adam chuckled, and slowly rose to his feet.

"But...but I..."

"Have run out of excuses," he interrupted and placed a callused hand on her cheek. "Do you know how much it hurt to get on bended knee for you, Belinda Graber?" His smile was infectious, making her smile too. It didn't matter if she worried that she wasn't good enough for a man like him. All that mattered was that Adam thought she was enough, enough to bend though he still wasn't fully healed, and enough to buy her paints and propose marriage to her in front of those close to them just to please her. Amish men didn't do this, she recollected.

"Go ahead and answer the man, so we can get this house marked out." Mica's deep voice penetrated the moment.

"House?" Was that what Ivan and Tobias were doing here? Marking out a house?

"We're going to need one, ain't so?" Adam turned. "I can spread out the hives good. I made a few arrangements to rent some to a few neighbors too."

"So you'll have your hundred hives." He nodded. "And the ground here is perfect."

"Perfect for what?" she asked.

"Our flower farm," he said, matter of fact. "I can see rows of lavender trailing the drive and catching the breeze. People will smell it for miles. Tulips in spring, in every color possible. Down there," he motioned toward a dip in the earth, "a pond to keep everything watered. Over there," he pointed south, "the biggest sunflower field in Indiana."

She could almost see it. If not for the tears that blurred her vision, she would have seen it as clear as he described it.

"And best of all, Marcy will send a driver out to you, four days a week during peak season, and neither of us will have to deliver. We can stay right here, working together, loving one another." *On her flower farm, the one she had always dreamed of.*

"You're building me a flower farm?" Belinda swiped a tear from her cheek. She didn't care that her siblings were there, wouldn't have cared if the whole town had gathered to watch. Control and reasoning were no longer present. She wrapped both arms around Adam's neck and kissed him straight on the mouth. When they pulled apart, Adam leaned his forehead to hers, whispered another "I love you."

"My honey, your flowers, our love, will be more than enough for a family." What a life she would have, with this man. His passions were so purposeful and promising; their livelihoods were equally connected. To think it all started with a neighbor in a fix and a brother who volunteered her up. Belinda shot a quick, grateful glance toward Mica, and then turned back to face her future.

"I love you too, Adam Hostetler, and"— she lifted her chin in utmost confidence as excitement ran through her veins—"I'm ready for this adventure." Belinda had never been more ready for anything in her life. "But Daed might need to know your intentions," she playfully added.

Adam chuckled. "Over the phone, he seemed right pleased to know I had fallen in love with his *dochder*. It seems that Hattie has always wanted a September wedding." He grinned so irresistibly that she had to kiss him again.

Someone cleared his throat. Belinda blushed as she pulled away. Who would have thought her so spontaneous and care-less, kissing a man in front of others? The old Belinda would have been embarrassed, but today, she didn't care. She had wasted enough time not kissing Adam. "What kind of woman would want to marry a bee farmer?" he whispered, green eyes sparkling.

"One who doesn't like smelling mucked-out stalls all day," she teased.

"And one who loves singing to bees, growing flowers, and baking honey cookies," he suggested.

How had she become so blessed? A future that had only lived in her imagination was now here, right in front of her, waiting to be lived. She couldn't wait to get started.

Gazing into his eyes, she said, "And one who loves you."

The End

About the Author

Raised in Kentucky timber country, Mindy Steele writes Amish romance peppered with humor, using rural America and its residents as her muse. Steele strives to create realistic characters and believes in engaging all the senses to make you laugh, cry, hold your breath, and root for the happy ever after ending. A hopeless romantic with a lyrical pen, she hopes readers will find something of themselves within her pages.

Bee Sting Cake for Two

In *An Amish Flower Farm,* Belinda helps Adam with his honey business... and he's amazed that no matter what she does, she never gets stung! Before long, this bee charmer is charming Adam, too. This cake is inspired by their sweet story. It's the perfect size to share with anyone you love.

- **Prep Time:** 15 minutes
- **Cook Time:** 30 minutes
- **Serves:** 2

Ingredients

- 1/3 cup milk, room temperature
- 1/2 cup unsalted butter, room temperature
- 2 large eggs
- 3/4 cup all-purpose flour
- 2 tablespoons granulated sugar
- 1/2 teaspoon salt
- 3 tablespoons honey
- 2 cups flour

Preparation

1. Preheat oven to 400°F.
2. Coat a 9x13 cake pan with non-stick cooking spray.
3. In a medium bowl combine milk, butter and eggs.
4. Gradually add in sugar, flour and salt. Mixing well.
5. When batter is smooth, add 3 tablespoons honey and continue to mix.
6. Place the dough in a bowl, cover with plastic wrap and let rise for an hour.
7. Bake 25 to 30 minutes.
8. For the topping:
9. Combine 1 cup of almonds with 1/2 cup

granulated sugar and 4 tablespoons honey, stirring well.

10. Apply to top of the cake in layers; you will lose some in the process but continue adding layers until you run out.

Thank you for reading
An Amish Flower Farm!
If you enjoyed the story, please
support the author by leaving
an online review.

You might also enjoy these books
from Hallmark Publishing:

Rescuing Harmony Ranch
A Simple Wedding
A Country Wedding
Country Hearts

Turn the page for a bonus excerpt from

RESCUING
Harmony Ranch

A feel-good romance
from Hallmark Publishing

USA TODAY **BESTSELLING AUTHOR**

Jennie Marts

This night was too beautiful and they were having too much fun, laughing and teasing each other, to dredge up the old hurts. She wanted to enjoy the moment, enjoy the time they were sharing now. She liked having him back in her life and didn't want to ruin what they had now by fighting about what they'd lost then. It might have been cowardly, but they'd have time to hash things out later, when the moon wasn't shining in the twinkling reflections on the pond and the air wasn't full of night sounds and possibilities.

"I'd like that too," she said, determined to keep things light. She pulled out her phone and accepted his friend request. "Done. We're friends again."

"If it's on Facebook, it must be true."

"See, now you're getting the hang of it." She pulled up a picture she'd taken earlier of the blacksmith shop and showed him how to post it to the ranch's page. She typed in a caption about a "must have" secret item the blacksmith was creating that would be available to purchase tomorrow night, which visitors to the festival would go crazy for. "There. See how we've created excitement and consumer interest by letting them in on a secret item that everyone is going to want to buy?"

"I don't know that a candle in a jar is worth all that hype."

"It might not be if we'd just posted a

picture of it, but now visitors will be eager to see what the secret item is. And when they see them lit up and glowing around the pond like this, they will snap them up. Trust me. This is my job."

"That didn't seem too hard. But just so you know, I only plan to post stuff about the ranch. I'm not planning to ever share *anything* about my personal life. It's nobody's business what I ate for breakfast or where I'm spending my time or who I'm spending it with."

"Because you don't want people to know how much time you actually spend with your dog?" she teased.

He chuckled. "The dog probably cares about that more than I do. But I'm just saying, you will never, ever see me post anything personal. Even if I were on fire, and it was the only way to call the fire department. It's still not gonna happen. I'd rather burn."

"Okay. Okay. I think you've made your point." She nodded at his phone. "Anything else I can show you on your newfangled contraption?"

He tapped the screen to get the apps to light back up. "Yeah, actually. I haven't quite figured out the camera. Can you show me how to take a picture of something and then fix it up?"

"Sure." She opened the camera app and showed him how to snap a picture, then held his phone up. "And this is how you take a selfie. Just in case you want to snap a pic of you and Savage." She laughed as she pulled a silly face and snapped a few selfies, then wrapped her arm around Mack's shoulder and pulled him into the screen's view. She leaned her head into his and snapped another pic, then nudged him in the side until she finally got him to smile for one.

She was glad to be laughing and teasing with him again as she showed him more features of the camera, explaining the aspects of each as she thumbed through the different options. "This is how you record a video." She pressed the button and did a quick video of herself waving into the screen. "Hi, Mack." Passing him the phone, she said, "Now you try."

He took the phone and was playing around with the options when a new song came on the radio. Both of them stilled.

Jocelyn swallowed at the sudden emotion in her throat. The notes of "their song" drifted into the air and settled around their shoulders like a warm blanket on a cool evening. "It's crazy to hear Chase Dalton on the radio. Remember when we heard him singing this song at the county fair? He was only a few years older than us and just starting out, and now he's a huge country music star."

Mack studied her face, as if trying to see if she remembered the significance of the song.

How could she forget? It was their first dance, on the night of their first kiss. The night everything changed for them.

"Yeah, I remember," he said. "I remember everything."

Her voice lowered to a whisper. "So do I."

He set his phone down, carefully resting it against the radio so it wouldn't fall, then held out his hand. "Wanna dance?"

Her heart tumbled in her chest. Without analyzing the moment or thinking it to death, she simply put her hand in his and let him lead her to the edge of the pond and pull her into his arms. He was taller now, but she still fit perfectly against him.

Stepping into his arms felt like coming home again.

Read the rest!
Rescuing Harmony Ranch is available now.